JOHN PUTNAM THATCHER

"One of the very few important series detectives to enter the field. . . . A completely civilized and urbane man whose charm is as remarkable as his acumen. . . . I keep saying 'urbane, witty, faultless, delightful'; what other adjectives is one to use for Lathen's precise blends of formal detection and acute social satire?"

—Anthony Boucher, *The New York Times Book Review*

EMMA LATHEN

"She is peerless in style, wit, inventively credible plotting and character bits."

—Dorothy B. Hughes, *Los Angeles Times*

"The pseudonym of 'Emma Lathen' serves a pair of good wits who have . . . made guaranty trusts, banks, and accounting companies an exciting background for big-business deviltry, and [have] become . . . the best successful female duo in this field."

—Alice Cromie, *Chicago Tribune*

A STITCH IN TIME
was originally published by
The Macmillan Company.

Books by Emma Lathen

*Published by POCKET BOOKS

A Stitch in Time

Emma Lathen

A POCKET BOOK EDITION published by
Simon & Schuster of Canada, Ltd. • Markham, Ontario, Canada
Registered User of the Trademark

A STITCH IN TIME

Macmillan edition published 1968

POCKET BOOK edition published August, 1975

2nd printing.........June, 1975

Standard Book Number: 671-80046-9.

Library of Congress Catalog Card Number 68-17201.

This POCKET BOOK edition is published by arrangement with Macmillan Publishing Company, Inc.

Front cover illustration by John Melo.

Printed in Canada.

Contents

1 Medical History

Wall Street is the money market of the world and its outward trappings of power are plainly visible. Proud bastions rise from high priced curbs with glass walls, contemporary decor and pampered foliage to bespeak financial might. From Brooklyn to the Bronx, whole armies of men and women are drafted to service Wall Street by carrying papers, typing letters and answering telephones. On occasion, one of the grandees of the street can be sighted, the healthy tan of his countenance marking him out from the pallid herd of the common folk.

In an era which puts a premium on visual communication, the face of Wall Street is entirely satisfying.

John Putnam Thatcher came to this conclusion one damp May afternoon as he strolled back to his own particular outpost, the Sloan Guaranty Trust—third largest bank in the world. Possibly a leisurely lunch explained the idle tenor of his thoughts, more possibly it was the inexplicable lull in his duties as senior vice-president of the Sloan and head of its Trust Department.

On the other hand, it might have been native tenacity. Thatcher was still trying to find something good to be said for the new Sloan Guaranty Trust, an opulent palazzo of glass, marble and brass that had replaced the stately and venerable edifice on Pearl Street where Thatcher's banking had begun many years earlier.

Undeniably, the new Sloan looked impressive.

But, Thatcher thought as he proceeded unhurriedly in the midst of desperate secretaries returning to their desks in frantic hobbled dashes, this cosmetic effect was misleading. Wall Street's power is not embodied in its profligate real estate, in its streams of myrmidons or even in its throbbing pulse of activity.

These, after all, could be duplicated on Seventh Avenue. Or, if modern architecture were the nub of the matter, in Dallas, Texas.

No, the real power on Wall Street lurked unseen behind this façade, in the hands of men who could make one telephone call and raise the price of steel. They did this, as they shook hands on four-million-dollar deals, very calmly indeed.

Tom Robichaux, thought Thatcher, entering the Sloan

7

lobby, was a case in point. Robichaux, an investment banker and lifelong friend, had been his recent companion at lunch.

As this protracted meal had testified, Tom Robichaux was markedly untouched by the tensions of high finance that etched lines in the faces of his subordinates at Robichaux & Devane. He had even found it difficult to summon passing interest in the bond issue of a sports arena outside Boston, the ostensible reason for their meeting.

"I'll send this prospectus over to Bowman," Robichaux had said, critically studying his steak *au poivre*.

"Fine," Thatcher replied. He had sensed a certain abstraction in Robichaux, but ingrained caution kept him from explicit inquiry; all too frequently his friend's preoccupation signified another change in marital status. Over the years John Thatcher had perfected an all-purpose response to tidings of divorce, marriage, alimony, alienation of affection suits and remarriage which conveyed sympathy devoid of any desire for detail.

"Are they thinking of an enclosed arena like the Houston Astro-Dome?" he asked.

Robichaux seemed to have forgotten what they were talking about.

"The Boston bond issue," Thatcher prompted.

Robichaux grounded his coffee cup decisively.

"To tell you the truth, John," he rumbled after close scrutiny of the adjoining tables, "I've got a little problem.
. . ."

The rest of the conversation was devoted to a conflict between Robichaux and the current Mrs. Robichaux, a Melinda who had hitherto escaped Thatcher's notice. Melinda, Thatcher concluded, was decidedly original. She did not want diamonds, ermines or Balenciagas. She wanted an island.

" ' . . . so I said that Gardiner has an island because he inherited it, for God's sake!" Robichaux reported indignantly. "He didn't buy it! You don't buy islands around Manhattan!"

Thatcher reflected on this as the Sloan's elevator bore him up to his offices on the sixth floor. Tom was right. A prudent man contented himself with buying stocks and bonds, industrial parks and warehouses of cocoa beans. That was what Wall Street was for.

Within the hour, Thatcher was to learn that money could take even more mysterious forms than he thought.

Together with one of his junior trust officers, he was reviewing the affairs of a hydrofoil company hovering on the brink of bankruptcy. Suddenly they were interrupted by sounds of raucous merriment from the outer office. Thatcher's eyebrows rose in mute question; young Kenneth Nicolls showed more open surprise.

Just as Tom Robichaux could carry out chancy deals for a million dollars without evincing strain, so the Sloan Guaranty Trust was in the habit of conducting profitable operations without audible gales of hilarity.

Both Thatcher and Nicolls knew that these sounds were not emanating from clerical minions. The outer office was guarded by Thatcher's secretary, Miss Corsa, a young woman clearly designed by nature for the motto: *We are not amused.* Rose Theresa Corsa believed in decorum and propriety to a degree that sometimes oppressed Thatcher, and she was fully equal to the task of suppressing indecorous yelps from messenger boys.

She could keep Kenneth Nicolls in line, too.

This meant that the rioters were so exalted that Miss Corsa was powerless to impose her own standards. Considering her attitude to her employer, that boiled down to two starters—the Chairman of the Board and the President of the United States. Lesser mortals would need nerves of steel.

"We've got to find out about this," Thatcher said, rising to throw open the door and advance upon the scene.

The disturbers of Miss Corsa's peace were two middle-aged men. One of them, his elegant form topped by a Homburg, was applying a handkerchief to eyes streaming with the force of his glee. He was promptly overcome by another paroxysm.

"Better than a fifty-fifty chance!" he crowed. "It was beautiful! Unbelievably beautiful! And Chisolm . . ."

He became speechless at the memory.

His vis-à-vis seemed to understand him, if Thatcher and Nicolls (and Miss Corsa, for that matter) did not. Sitting in a chair, doubled over in pleasurable agony, three hundred dollars' worth of discreet tailoring hooted triumphantly:

"Chisolm's face! If I die tonight, it will be worthwhile!"

"I think," said Thatcher to Nicolls, "I think that we can abandon hydrofoils for the moment while I deal with this."

This dismissal was unfair and Thatcher knew it. On the other hand, he did not want junior members of the staff present while their elders and betters were losing control.

Obediently, if regretfully, Nicolls departed, leaving Thatcher to survey the intruders. Despite tears, bellows, backslappings and incitement to further delirium, he recognized the two figures.

The Homburg hat, now pushed back to a regrettable angle, crowned his second-in-command, Charlie Trinkam. Trinkam, the most ebullient trust officer of the Sloan, had always been notorious for the gaiety he brought to a vigorous bachelor life, but so far he had not broken down during office hours. The tailoring encased the form of Paul Jackson, one of New York's flourishing trial lawyers.

The strangest feature of the whole business was that both men seemed sober. Perhaps, not so strange, Thatcher had seen them both drunk and exercising more control than at present.

Charlie Trinkam finally acknowledged his superior's presence. Clutching at a desk for support, he gasped:

"Oh God, John, you missed the scene of the century!"

Banishing everything but mild curiosity from his voice, Thatcher said:

"What have I missed? What have you two been up to?"

A diabolical smile crossed Paul Jackson's lips.

"Freebody v. Atlantic Mutual. To both questions."

Then it all came back to Thatcher.

Pemberton Freebody had been a wealthy and childless widower, living out a comfortable old age at the Waldorf Towers until the onset of cancer. Freebody contemplated the lingering pain and indignity in prospect. Then, without undue regret, he put his affairs in order, named the Sloan Guaranty Trust as executor of his estate, got into his Cadillac and drove safely and slowly out the Long Island Expressway to a small wooded area he remembered from his distant youth. There he punctiliously affixed a note to the dashboard, proceeded into the trees and shot himself in the chest.

At this point, Pemberton Freebody's plans went awry. A passing truck driver was alerted by the shot. Braking abruptly, he plunged into the woods to find the old gentleman still alive. Forthwith giving the lie to theories about the alienation of our times, he slung the frail body into a fireman's lift, hurried back to the highway and sped to nearby Southport. At Southport Memorial Hospital, emergency stations were manned, the chief of surgery summoned and every resource of modern medicine brought in to play. Despite the intervention of these well-wishers,

Pemberton Freebody finally did manage to die—four days later. He had not escaped the indignities, but at least he had never regained consciousness.

So exit Freebody, and enter the Freebody estate. The bulk of it had been left to the newly formed Institute for Cancer Research at Hanover University. Included in the large estate was a hundred-thousand-dollar life insurance policy with the Atlantic Mutual Insurance Company. Atlantic Mutual quickly informed the Sloan that the suicide invalidation clause of the policy was still in force; Hanover would have to do without this particular one hundred thousand dollars.

Almost immediately, Atlantic Mutual came up against three powerful forces. First was Hanover's deep disappointment. It was delighted with the amount it had inherited, but it still regretted that one hundred thousand dollars.

"For cancer research, we need every cent we can get!"

Second, came Charlie Trinkam's native instinct to spread happiness. More as a theoretical exercise than anything else, he had said: "Of course if we hinted that we were willing to go to court, we might get some sort of settlement. . . ." After that, as Trinkam himself was the first to admit, he lost effective control of the situation.

Third, the trial lawyer chosen to lend substance to this hint was Paul Jackson. Trinkam had reported this to Thatcher.

"When Hanover insisted we retain Paul Jackson—well, John, I figured there'd be a laugh or two in it, if nothing else."

Thatcher had asked why Jackson, a noted criminal lawyer, had consented to take the case.

"He likes to get his teeth into insurance companies."

Recalling these words as he ushered the two men into his office past Miss Corsa's frosty disdain, Thatcher could only suppose that Jackson's teeth had found a nice, solid grip.

"You should have seen it," Charlie Trinkam murmured once again.

"Well, I didn't," Thatcher announced tartly. "Suppose you tell me about it."

His professional instincts roused, Paul Jackson leaned forward:

"It's really quite simple. Atlantic Mutual put on its suicide defense. The usual thing, rounded off with the people from Southport Memorial—the hospital where Freebody was taken. A couple of nurses and the surgeon who cut out the bullet."

"Beautiful, just beautiful," Trinkam provided a slight accompaniment.

Jackson grinned an acknowledgment.

"Then I got started, cross-examining Dr. Martin, the surgeon. And was heaven watching out for us today! He was perfect, an arrogant cocksure bastard who wanted to tangle with me." He turned for an aside to Trinkam. "I don't know what was bugging that guy but we couldn't have asked for anything better."

"You played him like Paderewski."

"Martin's built to be a keyboard!" snorted Jackson. "All he wanted to do was contradict me. I could have gotten anything from him. But what I got was the jackpot. It all boils down to his saying two things. First, I wanted to know why the hell they operated—if the man was on his deathbed and nothing could save him anyway. Martin snapped right back at me: *The patient had better than a fifty-fifty chance for recovery. The bullet was nowhere near the heart. I operated to improve his chances.* All very lofty and professional. Everybody in the courtroom was hating Martin already."

"Except us," Charlie said irrepressibly. "We were ready to take up a collection for him. Then Paul really twisted it home. Asked why Freebody died if the chances were so good. And he answered—"

"Let me," pleaded Jackson. He held up a hand and seemed to be quoting holy writ, "Martin said: *The operation was perfectly successful. But the patient was seventy-six years old, and dying of cancer. He was an aged and enfeebled man in no condition to withstand any unusual or extended strain.*"

Jackson stopped and looked across at Thatcher with a broad grin.

Thatcher did not hide his restiveness. "I have grasped the fact that Martin said exactly what you wanted him to say. I can even see that something else is coming. But until I know what it is, I'm outside this ring of self-congratulation."

Nothing could ruffle the high spirits of his visitors. Charlie Trinkam took a deep breath and delivered the denouement in one long stream.

"Then Dr. Martin stepped down and Paul called the

man who did an autopsy on Freebody for us. The autopsy revealed that seven hemostatic clips had been left in the body!"

Jackson and Trinkam grinned at Thatcher like two imbeciles.

"Now wait . . . let me get this absolutely clear," he said. "You mean we now have a case that Freebody did not die as a result of shooting himself, but as a result of these hemostats?"

"That's it!" Jackson sang out. "And the beauty of it is that DeLuca, the expert we hired for the autopsy, refused to give an opinion as to the cause of death. He wouldn't swear it was the hemostats—but he wouldn't swear it was the bullet, either. DeLuca, by the way, is a big gun in postmortems."

"The whole thing seems to have gone beautifully," said Thatcher not stinting his praise.

"We were lucky in our man. If the surgeon had been a remorseful young resident, we might not have had it so easy. But this Martin is pure poison. You should have seen Chisolm's face when he realized what he was stuck with."

"Who's Chisolm?"

"He's the lawyer for Atlantic Mutual. This Dr. Wendell Martin, the surgeon, is his witness. Couldn't be worse." Paul Jackson smiled beatifically. "And the jury is going to see a lot of Dr. Martin, believe you me."

"Where do things stand now?" Thatcher asked.

"Oh, Chisolm got an adjournment. To do research, he said. What else could he say? He was flabbergasted!"

Thatcher said that he could understand and, in fact, sympathize with this.

Paul Jackson, however, was too deep in hilarious speculation to pity his fellow attorney.

"You know what they'll do, don't you? They'll beat the bushes trying to find doctors willing to say they always forget seven hemostats! And is Chisolm going to have a hard time! I can just hear the doctors! Every one of them will swear that he's never known of seven hemostats left in a patient. No experience with it at all. . . ."

Since Jackson showed signs of giving way again, Thatcher intervened.

"What about the hospital—at Southport, was it? Will they support the doctor?"

Jackson pursed his lips thoughtfully and continued his predictions.

"As soon as Southport Memorial Hospital realizes what's hit it, they'll lower an Iron Curtain. Nobody will know anything—or remember anything! Oh, we're still not home clear on this case, John. But we are a lot closer than we were yesterday."

Jackson sighed dreamily.

Charlie Trinkam was ready to pass judgment here and now. "I've got to hand it to you, Paul. You've really set the sparks flying!"

2 Heartburn

If it was sparks at the Sloan Guaranty Trust, it was more like a forest fire in Southport, Long Island. Southport Memorial Hospital was one of the town's proudest possessions, so it was only natural that in Segal's Drugstore, in Muriel's Bake Shop, in the park and the bus stop, nothing else was discussed.

"Isn't it awful!" Southport asked and reasked. "Just awful!"

The medically devout then moved on to a litany featuring illustrations culled from their own operations.

Southport's Christian Scientists shook their heads more in sorrow than in anger.

"Seven hemostats!"

"Hemostats, nothing! Do you remember that rubber glove two years ago?"

Only a few professional optimists in the Chamber of Commerce were able to dredge some satisfaction from the metropolitan press coverage. "Well, this sure puts Southport—and Suffolk County—on the map!"

There was some merit in this observation. In 1925, Suffolk County had been much as it was during the American Revolution. Fifty miles stood between the easternmost portion of Long Island and Manhattan. Behind this buffer, Suffolk County slumbered in agricultural languor, cultivating potatoes, ducks and market produce. Its rural fastness suffered only one annual interruption during the brief hysteria of summer vacations, but otherwise Suffolk County was unaffected by the vast population of New York City. A geographic truism explained its protection: fifty miles is too far to go to work.

World War II changed all this. Work came to Suffolk County. The sandy soil began to produce aircraft, gyroscopes and secondary radar instead of asparagus. With the work came workers, and soon the potato farms were giving way to housing developments. Following hard on the heels of these consumers was free enterprise, in the form of shopping centers, discount houses and used-car lots. The great suburban ball was rolling.

The stage props for *Freebody v. Atlantic Mutual* arrived with another phenomenon. Having been provided with jobs, houses and stores, a multitude of Americans still found time hanging heavy. Despite a forty-hour week earning money (rather restful on the whole), despite a fifty-hour week spending money (totally exhausting), people still managed to divorce each other, abandon their children, commit crimes, read books, play tennis and get sick.

There was an anguished wail for social services. Authority, slower off the mark than entrepreneurs, belatedly recognized the need for more schools, marriage counselors, libraries, courts, jails, parks, social workers and hospitals. New agencies proliferated like fruit flies; old institutions donned new paint and flexed their muscles.

Among the older institutions struggling with the population explosion, none had been more successful than Southport Memorial Hospital. Originally built in 1927, Southport Memorial was remodeled in 1949; a new wing was added in 1959, and by 1966 a full-scale expansion was projected.

It was, Southport learned, one fund drive after another.

Expanding with the hospital was the medical staff. Nurses, orderlies, analysts, X-ray technicians, laboratory specialists and nurses' aides jostled for parking space. The top of the totem pole was, of course, reserved for the doctors—obstetricians, internists, surgeons, neurologists, endocrinologists, gynecologists, dermatologists, pathologists. Many specialties and many men. But, as in any hospital, the doctors who really ran things could be numbered on the fingers of one hand.

Two of them were showing the flag, as it were, at Segal's Drugstore. On the whole, they were giving a fine performance of men oblivious to the vulgar gossip around them.

"That's him, isn't it?" the customer at cosmetics hissed at the salesgirl. "Martin, I mean. Over there, at the tobacco counter."

The clerk emerged from under the counter and looked across the store.

"That's him, all right. The short one. The big man with him is Dr. Wittke, the head of the hospital. Dr. Wittke's a real gentleman."

"Did you read about what Dr. Martin did? I tell you! Imagine leaving all that junk in that guy. Killed him just as if he put the bullet in him, that's what I say!"

The salesgirl lowered her voice confidentially. "Listen, nothing Dr. Martin does would surprise me! He's always rushing around and snapping someone's head off. He probably leaves things in his patients all the time!"

This libel was the result of personnel practices at Segal's Drugstore. At lunchtime, the salesgirl covered the tobacco stand, and Dr. Wendell Martin was particular about his cigars.

At the back of the store, a salesman from one of the big drug houses was deep in knowledgeable talk with Harry Segal, who was Sid's younger boy.

"I see Dr. Martin got himself in hot water," he said.

"He's sure making the headlines," Harry agreed neutrally.

"He'll find some way to duck the whole thing," the salesman said with a knowing smile. "He's a smart cooky when it comes to taking care of old Number One."

Harry looked up from the price list. "I didn't know you knew him."

"Met him a couple of times," said the salesman. "I don't deal with him, thank God! Give me the druggists any time. You can have doctors!"

Harry smiled carefully.

"Still," the salesman continued, "I saw Martin yesterday just after he got back from the trial."

"Oh?" Harry abandoned the price list and leaned forward. This was the closest he had come to an eyewitness report.

"Yeah. I was over there at the hospital pharmacy. Not that I ever sell them much. They're as bad as you. All the doctors want to do is cut, cut, cut. Boy, if they made as much money from prescriptions as they do from operations . . ."

"Martin? What about him? You saw him?"

"Sure. I was just packing things up when he came sailing in. So help me God, he was purple! Looked like he was going to have a stroke. Of course, at the time, I didn't know what was the matter. . . . But Boy! When I read the evening papers—well, if he looked like that by the time he got back here, I hate to think of what he looked like in court."

"It would upset anybody," said Harry.

"Upset, hell, he was mad! Slammed the door to his office—like a cannon. But one thing I'll say for him. He sure got busy. Right away, the loudspeaker was blasting away for Dr. Wittke and Dr. Neverson—and you know what that means."

A STITCH IN TIME

Harry shrugged. "Oh, the big shots will take care of it. Now we're going to need a thousand units——"

"A thousand units! You're crazy! You gotta stock at least five thousand...."

At the soda fountain, three middle-aged women argued over sundaes.

"I don't care what you say," the center woman announced defiantly. "Just because you work in the hospital kitchen you think you know all about the doctors. Well, I work there too!"

"What's the kitchen got to do with it, anyway? It's in the papers, right there in black and white. They wouldn't say that Dr. Martin killed that man if he didn't!"

"Papers will say anything! All I know is, when Burt had the gall bladder, Dr. Martin was marvelous!"

Her companions scoffed.

"It's two years now and you've forgotten all about it. Day after day, you kept saying how Dr. Martin wouldn't tell you anything. Wouldn't talk to you—or to Burt!"

"Who wants a doctor to talk?" she demanded unanswerably. "You want he should do a good job. And in two years, Burt hasn't had a day of trouble—knock on wood!"

Ceremonially she knocked twice on the formica counter.

At the candy counter another viewpoint was being aired.

"Well, as soon as I saw that story, I called our GP," said the man, holding out a five-dollar bill absently. "I put it on the line! Faulkner, I said, I'm holding you responsible. I won't have Dr. Martin within ten feet of Alison!"

"But I thought you said Alison and the baby were coming home day after tomorrow," the other objected. "Why should a surgeon go near her?"

The new father accepted a beribboned two-pound box of Whitman's and swelled protectively. "Let him try!"

At the cigar counter, Dr. Wendell Martin was continuing his thoughtful inspection of the stock, deaf to the conversations around him and untouched by the atmosphere. Sid Segal waited patiently, his shrewd eyes partially hooded by drooping eyelids. The tableau was not wasted on him. Nothing ever was.

Dr. Martin's companion, Dr. Philip Wittke, did not smoke. But Dr. Wittke had felt it politic to accompany Wendell Martin on this expedition as a public demonstration of professional solidarity.

"Of course, this notoriety is unpleasant for all of us,"

Sid." He shook his head sadly. "But that's the way things are these days. Journalists have no qualms about exploiting misery to provide sensationalism."

"It's tough, Doc," said Segal.

Wittke drew a deep breath and allowed his volume to expand slightly. Nothing obtrusive, Segal noted appreciatively, but enough so that anyone could overhear him.

"I always tell young men just starting their medical careers that they have to realize every hospital is going to have a certain number of terminal patients. We'd like to save them all, we do our best, but in the end it's in Other Hands. In the first shock of loss, you have to make allowances for the survivors. We have all of us faced hysterical accusations and other unpleasantness, from time to time. But I tell my boys that the thing to do is to be patient, and remember that time is the only healer."

If Sid Segal found it hard to visualize Hanover University rending its face and tearing its clothes in grief for Pemberton Freebody, he kept the thought to himself.

Wendell Martin finally finished preparing a cigar and stuck it jauntily into a corner of his mouth. A moment later, fragrant smoke enveloped the threesome. Dr. Wittke's voice continued from somewhere within the cloud. "The important thing for a doctor is to know that his colleagues support him," he said, coughing slightly. "They're the ones who've seen his work, who know how he responds to pressure. Only his fellow doctors can value a fine professional. And that"—here he weakened slightly and looked beyond Segal to the larger audience—"that is what we have at Southport Memorial! A fine group of dedicated professionals, proud of each other, standing shoulder to shoulder!"

"Standing shoulder to shoulder," said Sid Segal, "that's always a good idea."

Wittke indicated accord, glanced at the wall clock and gave signs that he and Dr. Martin had to return to their great work of healing. Their departure, dignity itself, did not end discussion of them.

Waiting for the light, Wendell Martin was disposed to grumble.

"I don't know what good that did," he said sourly.

Paul Jackson might wonder what was producing Wendell Martin's sourness, but Philip Wittke did not. Wendell Martin's sourness was nothing new. Unfortunately, Wittke reflected as they crossed the street, it was allied with a positive genius for alienating people—as Martin's lamentable performance on the witness stand demonstrated. He debated suggesting a more cooperative stance in future courtroom appearances, then rejected the notion.

Dr. Wendell Martin did not react favorably to even the sanest suggestions. Short, stocky and abrasive, he was Southport's chief of surgery; in the hospital, his word was law, his opinions valued and his foibles deferentially pandered to. Small wonder that he acted and thought like a dictator.

Dr. Wittke, who liked power as much as the next man, was another one of Southport Memorial's titans, but he eschewed the Napoleonic manner. In part this was temperament: Wendell Martin did not mind having people hate him. Dr. Wittke liked to be liked.

Still, as they strolled up the drive to the entrance, he had to conclude that Wendell Martin's unshakable self-assurance was an advantage at the current juncture of affairs.

Wittke shot a glance at him. Wendell Martin was strutting along, as if he had not left seven hemostats in Pemberton Freebody. It might have shattered a lesser man; it would have shaken Dr. Philip Wittke. Dr. Wendell Martin was simply angry, angry at the demands made on his time, angry at the presumption of the lawyers, angry at Pemberton Freebody for having died.

Well, it takes all kinds, Philip Wittke decided, smiling at Mrs. Stosser, the director of nursing, who was hurrying back from lunch. For himself, power—even unlimited power—at Southport Memorial was not enough. Philip Wittke looked to wider horizons. The profession knew that he ruled Southport Memorial Hospital's Executive Committee and controlled the outside doctors who wanted hospital privileges. More than once unfriendly voices had accused him of using this power to discipline doctors whose views on medical insurance and group medicine did not have the imprimatur of orthodoxy. But footing criticisms did not bother Philip Wittke; his election, some years earlier, as delegate to the national convention of the American Medical Association had heralded his arrival in the bigger world of medical politics. The Wittke Clinic was being run—and very successfully—by his two sons these days; the elder Dr. Wittke had become a familiar figure on the public platform and the television discussion show, either appealing for funds or denouncing Medicare.

He cultivated a confident, genial voice and silver hair, both calculated to contribute to his aura of massive distinction.

Lowering that confident voice slightly, he said, "Well, Wen, I am glad that you've agreed to have a little talk with Roy and me. It should be most helpful."

Martin gave a snort of impatience. He had never been guilty of considering any well-being other than his own, but Wittke had convinced him that his Southport colleagues had a vested interest in the disposition of *Freebody v. Atlantic Mutual*. It was characteristic of the man that he thought of the forthcoming conference in terms of his own needs and desires.

"All right, Phil. But I'm going to want a strong statement of support. And while we're at it, we may forward a protest to the medical association about that postmortem. . . ."

Wittke evaded a reply. This was no time for Dr. Wendell Martin or Southport Memorial to be protesting anything. He wondered if Martin could be brought to see this.

"Another thing!" said Martin imperiously as they strode into the lobby. "When the trial is resumed, they're going to call those nurses! Now I want to make it clear to them what their duty is. . . ."

He had not bothered to lower his voice, despite visitors in the waiting room, two young doctors glancing with masked curiosity in their direction, the girl behind the desk. This sublime indifference to the needs of the moment nettled Philip Wittke, but with an effort he contemplated the harangue that Martin could be expected to inflict upon the nurses who had assisted during the Freebody surgery. Repressing a shudder, he masterfully led the way to the privacy of the office corridor, then said:

"Yes, although on the whole I feel that perhaps your talking to Doyle and Gentilhomme might well be . . . er . . . misrepresented by the lawyers. You know lawyers. Why don't you let me have a word with them?"

Wendell Martin halted outside his office and narrowed his small eyes at Wittke.

"All right, Phil, you talk to them. Just be sure that you get them to understand—completely!"

"I think," said Dr. Philip Wittke authoritatively, "I think I can promise you that they will!"

3 Symptoms

By this time a number of lawyers and doctors were mobilizing to fight *Freebody* v. *Atlantic Mutual* if it took all summer. None of the lawyers, and only a few of the doctors, underestimated the magnitude of the engagement. It was the clear destiny of those seven hemostats to become as hotly argued as if they moved in interstate commerce.

At Jackson & Jackson, Paul Jackson directed a large stable of legal yearlings through grisly precedents, himself lunched steadily with Dr. Edmund Knox and other medical bigwigs from the Institute for Cancer Research and, as he reported to John Putnam Thatcher, unearthed proof that any medical treatment beyond prescription of two aspirin tablets was grossly overpriced and probably potentially lethal.

"What are our chances?" asked Thatcher, upon whom medico-legal anecdotes were beginning to pall.

The phone temporized. "Well, we've still got Wendell Martin going for us," it said. "He'll be a big help. But the hospital is backing him. I'll have to fight to get a word out of anyone. Oh, say, seventy-thirty!"

On the opposing shore, the Atlantic Mutual Insurance Company, in the persons of its Eastern Manager, Dexter Loomis, and its counsel, Andrew Chisolm, was also performing prodigies of research. Telephone calls flowed out of obscure clinics in hunting areas, several recuperative miracles were dusted off and readied for citation, and some extremely plain talk was directed at Dr. Wendell Martin. But, as Andrew Chisolm was the first to admit, with seven hemostats going against you, it would be foolish to offer any odds.

Nor was the cooperation being offered by Southport Memorial Hospital enough to make him alter this assessment.

"No," said Dr. Wittke to the phone, "it's no trouble. I'm having a small conference this afternoon—quite informal. We'll talk things over and reassure Wendell that Southport is supporting him—"

The phone erupted.

"Yes," said Dr. Wittke soothingly. "Wendell can be difficult—a fine doctor, of course—but we'll try to talk sense to him. You will be happy to know that I've had a friendly

22

little chat with Mrs. Doyle and Miss Gentilhomme—the nurses, you recall. They are fully alive to their professional obligations."

He listened for a moment, then more sharply said, "Yes, we fully realize that it will do Southport Memorial no good . . . yes . . . I think I can say that everything here is well under control."

So began a week of surprises. To lawyers and doctors, *Freebody v. Atlantic Mutual* might appear to be a question of fact and logic. But, in addition, it touched many corners of many lives. This, as John Putnam Thatcher could have foretold, guaranteed the intrusion of antic, authentically human unpredictability. By the time *Freebody v. Atlantic Mutual* resumed, nothing—and no one—was well under control.

Dr. Wittke wished to speak to Dr. Martin and Dr. Neverson—a summit meeting in effect; since this was the triumvirate that dominated the hospital. To allay any such impression, Dr. Wittke suggested meeting in his home, a majestic structure commanding a wide view of great South Bay from its acre of ocean frontage on Southport's choice Rocky Point.

They sat in the large sunny room overlooking the bay. Roy Neverson, the youngest man present, gazed idly out at the sparkling waters and repressed a sigh. A beautiful day to be out in the boat!

He glanced down at the watch contrasted against his darkly tanned wrist. Thirty minutes already, and they were still where they had been when they started!

Neverson forced himself to sit still. He had made his mark early; it had taken just ten years to fight his way from resident to the best internist at Southport.

He hadn't done it by sitting around trying to reason with Wendell Martin, a waste of time if there ever was one. On the other hand, he had not made it to the top by letting his opinion of the chief of surgery show.

"This court case shouldn't pose a serious threat," he said. "But we have to decide how to handle it."

"What is there to decide?" Martin burst out. "You know you have to back me up. Loomis and Chisolm have explained the whole thing. I don't know why you got us out here, Phil."

A short, brutal gesture transformed the gracious room into a tawdry pool hall.

Wittke retained his equanimity. He felt it proper to shoulder the burden of the conversation, but realized that his platitudes were not piercing Wendell Martin's armor. As he downed his cup of coffee, he shot a quick glance at Roy Neverson.

Neverson hitched himself forward. Trying hard for friendly frankness he said:

"Look, Wendell, Southport *is* backing you! That's already been decided! Nobody is testifying—except the nurses! We haven't answered any questions—and we won't! But Phil and I want to be sure you realize that this isn't simply a malpractice suit with some John Doe trying to make hay out of a little slip. It's the Sloan Guaranty Trust and Hanover University—with the most expensive lawyers on Wall Street Under the circumstances, you see, this is bigger than a question of professional support. . . ."

He discovered that he was talking slowly and distinctly. Wittke, at any rate, nodded measured approval.

Wendell Martin glared at him.

"For God's sake! You make it sound as if they're the only ones involved. What about Atlantic Mutual? Don't forget them! It's their job to look out for us! And let me tell you, I'm going to give them hell! I'm their witness, after all! And look what they let me in for . . ."

For a moment, Wendell Martin's view of his place in the universe stupefied his companions. Although there was a gap of thirty years between them—and all that implies in style and substance—Neverson and Wittke found their eyes meeting.

Wittke cleared his throat.

"Now, Wen, I don't like to hear you say that about Atlantic Mutual. They're some very fine people over there. And we must remember that they do have some grounds to be . . . er . . . less than happy with you, at the moment."

Inwardly, Neverson grimmed. This was Wittke at the top of his form. Not many people could take so Olympian a view of seven hemostats.

Martin did not see it this way.

"They're not pleased?" he repeated in outrage. "What have *they* got to complain about?"

"One hundred thousand dollars," Neverson could not keep from retorting. "Now look, Wen, you're not the only doctor they'll call—"

"So what!" Martin snarled.

Neverson made another effort to keep his voice steady. "So that means, the questions haven't started yet?"

Despite himself, the sentence came out like a bullet. He turned to look at the bay again. "That's what we want you to realize. The longer this goes on——the worse it's going to be. There's going to be publicity, and more questions——and it's going to be tough on you, and on us. It could be disastrous." He paused. "The sooner this is over, the better!"

Again Wittke waded in.

"The important thing for us is to maintain a united front,"

"Of silence!" Roy Neverson was urgent. "Look, Wen, we realize that you're taking the knocks. But we've all got to keep as quiet as we can. We don't have to say who was in the hospital, what they were doing, or what we were doing. Unfortunately," he added almost unwillingly, "we're stuck with those damned hemostats!"

The last words undid his good work. Martin was affronted.

"Those hemostats could have happened to anybody!" he snapped, pushing cup and saucer away. "Phil's a surgeon. He understands!"

Whatever Phil understood was interrupted as a melodious gong echoed through the house.

For a moment, naked consternation leaped into his eyes. "Who could that be . . . Virginia is out . . . didn't say anything. . . ."

"It's Dr. Bullivant, Dr. Wittke."

The housekeeper stood on no ceremony. With so many doctors present, what did one more matter?

Edith Bullivant was in the doorway, gazing at her colleagues with her usual placid and maternal good will.

"Coffee? Well, I call that nice!"

"Yes of course. . . ."

Philip Wittke, notorious for his sangfroid, was not equal to Edith Bullivant. She sailed past him. Patients found her reassuring; young nurses were known to refer to her as "Aunt Edie." Without haste, she sank into a comfortable chair and expelled a sigh of relief. Then, with small delicate hands that were surprising in so substantial a woman, she accepted a cup of coffee with unstudied graciousness.

"What a day!" she remarked humorously. "I had a terrible breech delivery this morning. Well, you don't want to hear about my little troubles, do you? Thank you, Phil, just sugar, please. I wanted a word with you"—she smiled brilliantly at Martin and Neverson—"and they said that you'd gone home!"

An indistinct noise from Wittke led her to add: "And I remembered how you—and Wen and Roy—like to have your business meetings here!"

"Oh yes," said Dr. Wittke.

"I'm not interrupting you, I hope," said Dr. Bullivant gently.

Wendell Martin could barely restrain a growl, and Dr. Bullivant's voice grew more emphatic.

"Although, of course, you—we—all have a lot to talk about now, don't we?"

"Dammit—" Martin began.

Swiftly, Roy Neverson cut in, although he was somewhat amused by the womanly ruthlessness of Dr, Bullivant. "Yes, Edith. We're just agreeing that the best thing for us to do—in connection with this case of Wendell's—is to help it die down, fast. We've agreed that we won't have anything to say, to lawyers or newspapermen."

There was nothing in this speech to give Dr. Bullivant food for thought, yet she knit her face fine brows. When she did speak, it was in a heavily practical tone.

"Have any of you thought what will happen if somebody comes up with Harley Bauer?"

There was an appalled silence.

Both Martin and Wittke stared at her.

"That's one for the old girl," Roy Neverson thought silently.

"I mean it won't look good, will it?" she asked the room at large. "In fact, it could look quite bad."

Harley Bauer had been, until very recently, Southport Memorial Hospital's pathologist. He had been dismissed. Wendell Martin recovered himself. "What does Harley Bauer have to do with anything! This isn't a case of a questionable operation, let me remind you, Edith! There was a perfectly simple medical situation, and there's a perfectly simple medical question as to the cause of a patient's death! There's no need for a pathologist's report. This is not an investigation into *your* medical practice!"

The naked animosity in his voice left Dr. Bullivant untouched.

"We don't want to get involved in old quarrels now, do

we, Wendell?" she asked sweetly. "After all, you have enough to worry about. . . ."

Wearily, Roy Neverson tried to salvage the discussion.

"That's the point I'm making. On the whole, the best thing is to let other doctors dispute about what killed Freebody. We should keep quiet!"

"And cooperate with the people at Atlantic Mutual," said Dr. Wittke quickly. His immovable hostility to group insurance did not preclude approval of joint action in other areas.

"That's right," said Roy Neverson, still trying to sell the idea to Martin. "Let Atlantic Mutual fight with the Sloan! The two of them can slug it out by themselves. We don't want them nosing around here! Right?"

There was probably no possibility of success for his appeal, but Dr. Bullivant assured its failure.

"Unless, Wendell, you decided to modify your opinion?"

Martin paled in rage.

"You mean, say that I killed Freebody? Would you?"

Dr. Bullivant sipped her coffee. Then, quite deliberately, she said: "You practically have said so, you know!"

In a voice that was choked, Martin spoke as he jumped to his feet.

"I've had enough of this! And thanks for the coffee, Phil!"

He had slammed out of the room before anybody could move.

"Isn't it fortunate," said Edith Bullivant quietly, "that he has a devoted wife to go home to."

Roy Neverson's wife and two children were now living in Michigan, not Long Island. But he did not rise to Dr. Bullivant's bait.

"Isn't it?" he agreed. "Well, I'll be pushing on. . . ."

"I hope I'm not driving you out," said Dr. Bullivant cheerfully.

"No, I think we said what had to be said," Neverson paused before the final thrust. "And, Edith, give my regards to Giles."

Wendell Martin's devoted wife heard him before she saw him.

"Lucille! Lucille!" His voice resounded through the sprawling ranch house and reached her as she was bending over her golf bag, putting new balls in the pocket. Without hesitating, she put them aside and hurried into the living room.

Her husband stood before the built-in bar, brandishing a bottle in one hand.

"Lucille, there's no soda water!"

In the hospital this would have been a vicious accusation. Here, in his own home, however, Wendell Martin's disappointments with the world put a faint plaintive edge on his voice.

"Oh, Wen, wait," said Lucille Martin reassuringly. "I've got one in the kitchen."

When she returned, he was sitting on the sofa.

"It won't be cold," he said angrily.

Without comment, she made him his drink. Then, making herself a much weaker one, she reminded herself to call Natalie and beg off golf this afternoon.

"Are you going out?" Martin finally asked.

"No," said Lucille Martin serenely.

He looked at her suspiciously.

"If you are . . ." he began.

Lucille Martin was too experienced to fall into this trap. Instead, she asked what kind of day he had had.

"What kind of day would you expect?" he asked. "First, I've got those damned fools at the insurance company on my back. Then Wittke and Neverson keep talking nonsense. And that damned Bullivant woman . . ."

As he warmed to his narrative, Lucille Martin unobtrusively refilled his glass, occasionally murmured agreement or, simply, comprehension and continued to look faintly indulgent. A smartly outfitted blonde with a clear fresh complexion and untroubled eyes, she managed to maintain an atmosphere of healthy calm despite Martin's endless complaints and outbursts.

" . . . all that woman does is try to shaft all of us! She's so jealous she's green!" he concluded, sounding almost cheerful.

"I've never liked her. Or that husband of hers!" Lucille Martin lied. She neither liked nor disliked the Bullivants; she simply never thought of them. Her attention had remained centered on the children when they were still at home; now it was focused on running a house smoothly and efficiently.

And coping with Wendell.

"It isn't a question of liking them," he began happily.

Unfortunately, at this juncture the maid entered the room with a vase of flowers.

"Why wasn't the soda water put on ice?" he snapped.

"Wen——,"

"No, Lucille, I don't see why you should be worried about these things. What's the girl for? And"—he was growing more excited—"look at the condition of these glasses! My God! Where were you brought up! Haven't you ever heard of infection? You can damn well take this whole tray back to the kitchen and wash them again. I don't know what you do with your time. And see that they get clean this time!"

Lucille watched the girl retreat to the kitchen. Despite desperate sniffing, the sobs started at the door. Well, it was another toss-up. Would the extra five dollars a week—plus choice culls from Lucille's wardrobe—balance Wendell?

On the whole, she thought not. Gladys had been snapped at just once too often.

Well, that would give her an occupation for the next few weeks. Finding a new girl.

Running Wendell Martin's house smoothly and efficiently was no small task.

4 Exploration

John Putnam Thatcher knew nothing of Lucille Martin's domestic problems, but within days he was privileged to learn that running a trial smoothly and efficiently with Dr. Wendell Martin on the premises was no picnic, either.

Paul Jackson fixed his eyes on the witness.

"Dr. Martin, I put it to you that on the basis of your own testimony, Pemberton Freebody—quite apart from his gunshot wound—would have been unable to survive the strain imposed by the presence of seven hemostatic clips for over four days."

"Put it any way you want!" Martin snapped. "That man died of his wounds, and my operation had nothing to do with it!"

"Is it not a fact, Doctor, that the patient had begun to recover the morning after the operation? That he suddenly collapsed that afternoon, as if affected by severe strain?"

"You can't tell how a patient will react to major surgery. In nine cases out of ten—"

Jackson was peremptory.

"You must be more responsive, Dr. Martin. I am not asking for a generalization about what *most* patients do. I am asking what the late Pemberton Freebody did."

"In my opinion—"

Again Jackson cut in.

"I am not asking for your opinion, Dr. Martin. I want the facts."

"What kind of facts? You're asking me for an opinion as to the man's condition."

"Isn't it true that the patient's pulse, blood pressure, temperature and breathing were adversely affected the day after the operation? Isn't it true that, before this, there had been marked improvement?"

"If you know so much—"

Paul Jackson appealed for assistance. "I must request the defense to keep its witness in order."

"Perhaps I can perform that duty," the judge intervened. "Dr. Martin, I shall remind you that you have sworn to speak the truth and the whole truth. You must answer these questions!"

Wendell Martin crossed his arms.

"I'll answer reasonable questions," he declared. "These

questions are out of order. They're a violation of medical ethics——"

The gavel slammed down.

"In this court," the judge said severely, "I am the arbiter of the propriety of counsel's questions, Doctor."

"I'm not going to let him——"

Gavel, gavel.

"I think," said Thatcher in an undertone to Trinkam, "that this round is ours!"

"Now, Mrs. Doyle, as chief operating room nurse, you were present throughout the operation on Pemberton Freebody, performed by Dr. Martin?"

Mrs. Doyle stared at Jackson coldly. Her navy-blue linen sheath, like her bright blond hair, was beautifully disciplined. But Mrs. Doyle did not suggest hospital austerity; her figure, well-fleshed if mature, was displayed to advantage. Cosmetics and costume jewelry had been applied with a lavish hand.

"Yes, I was," she replied. Her voice, like her person, held the hint of boldness in reserve.

"Then, can you tell us how many hemostatic clips were inserted by Dr. Martin during the operation?" Jackson asked.

"I don't remember."

Jackson raised his eyebrows. "Oh come now, Mrs. Doyle. Do you mean that a nurse of your experience did not note such an important factor?"

"I don't remember."

"Can you tell us how many hemostatic clips were removed from the patient at the conclusion?"

"I don't remember."

Alice Doyle kept her eyes fixed straight ahead of her expressionlessly.

"Can you tell us how long the operation lasted?"

"I don't remember."

"Tell me, Mrs. Doyle," said Paul Jackson, passing from sarcasm to a certain playfulness, "can you remember whether Dr. Martin was present?"

Mrs. Doyle narrowed her eyes in dislike. She was under orders not to abandon the security of mechanical response, Thatcher was willing to bet. But she was clever enough to yield fractionally to pressure. A tremor crossed her carefully schooled features.

"Yes, Dr. Martin was present."

"And, I presume, Pemberton Freebody as well?" But Alice Doyle had recovered the hard unforthcoming tone.

"That is correct."

Paul Jackson appraised her for a moment, then turned away, speaking almost casually, "Now, on the first day of this trial—before we learned the results of the autopsy performed on Pemberton Freebody—you told us about the condition of the deceased when he was being prepared for surgery. You also described his condition during and after the operation. You agree that you did so?"

Mrs. Doyle could have been miles away. "That is correct."

There was nothing playful about Jackson now.

"But today, Mrs. Doyle, you claim you don't remember who was present or what instruments were used. You don't remember what was done to recover clips and sponges. Even though these things are your responsibility—and the condition of the patient is not?"

The nurse was as emphatic as Jackson.

"That is correct." Her words were evenly spaced.

Jackson moved his shoulders lightly.

"Thank you, Mrs. Doyle, that will be all. Thank you for your cooperation."

"And that round?" Charlie Trinkam asked. Thatcher thought for a moment, "Let's call it a draw!"

But Paul Jackson professed satisfaction with the morning's work when he joined John Thatcher and Charlie Trinkam for lunch. His enthusiasm was so infectious that he managed to convince them to remain for the afternoon session, promising developments with a high entertainment value.

"And dollars and cents, too, I trust," Thatcher remarked. "Otherwise, I've had enough of well-rehearsed nurses."

"Sometimes," said Jackson with gusto, summoning a second round of drinks, "sometimes the rehearsal is perfect, but the performance is lousy!"

On this enigmatic note, the conversation turned to the unmanning behavior of an outstanding investment analyst who had recently withdrawn to a Trappist monastery.

Andrew Chisolm, Dexter Loomis and the assembled representatives of Atlantic Mutual Insurance Company enjoyed no such surcease. Moreover they had charges to chaperone.

Loomis slid into heartiness as he approached the Southport contingent at the back of the courtroom and suggested one large luncheon table. That table would not have to be overlarge, since the Southport group at the trial was limited to Dr. Martin, the nurses, and a Dr. Kroner, who had been present in the Emergency Room when Pemberton Freebody was carried in.

This was not pure chance; Paul Jackson was lavishly inviting all interested parties—from the Sloan to the Red Cross—to drop in on the trial. Atlantic Mutual was not. Indeed, a very frank exchange with Dr. Wittke had produced consensus: Southport Memorial Hospital should keep its nose to its own grindstone and boycott legal byplays at the New York County Courthouse.

Unfortunately, Loomis's suggestion foundered, as had so much else, on the idiosyncrasies of Dr. Wendell Martin.

"No," said a stripling from the insurance company, still peering around the crush outside the courtroom, "I don't see Dr. Martin, sir."

"Well, we'll just go on to lunch," said Loomis briskly, aware of the perils raised by increasing public interest and journalistic coverage.

Not that he looked forward to lunch. Chisolm had cravenly begged off, pleading the need for further research. This left Loomis with an ill-assorted group of guests. There was Mrs. Doyle. A quick look told him that Mrs. Doyle was still nursing the bruises from Paul Jackson's rough handling. Moreover, to Dexter Loomis, Mrs. Doyle was not—quite—ladylike. Handsome, yes. Well turned out, yes. But not what he would call a lady.

The second nurse, Miss Gentilhomme, was a a pale depressed girl in a limp seersucker suit. Her plump shining face was innocent of the rouge and lipstick so luxuriantly evident on Mrs. Doyle. Perversely, this did not hearten Dexter Loomis.

Dr. Kroner (Karl, according to Dexter Loomis's notes) was courteous, gentle and totally nondescript. He was not proficient in English.

"We'll just go off and enjoy ourselves without Dr. Martin," said Dexter Loomis robustly.

If Dexter Loomis enjoyed lunch, he did it alone. Mrs. Doyle, after three martinis, remained edgy. Miss Gentilhomme refused a drink in a frightened voice suggesting either awe of her surroundings or terror of her forthcoming appearance on the witness stand. She remained dumb. Dr. Kroner's desire to please foundered on the language barrier.

"Very nice indeed," said Loomis desperately, signaling for the check. "And, Miss Gentilhomme, there's nothing at all to worry about. . . ."

The worst was yet to come. His aide hurried up, bad news writ large on his face.

"I've located Dr. Martin," he announced breathlessly. Mrs. Doyle and Miss Gentilhomme stared; Dr. Kroner leaned forward eagerly.

"I hope he's had lunch," said Dexter Loomis, who hoped something else.

"He hasn't," said the aide. "He's been in the corridor, giving every newspaperman in New York an earful."

"He's *what?*"

"Been talking for about an hour," said the aide, relishing the magnitude of the disaster. "I got Chisolm to shut him up finally. But from the way the reporters set off—I think Dr. Martin got a lot off his chest."

"The goddam fool!" But this cry, Loomis kept to himself.

The same thought was expressed aloud by one of his guests.

"Dr. Martin," said Dr. Kroner with great care, "Dr. Martin is not always wise."

Dr. Martin's confidences to the journalists, suitably edited, were rushed into the afternoon papers. A number of people read them with interest.

At the office of the District Director of Internal Revenue, a young man checking a file nodded to his superior.

"You were right. We do have this Dr. Wendell Martin down as due for an audit."

His superior read further. "Holy Christ! He says he does hundreds of operations a year . . . listen, have an examiner call for an appointment. My God, I thought the first thing they taught them in the medical school was to keep their mouths shut. . . ."

"And ask for payment in cash!" his subordinate added.

"Now, Will, you're getting cynical!"

At the office of the American College of Surgeons, telephone calls alerted a gray-haired man. He read, and did not like what he read.

"But why won't he say anything about who refers patients to him?"

"I can guess," said a colleague.

Gloom descended. "The whole world can guess he's milking kickbacks," the gray-haired man mused. "What about a word to the wise?"

"To Wendell Martin? You're kidding."

The local medical association felt the need to act more imperatively.

"I don't like this. Martin is giving the whole profession a black eye. Now, who do we have at Southport? Wittke, isn't it? Can't he give Martin some advice?"

"He'd better try!"

Even as far away as Wilmington, Delaware, the afternoon papers were making themselves felt. Albert Martin, Wendell's brother, listened to the account read over the phone to him, whistled, then rang off.

"No brains. That's Wen's problem! No proportion. He wants to take on the whole world."

He drummed his fingers on the desk for a while, debating a telephone call to Lucille.

In her way, Lucille Martin could manage Wen, he knew. Certainly better than he could. But Lucille had always confined herself to house and home. As a matter of policy, she chose to remain ignorant of Wendell Martin's business.

Al envied her, at the moment. Then he started running down a list of names. Wittke, Neverson, Bullivant . . .

Dr. Harley Bauer was bubbling over about a young Puerto Rican mother who had managed to have twins in a shopping center when his wife called.

"Harley!" she said excitedly. "Your Wendell Martin has got himself into an awful jam!"

Dr. Bauer, still full of little Jesús and Anastácia, had to ask her to repeat her remarks.

"Oh, Harley," his wife wailed in mock despair. "You are absolutely the only man in the world who could forget someone who got you fired!"

"Now, hon," he said. "I didn't forget. What is it?"

"Get a paper!" she directed him. "And what time will you be home tonight?"

Harley sent his nurse out for a paper and snatched a

moment (between a tricky thyroid condition and a small staph infection) to read the details, shaking his head as Dr. Wendell Martin's intemperate outburst unrolled before his eyes.

"Boy," he said. Suddenly, something in column two captured his attention. Since he was by nature gregarious, he drifted out of his office across the hall.

"Stan, you read this about Dr. Martin?"

Dr. Stanley Fink's dental offices were almost as spanking new as Dr. Bauer's.

"You mean your esteemed colleague who left the stuff in that patient?" Fink asked, disengaging himself from an open mouth. He moved to the doorway. In his waiting room, Harley Bauer was now reading aloud.

"Yeah . . . say, listen to this! February 17 . . . you know what that means?"

"Just a few minutes, Mrs. Ober," said Dr. Fink, firmly closing the door on his equipment-festooned victim. "No, what?"

"That's the night that I got bounced from Southport!" said Bauer.

Fink plucked the paper from him and read avidly. "You mean this jerk really was your colleague?" he asked. "He must think he's God Almighty! He wants to take on everybody. Listen to this! He's going to sue the AMA and demand a public apology from Hanover! On top of that, nobody's got any right to ask *him* questions about anything!"

"That's Martin, all right. He was chief of surgery out at Southport. He got me fired as pathologist."

Fink remembered the details of this operation. "February 17? He fired you the day of this operation? So he was upset. That's why he left the kitchen sink in this poor guy." Bauer was too engrossed to respond to the habitual mockery.

"Wendell Martin upset? Why should he be?" he said, rescuing his paper and turning to an inner page. "I was the guy that got canned. And believe me, Martin was tickled to do it. He was always out to get me . . . him and that Bullivant bitch. I told you . . ."

Stanley Fink's interest in non-dental matters was limited. However, with his customary good sense, he pointed out that this might have been a blessing in disguise. Bauer's new practice was getting off the ground nicely; it would do a young man no good to be associated with any hospital currently rating Southport's headlines.

"I mean," he amplified, reading one aloud, " *'Southport Mem Operation Challenged.'* "

He cocked his head. Muted voices from his office suggested restiveness or worse on Mrs. Ober's part.

Bauer, however, was deep in his own thoughts. His open, normally good-natured face was solemn.

"I can't help wondering if there isn't more than a coincidence here."

Fink asked what that was supposed to mean.

"I told you about . . . the trouble," Harley said.

"Yes," said Fink. "Listen, I've got to get back inside. Why don't you and Joan drop by for a drink tonight?"

"It might be a good idea for me to run out to Southport, just to see what's going on," Bauer continued. "That way I could get the real lowdown on Martin."

Dr. Fink shook his head sadly. "Always afraid you'll miss something, Harley," he said reprovingly. "Remember, curiosity killed the cat."

But Bauer protested that Southport Memorial Hospital held no further dangers for him. This time Wendell Martin couldn't get anybody else to take the rap for him.

Fink shrugged. "You may be right," he said, opening the door to his office. "You still have friends out at Southport, don't you? Here we are, Mrs. Ober. I think we're just about ready now. If you'll just open a little wider. . . ."

Dr. Fink did not hear Harley Bauer's response to his observations.

"I've got friends out at Southport," said Harley Bauer slowly. "But I've got enemies, too."

An apprehensive Marie Gentilhomme finally mounted the witness stand. John Putnam Thatcher, whose partisanship had sharply defined limits, watched with pity. Lambs always had this effect on him.

Paul Jackson, ostensibly mellowed by an excellent lunch, smiled.

"Miss Gentilhomme, were you present at the operation on Pemberton Freebody?"

Trying to emulate the spartan conduct of her elder, she quickly said:

"I don't remember."

The ripple of laughter through the courtroom surprised her into blushing.

Paul Jackson became a comforting father figure.

"I'm confusing you," he reproached himself. "Now, let's start farther back. How long have you been qualified as a registered nurse, Miss Gentilhomme?"

"For nine months, sir. Since last September."

"And how long have you been employed at Southport Memorial Hospital?"

"Since January."

"So, on the night of February 17, when Pemberton Freebody was brought into the hospital, you were on night duty, weren't you?"

Silence.

"Come now," he said gently. "You have already told us that you were."

"Yes," she said, sounding scared.

"And did you see the patient before he was brought into the operating room?"

"Oh, no!" The truth and her relief was transparent.

"But you saw him in the operating room?"

"I don't remember."

"Oh, now, Miss Gentilhomme, you must have noticed him."

Miss Gentilhomme was younger and more vulnerable than Mrs. Doyle.

"Well, I did just notice him."

"Where were you throughout the operation?" Jackson asked with flattering interest.

"I was removing instruments from the sterilizer, bringing them to the table and taking them away. Most of the time, I wasn't even at the table."

"But when you were—I suppose you glanced at the patient?"

"I . . . I don't know."

Lunch had not really mellowed Paul Jackson. The questions were coming faster now and the witness, showing confusion, was trying hard to distinguish between innocent questions and questions about the patient. Jackson helped her to her destruction by snapping his queries about Pemberton Freebody, and relaxing the pace on others.

"You were too busy with the instruments?"

"Oh yes! I barely saw the patient or the doctors!"

"You were busy bringing instruments to the table and removing them, too?"

"Yes, sir!"

"And you started to take things away after the bullet had been removed from the patient?"

"That's right," she said, shying again at the word "patient."

"So you did notice when that part of the operation was finished, didn't you, Miss Gentilhomme?"

"Only because I started taking things away. But honestly, I wasn't noticing the patient!"

Jackson seemed to yield to the pleading in her voice.

"All right. But if you weren't noticing the patient, perhaps you were noticing what Dr. Martin and Mrs. Doyle said about him. You did have to listen, didn't you—so that you'd know what instruments were wanted?"

"Yes, but I didn't really pay attention—not unless it was about the instruments." Marie Gentilhomme had her moment of innocent triumph.

"And when you began taking the instruments away, Miss Gentilhomme, when did you first notice that hemostats were missing?"

The lawyer's voice was free from tension as he asked this critical question. He reproduced the slight decrescendo that Marie Gentilhomme had come to associate with safety. Without missing a beat, she fell into the trap.

"I didn't notice until Mrs. Doyle told Dr. Martin."

"And what did Dr. Martin say?" Jackson asked casually. Mentally he, Charlie Trinkam, John Thatcher (and the judge as well) were anathematizing the spectators who let their gasps become audible.

"He said not to bother him because he'd made his own count, and anyway he'd completed the sutures. . . ."

Abruptly, Miss Gentilhomme's hearing caught up with her speech. A hand flew to her mouth as the echoes of her last two replies hung in the now-silent room.

Paul Jackson spoke with quiet, deadly calm, repeating the substance of her replies.

"So, while the patient was still on the operating table, the chief operating room nurse, Mrs. Doyle, drew the surgeon's attention to the discrepancy in the hemostat count. And Dr. Martin told her not to bother him because he'd already completed the sutures. That's what happened, isn't it?"

As he pressed her gently, the courtroom held its breath. All eyes were fixed on the shrinking figure in the witness chair.

Miserably she glanced around the room for help that would not come. It was a long time before she replied:

"Yes."

Thatcher saw Andrew Chisolm struggling out of a fog to protest. But Jackson hurried on to his stark conclusion too quickly for intervention.

"And what did Mrs. Doyle say?"

Too late, Marie Gentilhomme remembered her instructions.

"I don't remember!"

Five minutes later, Paul Jackson was speaking with firing-squad cadence.

"Your honor, I find it necessary—once again—to recall Dr. Wendell Martin."

5 Malignancy

Newspapers and life being what they are, the evening headlines were inevitable:

NURSE TELLS ALL

The violent exchanges between Wendell Martin and Paul Jackson, the increasingly thunderous animadversions from the bench, the testimony of two doctors from Massachusetts General Hospital (unable to give opinions about what seven hemostats would do since at Mass General, etc. etc.), even Pemberton Freebody, were relegated to small print. Marie Gentilhomme's unwitting disclosures catapulted her into brief notoriety.

NURSE SPILLS BEANS, said the tabloids the next morning with an unfortunate photograph showing a dazed Marie trying to hide behind Mrs. Doyle.

"Disgraceful," said Everett Gabler, oldest, primmest and most easily outraged member of Thatcher's staff.

"What is, Ev?" Thatcher asked idly, leafing through some research reports forwarded by Walter Bowman.

"This emphasis upon personalities," said Gabler austerely.

"Oh, I don't know," Thatcher replied infuriatingly. "Here's a situation where a doctor seems to have more or less killed a patient. And the hospital is engaged in a massive cover-up. Now *that* may be disgusting. But it seems excessive to react to the American press. Under the circumstances, they come out looking fairly good. After all, Ev, they have neither slaughtered anybody, nor condoned such slaughter."

Everett Gabler, like Miss Corsa, had developed selective hearing when it came to John Thatcher's whimsies.

"Constantly focusing upon trivialities," he muttered, turning to page four.

But Gabler was wrong. It was not trivia which the newspapers had fastened upon. To lawyers like Paul Jackson, Marie's testimony was a small brick in the great wall of evidence. But only lawyers, and coldhearted institutions such as the Sloan Guaranty Trust and Hanover University, are obsessed with items like one hundred thousand dollars. The world at large, and Southport in particular, found Marie Gentilhomme's revelations incomparably more dramatic than Wendell Martin's virtually uninterrupted histrionics—and almost as engrossing as the question of why Pemberton Freebody had died. Marie was young; not beautiful (despite the newspapers who ignored her solid contours and undistinguished features to describe her as slim and lovely), but young. This, spiced by the distress she could not hide, was enough for the vast majority of the newspaper reading public.

In Southport, things were more complex. In the town, the first flurry of excitement about *Freebody* v. *Atlantic Mutual* had simmered down to a general, if ill-defined, feeling that a bunch of high-priced outsiders were trying to pull a fast one. Many Southportites had been born in Southport Memorial Hospital, many had consulted Dr. Wittke, many had had gall bladders removed by Dr. Martin. Familiarity, after all, breeds complaisance more often than it breeds contempt; Southport had buzzed for a while, then decided that it probably wasn't true. If it was true—well, these things happen.

Marie Gentilhomme forced Southport to think uncomfortable thoughts.

This was enough to justify headlines.

Inside the hospital, of course, feelings were bound to be stronger. Marie had committed a worse offense than killing a patient; she had let down the side and betrayed a doctor.

She had begun paying for her sins before she was clear of Manhattan.

"But everyone will know that you are not . . . that you could not . . . it was not your fault."

Dr. Kroner had been worried as he tried to comfort Marie.

She had sat in the corner of the car speeding back to Long Island, huddled as far as possible from Mrs. Doyle. The silence remained unbroken, except for an occasional comment from Dr. Kroner.

Dr. Martin would have had plenty to say. Fortunately he had been detained for further consultation with the lawyers. His red-eyed glare had boded ill for Marie; today Dexter Loomis and Andrew Chisolm were dogging Martin with a view to keeping his comments off the record, but there would be no such protection for Marie at the hospital tomorrow—despite Dr. Kroner's comfort.

They debouched him at the high-rise apartments on the

outskirts of Southport, and Marie was immediately given a more realistic view.

"Well!" Alice Doyle exploded in a harsh exhalation of smoke.

Marie flinched.

"I've got to hand it to you," said Mrs. Doyle raspingly. "You sure blew things sky high."

"I'm sorry, Alice. I . . . I got confused."

Furiously, Alice Doyle ground out her cigarette, slashed at the ashes marring her navy-blue sheath.

"Sorry? A lot of good that's going to do—now! Oh, for God's sake, don't cry! Here, here's your purse. Be a good girl and powder your nose. You don't want your aunt and uncle to worry."

Marie smiled weak gratitude and subsided.

Alice Doyle twisted and retwisted her gloves. "I told you! Wittke told you! Why couldn't you just say you didn't remember. . . . Now we're really in trouble. Oh hell!"

Marie listened, but Alice Doyle was talking to herself.

"This is really going to be rough. I don't know what they'll do, now." She woke to her surroundings and spoke with grim honesty.

"I just don't know what's going to happen to us—or to you, Marie!"

Her sentiments were shared in many quarters, among them, the offices of the director of nursing. Mrs. Stosser listened to the telephone first thing next morning with tempered resentment.

"Well, of course, Doctor, I *can* remove Nurse Gentilhomme from O. R. duty . . . yes, Doctor? But we're shorthanded as we are . . . yes, Doctor!"

The phone she was holding went dead. Mrs. Stosser pursed her lips. This was the third curt demand made for Gentilhomme's dismissal. As if nurses grew on trees! With the cunning of the cornered, Mrs. Stosser drew forth a large schedule and studied it.

If she took Gentilhomme out of the operating room and tucked her somewhere out of sight, say up in Ward Four, why, by the time this furor died down . . .

Without hesitation, she picked up the phone and dialed the number of the modest bungalow where Gentilhomme roomed with her aunt, her uncle and innumerable nieces and nephews. She reached Marie after some difficulties with Aunt Yvonne. In brisk, no-nonsense tones she gave the girl her new assignment.

Trust Gentilhomme not to understand!

"But, Mrs. Stosser, my uncle Dominic can't pick me up until eleven-thirty. If I get off duty at ten o'clock—,"

"You can wait!" said Mrs. Stosser. "This is no time for you to worry about commuting problems!"

Mrs. Stosser hung up, satisfied with her stratagem. She was as devoted to Southport Memorial Hospital as anyone else, but her primary job was to keep a nursing staff. And Marie Gentilhomme was not leaving—not until Mrs. Stosser was convinced that some other people weren't leaving first.

"And I just don't know what's going to happen!"

Through the arteries and veins of the hospital, from the outpatient clinic (in the basement) to Obsterics (sixth floor, new wing), similar uncertainty percolated. To a large extent it remained unvoiced; hospitals, like armies, have people working with those in whom it would be dangerous to confide. Doctor may talk to doctor—but not all doctors. The nurse network is beyond rational representation.

The only people on whom this hierarchy does not weigh heavily are the orderlies. At Southport, they were not talking about Dr. Martin—or Marie Gentilhomme—because they were not interested.

But hospital routine is one of the most powerful forces known to man, and it functioned at Southport Memorial. The work went on.

Early that evening, Harley Bauer, bouncing up the stairs and bursting into the main entrance, felt a pang of disappointment at the very normalcy that met his eyes. He and Joan had stayed up far too late discussing Southport Memorial. Indeed, it was almost like old times, he thought with a chuckle. When he had been on the staff, he had taken home his troubles—and what troubles they had been!

Perhaps that was why Joan had been so gleeful in writing dialogue for the tricky little exchange before him. She always felt things more than he did.

Still, here he was, back at good old Southport.

Harley Bauer paused, missing Joan's prompting.

On the surface, things hadn't changed. Two harried women were bedeviling the reception clerk, while three men and one small child sat dully in the waiting room. White-coated figures strode importantly in and out of elevators, past swinging doors. Beyond those doors, up on the floors above, carts were moving patients, trays were being loaded, nurses were sneaking smokes, labor was continuing, life was ending,

"Harley?"

Someone was genuinely glad to see him. Eagerly, Harley turned.

Sid Segal, incongruously gripping a package from which long plush ears protruded, had hurried up behind him.

"Good to see you again! I didn't get a chance to tell you how sorry I was you decided to leave."

Harley's departure, abrupt, involuntary and dramatic, had been the last uproar at Southport Memorial Hospital. At the time, he assumed everybody must be talking about it. And here was Sid, who knew everything. He hadn't known.

"It just goes to show," Harley Bauer thought he would tell Joan, "how they can hush things up!"

Could they hush up Dr. Martin's operation after what that nurse had said?

" . . . and your wife. Give her my regards. So, you're practicing in Garden City? Not a bad location . . ."

Sid was continuing, almost friendlier now than when Harley Bauer was dropping into the drugstore daily. Harley was unfeignedly glad to see him. In a world of great men, Sid was a note of humanity. He owned the drugstore and the whole business block adjoining, but he was not above delivering stuffed rabbits to small patients in the children's wing.

"You've come back to see your friends, Dr. Bauer," Segal suggested with a friendly prod and the flattery he always extended to even the youngest doctor.

Tactfully, Harley lowered his voice and confided: "I still haven't cleaned out my locker. While I'm here I thought I could see Dr. Wittke . . . or Dr. Martin, maybe. If he's here . . ?"

Segal knew about Harley Bauer's insatiable curiosity. Locker cleaning had waited until Southport Memorial had secrets to hide. He answered the question in Harley's voice.

"Oh, he's here. A little thing like a trial—what's that to Dr. M tin?"

With clumsy subtlety, Harley said, "He's carrying on as if everything were okay, huh?"

Segal became confidential. "Me, I'd stay away. If he asked me, I'd tell him to stay away. Let things die down. After all, this is only temporary . . ."

"I wonder," said Bauer, looking around.

Segal bent forward in interest, moving both of them slightly out of the traffic, to facilitate talk.

He was just in time. Like a majestic ship sailing into harbor, Dr. Edith Bullivant swept past them with her customary gracious greeting to the girl behind the desk. Even Segal rated a friendly wave.

Dr. Edith Bullivant looked straight through the substantial Harley Bauer, who gazed stolidly back.

But she had seen him. And, as she moved on, her expression was not pleasant. Edith Bullivant had been a doctor for more years than she cared to remember, and her natural talent for diagnosis had been sharpened. Unerringly, she knew that Harley Bauer was not simply visiting friends. As clearly, she saw that Wendell Martin had opened the door. Soon there would be other enemies of Southport Memorial gossiping, whispering, speculating.

She was hesitating at the door to her office when a familiar figure rounded the corner.

"Phil!" she called out.

Obediently, Dr. Wittke approached. "Edith," he said with a fair assumption of ease. "I've been looking in on a rather interesting multiple fracture. Young Jim"—his forty-year-old son and heir—"wanted my opinion. . . ."

Without qualms, she dismissed this. "I thought you said you were going to talk to that girl."

Wittke projected sorrow. "I did. Poor child, she was frightened by the lawyer. You know, yourself—"

She knew how genuine this sorrow was. Ruthlessly, she cut off further pieties. "Somebody had better do something," she said baldly. "If Wendell goes on the way he's going, we'll all be hurt. And as for that nurse, somebody better remind her that nurses don't talk about operations—to anybody!"

"An understandable sentiment." The smooth new voice was shaded with mockery.

Dr. Bullivant's eyes blazed but Dr. Neverson, who had come up behind them, ignored her.

"Phil, I have to talk to you," he said wearily. Dark circles under his eyes, a stoop to his shoulders, a crumpled jacket testified to fatigue and long hours.

"Now, wait a minute, Roy," Edith Bullivant began.

"This doesn't concern you, Edith," said Neverson in exhaustion. He set off down the hall, and the older doctor promptly followed. Wittke was no coward, but he was happy to escape Edith Bullivant. She was the only person in the hospital—possibly the world—who unnerved him. Although he did not realize it, she infected him with the chill of *déjà vu*: Edith Bullivant had many uncanny resemblances to Philip Wittke.

He followed Neverson to his own office, then tried to regain the initiative.

"Now, Roy," he said, settling at his desk, "I hope you're not going to complain about the nurse. I did what I could. . . ."

"The nurse?" Neverson asked vaguely. "Oh hell, that's the way the ball bounces. No, Phil, this is getting serious. Did you read what Wen said yesterday? Or for that matter, have you talked to Kroner about how he acted on the stand?"

Composedly, Wittke replied that he felt it prudent to evince no unusual interest in *Freebody v. Atlantic Mutual.*

Neverson slammed a tanned hand on the desk. "It's too late for us to behave like ostriches!"

Then, with an effort, he controlled himself. "Is Martin in? I'm going to talk to him. . . ."

"You'll be wasting your time," said Wittke quietly.

Roy Neverson believed him. Behind the pompous façade was a shrewd, calculating intelligence.

Wittke continued. "He is in, and in excellent spirits."

"Well, I'm still going to try to talk sense to him. . . ."

And he was out of the room.

Wittke watched him go unhopefully. If anybody could talk sense to Wendell Martin, the outlook would certainly be brighter. But Wittke prided himself on being a realist. Accordingly, he was worried. Deeply worried.

Dr. Wendell Martin on the contrary was not worried, Roy Neverson discovered. Perversely, he was exhilarated. The reason emerged.

"I finally got hold of that bitch of a nurse!" he said, eyes gleaming. "She's not so cocky now! I told her I'd have her blacklisted! She'll never get a job in a decent hospital again! She's got to go. I won't have her in my hospital. . . ."

Neverson found himself speaking slowly and distinctly once again: "We can take care of the nurse later, Wen. I want to talk to you about this publicity. . . ."

To himself, he was saluting Phil Wittke's astuteness; there was no use talking to Wendell Martin.

Martin looked through some papers quickly. "Just

checking my schedule next week," he explained. "The trial? Let me tell you . . ."

He did. He told Neverson what he was going to say, how he was going to make Jackson eat his words, how Atlantic Mutual would get on their knees to thank him . . .

When he stood in the corridor ten minutes later, Roy shook his head. Was Wendell Martin completely sane? He doubted it. And, despite an intelligence keener than many of his colleagues supposed, Roy Neverson was lost.

"I don't know what's going to happen," he said. "Might as well go home. . . ."

But home was no longer the house at the point with Julie and the children. It was an impersonal apartment. Perhaps this was what reminded Roy of one last chore.

He made his way to the desk on the fourth floor.

Marie Gentilhomme was the nurse on duty. Too late, Neverson tried to hide the irrational flick of irritation this caused him. Pale, moist-eyed, docile Miss Gentilhomme had not meant to add fuel to the fire.

Neverson took a deep breath while the girl looked up at him. Scared to death, he thought. Small wonder, after Wendell Martin chewed her out.

"Yes, Doctor?" she said.

He made his voice gentle. "Miss Gentilhomme, Dr. Myron is going to take a specimen from old Mrs. Guild this evening if he has time. He'll run the tests and bring the results up here. Now, if he does, I want you to call me. . . ."

"Yes, Doctor."

Even this grated. Roy Neverson was too tired and too worried to think clearly. He had to hang onto himself.

"If Myron brings the report up, I want you to call me. If I'm not in my office, call me at home. . . ."

"Yes, Doctor . . . ."

Abruptly, he turned on his heel and left.

Marie Gentilhomme looked after him blankly. Like most of the nurses, she admired Dr. Neverson's dark good looks. Like all the nurses, she knew that he was moody. And today, he was tense and tired.

And free to go home now.

There was no such escape for her, although a sick headache pounded her temples. She was still on duty. Earlier she had been grateful for this duty. Arriving at the hospital, she had shrunk from hostility at every corner. But almost immediately she was caught up in the unceasing demands made on the only registered nurse in Ward Four. Unimaginative by nature, she had no time to think about yesterday or tomorrow, as she checked on patients, ordered special diets, filled in charts, supervised the nurses' aides and ran errands for importunate visitors. The long day had wound slowly into evening, unnoticed under the impact of the endless chores.

But then Dr. Wendell Martin caught her in the elevator.

Marie shuddered, and touched her aching forehead, forcing a smile from Mrs. Perkins, who was passing the desk on her way to the bathroom.

Then, Dr. Bullivant had come up to check on one of her patients.

Even Dr. Wittke . . .

It was after ten o'clock when Marie came off duty. She was only dimly conscious of leaden feet and a sense of nausea. Mechanically, she checked the records on her desk for Nurse Dodd, who looked at her strangely but mercifully said nothing. Then she stopped at the telephone in the office and tried Dr. Neverson's number to report that Dr. Myron had left Mrs. Guild's report on her desk.

Numbly putting the phone down, she walked like an automaton to the elevator. She had an endless hour to wait until her uncle drove the battered car up to the parking lot entrance, but she could sink into the merciful oblivion of the Nurse's Lounge. She passed a telephone on the first floor without thinking about trying Dr. Neverson again, turned the corner and saw Alice Doyle sagging against a closed door. Dimmed lights exaggerated the shadows under her eyes; her rouged cheeks looked raddled. Here too was fatigue so deep that it obliterated personality. "There's been an accident . . . they're still bringing them in . . . farm laborers in a truck. Oh hell! Have you got a cigarette, Marie? I left mine in my car . . ."

"Going home?" Doyle asked vaguely.

Doyle would go back to Emergency in five minutes. Marie did not hesitate. "I'll go get them," she said.

Alice Doyle leaned back again and closed her eyes.

Marie's weary feet carried her down to the basement exit where a naked bulb cast harsh light over the stairs. She was edging toward the modest sedan that Alice Doyle always parked near the laundry ramp when she tripped.

"Wh . . . what!"

Suddenly frightened of the dark, of the fingers of light, of the massive building looming over her, Marie froze. Then, with an effort of will, she forced herself to look down.

She had tripped over an outstretched arm. Unsteadily, she squatted on her heels and peered into the shadow. It was a body. Part of the forehead sloped inward, crushed and bloody.

For a moment, Marie looked at death, as she had looked at death before. Then, slowly, awareness returned. Without moving, she looked in horror at the features.

This was Dr. Wendell Martin.

Although she did not know she was doing it, she opened her mouth and screamed, screamed, screamed.

6 Removal

These mechanical, inhuman screams stabbed into the lonely darkness of the parking lot. Almost before Marie Gentilhomme had relapsed into convulsive sobbing, Dr. Kroner, with Alice Doyle at his heels, was hurrying out of the basement entrance. And even as Dr. Kroner and Mrs. Doyle absorbed the macabre tableau, Dr. Philip Wittke joined them.

He took charge with complete authority. Dr. Kroner had dropped onto one knee beside the body. He looked up and reported what Dr. Wittke had already guessed: nothing more could be done for Wendell Martin.

Wittke turned to deal with Marie, who was half-struggling against the restraining arm of Mrs. Doyle.

"The last twenty-four hours have been too much for her," Mrs. Doyle said hoarsely.

"Take her inside and give her a sedative," Wittke rasped. Unconscious of Kroner's puzzled stare, Wittke did not move but continued to stare into space. Then, white-faced, he gave further directions, sharp and clear.

Thanks to these directions, when the state police arrived the body was still untouched. Lieutenant Joseph Perenna reported this to his superior several hours later.

"Not that I needed a doctor to see the guy was dead," he said. "Half his skull was crushed in."

He squinted, conjuring up a mental vision of the cordoned-off parking lot. Troopers guarded the entrance; the hospital staff had been shooed inside. Two cars had been positioned, their headlights beamed on the dead man. A steady drizzle had begun so that the fine raindrops clouded the converging cones of illumination. There had been little blood: it was soon washed away. The head—Perenna shook his own at recollection of the gruesome mess. The crossed lights had erased all shadow so that the body, spread-eagled on the path, looked two-dimensional, like a paper doll. One jacket pocket had been completely pulled out, presumably during a quick search; the pale lining showed up starkly against the dark gray of the victim's suit.

Perenna passed photographs of the scene across the desk.

The captain adjusted a pair of glasses and studied them closely. At the end of his examination, he frowned.

"Did our doctor have anything to say?"

"Nothing that isn't self-evident. An instantaneous death, almost. As for the weapon, it was smooth, rounded, quite narrow and heavily weighted. Any kind of metal bar would have done the job."

"And what about the people at the hospital? They have anything to say?"

Perenna shrugged fatalistically.

"At first they were too stunned to say anything. Then they started to gabble about why the police didn't stop all these muggings."

"They read too many newspapers," his superior grunted. "Southport isn't New York City. There aren't a lot of muggings here. In fact, I can't remember the last one."

The captain was silent for a moment as he prodded one of the pictures with a thoughtful forefinger. At length he asked a question.

"Anything strike you as strange?"

"Everything," Perenna said promptly. "It's the queerest so-called mugging I've ever seen. Our mugger wants to knock out his victim so he swipes him with a metal bar hard enough to crush his skull like an eggshell. Then he neatly removes a wallet from the inside breastpocket, but is so nervous he reverses an outside pocket where no man carries anything valuable. You could say he was just being thorough, except that he leaves an expensive gold watch in full view. He carries away both the weapon and the wallet, even though every fifteen-year-old punk knows enough to ditch the wallet fast. We may find it once it's daylight, but right now I'm willing to bet we won't. To top it all off, our mugger prefers working in a busy, lighted parking lot!"

"Not so busy, at that hour of night."

"A lot busier than a deserted side street!"

The captain nodded. "Yes," he agreed, "and there's another funny thing too. This Wendell Martin has been getting a lot of publicity. Too much. It makes quite a coincidence, his getting knocked off by accident. Hmm . . . who did you say that doctor was, the one who made sure the body wasn't touched?"

"Dr. Philip Wittke."

The captain consulted an exhaustive internal reference file on the personages of Suffolk County.

"He's one of the brass at the hospital. So, he's used to taking charge. On the other hand, he made damned sure we'd get the picture."

"You can't tell at this stage of the game. But how do you want this to go out to the newsboys? They'll be wanting something soon. Particularly with Martin being a name."

The captain's white teeth flashed in a sudden, humorless smile.

"That's no problem. Just tell them it's the latest in our rash of muggings. No sense in tipping our hand . . . yet."

Accordingly, the death of Wendell Martin was trumpeted to the world as a straightforward mugging. Reaction, for the most part, was correspondingly simple.

The Internal Revenue office immediately abandoned plans for an investigation of possible tax evasion. Overnight Wendell Martin had been transformed from monster to victim; more important, he was dead. Any discrepancies in his tax payments would be adjusted when his estate was closed. There was no longer any thought of prosecution.

Various arms of the medical profession announced public sorrow and breathed private sighs of relief. A troublesome problem had disappeared from their horizon.

Only at Southport Memorial was relief tempered by caution.

Philip Wittke cradled the phone. "That was the local medical association," he reported. "They're coming to the funeral."

"I hope they haven't confused Wendell Martin with the GP of the year." Roy Neverson sounded preoccupied. "The last thing we want now is a big public funeral!"

The blotter he had been toying with disappeared between his strong fingers to emerge a crumpled ball. He stared at it for a moment, then tossed it into the wastebasket before rising to pace back and forth before Wittke's desk.

"The quieter the better for us, Phil," he said.

"I know, Roy," Wittke too sounded absent. "But we certainly can count on the medical association. After all, they're as anxious as we are to avoid notoriety!"

"Are they?" Neverson asked softly.

Wittke had not spent a lifetime cultivating unperturbability to be disturbed by unanswered, and unanswerable questions. Firmly keeping his gaze on the window, he said:

"We all want the same thing, Roy. A dignified funeral for Wendell—to serve as a symbol of his professional achievements over a lifetime of service, instead of anything that reflects this last few weeks, and all the unsuitable publicity inspired by avaricious insurance claims."

Wittke made *Freebody* v. *Atlantic Mutual* sound like a teen-age orgy, Neverson thought. It was typical of him. Also typical was the unctuous ease with which he was simultaneously denying the existence of a problem, and pondering a solution.

Experience had taught Dr. Neverson that this curious technique rarely impaired the effectiveness of the solutions that Wittke ultimately produced.

Nevertheless, he could not restrain his impatience at a generation content to be clever without sounding clever. This, in turn, reminded him of something else.

"You're right, Phil," he said after weighing Wittke's words. "That's the line for us .to take. But one little thing—what about Edith Bullivant?"

Without seeming to, Dr. Wittke relaxed.

"Edith Bullivant is a sensible woman," he said. "She knows that we have to take the long view. That's something you younger men are sometimes apt to lose sight of. We—all of us here at Southport—we all want to remember Wendell as a valued colleague of many years standing. It's all a matter of perspective. And Edith, I am confident, even though she's not on the staff, agrees fully. So there is nothing for us to worry about any more—" He caught that unfortunate sentence in time. "Nothing at all to worry about. Except possibly—Lucille."

The uncertainty in the last comment erased the amusement dawning on Neverson's face.

"Lucille! My God, Phil, I'd forgotten about her! Do you think there's any likelihood that Wendell explained the situation to her?"

Philip Wittke was not relaxed now.

"I think Wendell would not have wanted to burden her with that kind of detail," he said, thinking aloud. "Which means that one of us should have a talk with her. After the funeral, of course. Unfortunately, Lucille and I have never really been close. Perhaps, Roy, you—"

Neverson was decisive.

"Oh no you don't! Not on your life. Lucille Martin has made it perfectly clear what she thinks of me."

He scowled for a moment, then looked up.

"And Phil, I don't think any of us should get involved with Lucille,"

Wittke, rather testily, asked what that meant.

Neverson became persuasive. "What about Al Martin? He's her brother-in-law, after all. It would be better, and a lot more natural, if *he* had a talk with her. Probably wouldn't have to go into detail at all. You know Al. He'll be coming up anyway to help out. He probably wouldn't want any of us interfering."

Wittke nodded. "Good idea, Roy. He is the best possible choice. And, as you say, that means that there's no real need for any of us to approach Lucille about business. In fact, we won't have to worry about Lucille at all!"

How mistaken he was, neither man realized until Dr. Wittke's secretary announced that the widow was on the phone. The danger was not apparent at first.

"Philip? Is that you?"

The voice was heavy and slow, almost drugged.

"Yes, my dear. I'm so glad that you called. When I tried to get you earlier, your maid said you were lying down. Quite the wisest thing for you at the moment."

"There's nothing else to do," said the lifeless monotone. "Wen is dead. Everything is over."

"Now, my dear, I know you feel that way now. It's only natural. The shock lasts a long time. But life goes on, and you must go on with it."

Philip Wittke was experienced with the recently widowed. The burst of angry denial usually sparked by this kind of consolation was beneficial. The important thing was to arouse an emotional response, any response.

Lucille Martin, however, was beyond the reach of such tactics. She did not argue or hit out; she merely asked, out of vast exhaustion, why he had called.

"I want you to know that you mustn't worry about the ... the arrangements. I'll take care of all the details, Lucille. I want you to feel that you can rely on me. Anything at all. Now, would you like me to speak with the undertaker?"

"The undertaker?" Mrs. Martin might have been hearing the word for the first time. "A man from Pfost's is coming here in about an hour. He said Wen had already arranged something."

"Then, I'll come right over, shall I? In about forty-five minutes?"

"It doesn't matter. I can't think about that sort of thing now. Nothing matters any more . . . nothing except punishing the man who killed Wen."

Wittke murmured sympathetically. "You don't have to worry about that, my dear. The police, I'm sure, will do everything possible——"

Lucille Martin interrupted him. Not quickly, not vehemently, but with a muted assurance that was almost terrifying.

"But the police are wrong, Philip. Wen would never have been mugged. He was always very careful. Somebody hated him and killed him. Somebody took Wen from me. And he was all I had."

A hint of sharpness entered Wittke's manner. He raised his eyebrows at Neverson, who was listening intently.

"Now, my dear, you mustn't say that sort of thing," he said. "I realize you're upset, but it can only make for unpleasantness, and you wouldn't want that."

"I don't care," she said simply. "Somebody murdered Wen, and they have to pay for it. I'm sorry if it will be unpleasant."

"Lucille!" Wittke was genuinely aghast. "I hope you haven't been saying—Well, never mind that, I'll come over right away."

The widow was very docile.

"Yes, you come right now, Philip. I'd like to talk to you. But I'm right. You'll see."

Wittke let out his breath as the receiver clicked.

"I just can't believe it, Lucille, of all people!"

"What's the matter?" Neverson asked.

Wittke gave him the gist of their conversation.

Neverson stared.

"That's incredible," he protested. "Of course, it's simply shock."

Wittke nodded mournfully. "You can't tell about sudden widowhood. Lucille always seemed so calm about Wendell. She was a good wife but you'd never expect her to go off the deep end."

Neverson hesitated before he spoke. Then he shook his head.

"I think you've got it wrong, Phil. True, she didn't act like an adoring bride. But she raised her children, and after they left home I think Wendell became her child. And she indulged him in a way she never indulged her daughters. If he stormed and raged, she was tolerant as if he were a spoiled child. But, by and large, she saw to it that what Wendell wanted, Wendell got."

Echoes of that automaton voice lingered in Wittke's ear and produced their own doubt.

"You could be right. That's what she sounds like—a mother who's lost a child. That's very bad."

Neverson brooded as he sat in silence. Eventually he came to an unpalatable conclusion.

"It could be very bad if she persists in this business about someone hating Wendell. Because you know the name that'll come to her mind? . . . Harley Bauer!"

Wittke's immediate reaction to this analysis was to reach for his hat. "Don't worry," he said confidently. "I'll quiet her down. She'll have forgotten this lunacy by tomorrow."

"I hope so," said Neverson, following him to the door. "All we need is to have Bauer in this mess. What if he talks?"

"Whatever his faults, Harley Bauer is a doctor." Wittke was at his stolidest. "We can count on him."

Neverson's equanimity was restored by this *volte-face*. Poor Philip must be feeling hard pressed, indeed, to defend Bauer. When they had first learned that Harley was joining a panel medical program, Wittke had apostrophized his conduct as unethical, unprofessional, un-American and downright communistic.

"Oh, I suppose so," he agreed. "Under normal conditions. But I hate to think of what he might say if the widow accuses him pointblank of murder."

"I'll take care of that."

"Fine. While you're at it, I intend to have a word with our other little troublemaker."

Neverson strode briskly toward the group at the end of the corridor.

Marie Gentilhomme was so busy listening to Dr. Kroner and Alice Doyle that she did not see Dr. Neverson until his voice at her elbow made her jump.

"Nurse! I want a word with you!"

She could tell right away that Dr. Neverson was in one of his difficult moods. He wouldn't yell, like Dr. Kroner sometimes did. Instead he would be terribly polite and cutting, every now and then pausing to give her a chance to reply, when he knew very well she couldn't.

"I left specific instructions that I was to be informed of

the results of Dr. Myron's test. Did you think that a twelve-hour delay would do just as well?"

"No . . . no, Dr. Neverson."

"I hope you understand how lucky you've been. The test result was negative."

"Yes . . . yes, I know that, Dr. Neverson."

"Yes, you knew it. The point, however, was that I should know it."

Marie was simply enduring. Horrible as this was, she could stand it better than Dr. Martin's savage bludgeoning. Her chin set stubbornly.

"If that test had been positive, an instant change in medication would have been required," Neverson was goaded to fury by her lack of response. "And may I ask why you saw fit to go off duty last night without leaving word with your replacement that I was to be informed?"

A third voice intervened.

"If you excuse, Doctor. I think you cannot understand." Dr. Kroner was prepared to struggle with the English language for the sake of justice. Laboriously he explained that Marie Gentilhomme had been given an injection and sent home in shock after her discovery of Wendell Martin's body.

"Under express instructions from Dr. Wittke himself."

"I see," said Neverson shortly. He had completely forgotten that it was Marie Gentilhomme who had found the body. "Very well, nurse. But if you intend to continue in this profession, you'd better harden yourself to the sight of physical injuries."

With that he turned on his heel and marched away.

"Whew!" breathed Alice Doyle. "I wonder what's eating him?"

"Thank you, Dr. Kroner," Marie Gentilhomme smiled shyly.

"One Bromo, it is," said Sid Segal. "Hard day, Alice?"

"The less days like this, the better Sid," replied Alice Doyle.

Cautiously she downed half the glass. Sid Segal, with years of experience, waited for exactly the right moment to resume the conversation.

"I suppose everybody's upset about Dr. Martin. Terrible thing. The police ought to do something about these muggings."

"Yes," Alice agreed absently, draining the glass. "But it doesn't help if people start acting up."

"The doctors?"

"You know what they're like."

Nurse and pharmacist exchanged a glance of perfect communion.

"On top of that, I hear that La Belle Dame Martin is making herself interesting. She claims it wasn't a mugging, it was murder."

Sid Segal clucked censoriously.

"Now that, that's not right. She can stir up a lot of ugly talk."

"Oh, I suppose they'll manage to shut her up. But it all adds to the atmosphere."

Collecting her empty glass, the druggist was philosophic.

"It takes a couple of days. Then it'll all blow over."

"My God, I hope so, Sid." Alice Doyle prepared to lower herself from the stool. "At least there's one good thing. We should stop hearing so much about that damned insurance trial."

"And where does Martin's death leave the insurance claim?" asked John Putnam Thatcher as Charlie Trinkam and Kenneth Nicolls assembled in his office to discuss the latest turn of events in *Freebody v. Atlantic Mutual.*

Trinkam was ready with his reply. "As far as information goes, Paul Jackson says that he has the two admissions he wanted from Martin—that Pem Freebody was not on his deathbed when he entered the hospital, and that the presence of the hemostatic clips would have been dangerous for him, quite apart from the bullet wound."

"Those are the tangibles," Thatcher nodded. "I presume there's an intangible as well."

"A very big one. The jury hated Martin so much that Paul figures every minute he was on the stand was so much money in the bank for us."

Kenneth Nicolls was pondering this cavalier treatment of evidence when Thatcher continued:

"Now, what about the hospital? Will they become more flexible now that they have no surgeon to protect?"

"Jackson doesn't think so," Charlie replied. "They've got their own reputation to protect. That nurse's testimony hit them hard. And, if you ask me, that's what really stuck in the jury's craw about Martin. They could have forgiven a simple mistake. They couldn't forgive the fact that Martin and everybody else in the operating room knew the patient was being wheeled out full of surplus metal."

Kenneth Nicolls was still trying to find his feet in the shifting balance of factors. "Do you honestly think those hemostats killed him?"

Trinkam shrugged his ignorance. "It's a cinch they didn't do poor Pem any good," he said cheerfully.

"We don't seem to be getting anywhere," Thatcher said with dissatisfaction. "The reason I called you in is that I've been getting cryptic phone calls from Dexter Loomis at Atlantic Mutual. I think he's putting out feelers for a settlement."

"Just wait," Charlie chortled, "Just wait until he finds out what Paul has up his sleeve now."

Thatcher waited with some misgivings. Alone, either Charlie Trinkham or Paul Jackson added a desirable zest to almost any commercial team. Hitched together, their combined *joie de vivre* might well run away with the carriage.

"Yes?" he inquired cautiously.

"Paul wants to see if he can get leave to amend the pleadings, to ask for double indemnity under the accidental death clause."

There was a moment's silence before Thatcher's wary response.

"It has a certain inspired simplicity. Does Jackson have anything to support this?"

"Oh, yes. His theory is that Pem would still be with us if he had been left to bleed privately in his little woodlot, as he had arranged to do."

"I see," said Thatcher gravely. "It was the ghastly mischance of being taken to a hospital that killed him?"

"That's it, in a nutshell." Charlie's grin broadened.

"Tell me, is he considering this seriously, or is it just part of his harassment program?"

"Well, there's no denying that insurance companies bring out Paul's sense of mischief," Trinkam conceded. "I think he would have been willing to give this one a serious try if he had Martin feeding the flames. Now, he's not so sure. He really needs something to take Martin's place."

Thatcher thought a dose of cold water might be beneficial.

"On a statistical basis alone, he is unlikely to find another Martin at Southport."

"No, of course not. Paul has something else in mind. He's got some people working out at the hospital. They're getting the names of patients that Martin had in the postoperative ward during the critical four days."

"And?"

"It seems that there's a lot of coming and going after an operation—doctors checking and consulting, nurses following through. Jackson thinks if he can get evidence that one more doctor knew about those hemostats and did nothing, we'll have it made."

Very slowly Thatcher nodded.

"I see. That would suggest almost a conspiracy against Pemberton Freebody. And we already have at least two nurses who knew of the situation. There might have been some talk. It would depend, I suppose, a good deal on how people felt about Wendell Martin."

Charlie was buoyantly optimistic.

"Well, you remember what he was like. He can't have had many friends."

7 Gall

Dr. Philip Wittke was not a sensitive administrator, but he was conscientious. The next few days were extremely busy for him. He rallied to the support of Lucille Martin, impressed his two sons into funeral preparations, established new safeguards for the hospital parking lot and gave a pep talk to the non-professional staff.

The doctors required a more personal touch. Pocketing his own inclinations, Wittke doubled the cordiality dispensed to outside doctors and took time for a public display of affability to Dr. Edith Bullivant, walking with her the length of a corridor and exchanging stately chaff about the population explosion in Southport's delivery rooms. Any nostalgia that Dr. Kroner might have felt for the medical circles of Europe was presumably banished by a cozy chat in which he was assured that Southport wanted to make him feel at home.

Nor was the nursing staff forgotten. Dr. Wittke found an opportunity to hope that Nurse Gentilhomme was recovered from her shocking experience and to convey a few words of warm appreciation to Nurse Doyle for unspecified services. Marie Gentilhomme, as was to be expected, was suitably grateful. Alice Doyle, on the other hand, jolted him severely by responding with a significant question about the forthcoming retirement of Mrs. Stosser, the director of nursing. (And Nurse Doyle was a woman he had thought he could depend on, too. Nowadays, no one seemed to do anything out of a simple sense of duty.)

These responsibilities discharged, Dr. Wittke was ready to call it a day. At this point, however, a worried group of inside doctors took him quietly aside and pointed out that the critical problem remained untouched.

"It's that damned insurance claim," said the chief of medicine. "If it wasn't for that, the publicity would be over after Wendell's funeral."

"But *Freebody v. Atlantic Mutual* doesn't concern *us*," said a surprised Wittke. "We have nothing further to tell them."

A resident neurologist corrected him. "We can't help being concerned. The way things stand now, there's still a legal quarrel over the cause of death."

Wittke prepared to join in the general anxiety. He was not sure that his colleagues were right. But he had long since grasped one facet of administration. A staff's morale was a reflection of what the staff thought. Whether they were right or wrong was largely irrelevant. Until Southport was relieved of the incubus of Pemberton Freebody, it was not going to be a happy ship.

"Not that there's much we can do about it."

Roy Neverson, who kept in touch with "the younger men" as Wittke called them, had been instrumental in arranging the meeting, but this was his first contribution; it was not calculated to raise any spirits. "Even if we all troop to the stand for the insurance company, we won't get support from other doctors."

There was a sound of gloomy agreement, suddenly interrupted by an exclamation from Philip Wittke.

"That may be the answer, Roy," he said reflectively.

"I didn't realize I was providing answers," Neverson said.

"You can't go on with a trial if you don't have a case. Wendell was the insurance company's medical testimony. Now they expect *us* to take his place, but what if we don't? Then, Atlantic Mutual will have to settle. Right?"

There was a respectful silence. Everyone realized that this was the answer, and that it could have been put forward by nobody else. Philip Wittke would have been quick to reject the suggestion that Southport Memorial wash its hands of Wendell Martin—if he had not thought of it himself.

Thus it was that one fine spring day found John Putnam Thatcher on the Southern State Parkway, rolling out to Suffolk County. Paul Jackson had been amused when he announced the conference.

"Of course it's irregular as hell," he admitted cheerfully. "After all, Wendell Martin was subpoenaed as a witness—and only Martin. Technically the rest of the doctors at Southport Memorial aren't involved, except maybe Kroner. But they don't understand that this isn't a routine malpractice claim. I think they plan to sweep the whole thing under the rug, just like one of their closed hearings before the AMA. And let me tell you, Atlantic Mutual doesn't like this meeting one little bit, but they're going along just to see what Wittke's got up his sleeve."

Thatcher said that he shared their curiosity.

"Me, too," said Paul Jackson. "Although I can make a pretty good guess."

At Southport Memorial Hospital's small, bright doctors' lounge (a faintly shabby collection of chintz-covered sofas and chairs, a small table and a free-standing blackboard), they found Atlantic Mutual represented by Dexter Loomis and Andrew Chisolm. Thatcher, Paul Jackson and Dr. Edmund Knox, from the Institute for Cancer Research at Hanover, represented the plaintiff.

Or, as Dr. Knox persisted in phrasing it, the beneficiaries.

Everyone could guess what Southport Memorial wanted. It wanted to be left alone. How they intended to achieve this goal, John Putnam Thatcher, for one, was eager to learn.

He did not have to sit through tedious preliminaries.

"I've asked Dr. Neverson and Dr. Kroner to be with me during our discussion," said Dr. Wittke, "so that you will see just how little information we can give you—especially now, after Dr. Martin's tragic death," he added, in case anybody missed the point. "Both of them were on duty the night that Mr. Freebody was admitted."

The mere fact that Dr. Neverson and Dr. Kroner were both able to maintain unconcerned silence at this point convinced the two attorneys present that Southport Memorial was not going to produce another Wendell Martin. The gathering nodded sober acknowledgment of Martin's death, and Wittke swept on to a disarmingly ingenuous conclusion.

"We'd like to be of assistance, but unfortunately we're no longer in a position to give you any information."

This was too much for Atlantic Mutual.

"As you must realize, Dr. Wittke, Al Chisolm said sternly, "this claim has now become an inquiry into the exact cause of the death of Pemberton Freebody. He was brought here directly after shooting himself, was operated on here, lived for four days and then died here. Thus, Southport Memorial Hospital is the only possible source of information as to his death. And, much as we all regret Dr. Martin's death, the patient was not in his exclusive care during the relevant period of time. Other people must have seen him."

Having relieved his feelings, Chisolm leaned back in his chair and fell to wiping his glasses savagely.

Philip Wittke frowned. One of the things sustaining him before this unpleasant interview had been his hazy assumption that he would be engaged in a tournament, championing the medical profession against the rest of the world. The arrival of Dr. Edmund Knox had destroyed that illusion—among others. The eminent Dr. Wittke was the product of a small private clinic and a small suburban hospital. In that environment he was a great success. But Edmund Knox was a name that conjured up the giant medical compounds of New York City, the recent Nobel prizes and the latest application of laser techniques to cancer surgery. Dr. Knox was material for *Time* magazine.

Dr. Wittke had counted on dealing with laymen.

He played his next card.

"Of course, Mr. Chisolm. The patient received constant care and attention from many of our staff. The initial examination in Emergency was made by Dr. Kroner."

The insurance brigade stiffened to attention. If Kroner was willing to say that Freebody was as good as dead *before* the operation, Paul Jackson would be left out in the cold. They turned hopefully.

The hope was very short-lived.

"Yes, this patient, I myself see," Dr. Kroner struggled manfully. "The bleeding I stop and I . . . I warn Dr. Martin to prepare himself for . . . for . . ."

"For an operation," Roy Neverson supplied helpfully. His voice was grave but there was amusement in his eyes.

Chisolm glared. No matter what Dr. Kroner was willing to say, he could never say it with any persuasive effect to a jury.

"May I ask a question?" Edmund Knox sounded happy. In fact, he sounded like a man who had just received a check for a hundred thousand dollars.

"Certainly, Dr. Knox."

Wittke didn't like the way his words came out. They were too damned deferential. But, he told himself, it is hard to hit the right doctor-to-doctor note with a man who has surrendered to the institutions. Everyone agreed that the individual practitioner was the backbone of the profession.

Dexter Loomis was also willing. "That's what we're all here for."

Thus encouraged, Dr. Knox got down to business. "We are happy to have heard Dr. Kroner's views. But the critical time in the patient's condition seems to have been during the four days after the operation. Who, besides Dr. Martin, was involved in the post-operative care?"

Across the width of the room, Neverson and Wittke exchanged glances. Thatcher, seeing this, was prepared to swear they had already prepared their tactics for the occasion.

"I was." Roy Neverson paused. "I was disappointed when he took a turn for the worse the day after the operation. He had been holding his own nicely until then. After that, he lost ground steadily."

Wittke took up the narrative. "Dr. Martin asked me to have a look also, because of my experience in the field," he said, momentarily forgetting Dr. Knox. "Everything humanly possible was done, but the patient did not respond normally to treatment."

"I see," Chisolm said tightly. He shook his head firmly at Dexter Loomis, who was at the boiling point, then stared balefully at the Southport contingent. Dr. Wittke and Dr. Neverson might just as well have said it outright. If pushed, they would testify that the patient had mysteriously started to fail as a result of Dr. Martin's surgery. "I see very clearly. You realize we'll have to call expert witnesses?"

"Naturally." Philip Wittke's cool voice invited him to try to find some. "On the other hand, with such an unusual and complex situation, many doctors may hesitate to answer hypothetical questions. Of course, I know nothing about such matters, but I would have thought that a settlement would be appropriate—where real doubt exists."

John Thatcher almost laughed aloud at Dexter Loomis's expression. It is not often, he reflected, that a third party intervenes to tell an insurance company it should settle with one of its policyholders. Particularly just after having kicked the insurance company in the teeth.

Chisolm's jaw was clenched so tightly, he was physically incapable of reply. But medicine is not the only discipline with professional loyalties. Paul Jackson, in his first observation of the day, took up cudgels on behalf of the New York Bar.

"The parties will naturally give consideration to the possibility of a settlement, as well as other courses of action. As you say, that need not concern the medical witnesses," was Wittke's rejoinder to this snub.

"Very fortunately,"

Strangulated speech had now become possible for Andrew Chisolm.

"There is one other way in which you could add to your helpfulness, Dr. Wittke," he said, heavily ironical. "At the outset, this case seemed so simple that we neglected to subpoena Dr. Martin's case records. I presume those records will be available when we require them. I would like your assurance to that effect."

There was a clear implication he wouldn't be surprised to find Wittke burning the files the minute his back was turned.

Dr. Wittke had long ago learned to let little unpleasantnesses like this slide off his back. Roy Neverson favored a more direct approach. Now he smiled openly.

"We thought you might be interested in those records. They're in Dr. Martin's office. As long as they haven't been subpoenaed, why don't you—all of you—come and take a look?"

Despite Atlantic Mutual's gnashing of teeth, John Thatcher and Edmund Knox were on their feet. They knew perfectly well that Neverson was feeding them ammunition. And an early glance at those records could be useful, if only to prepare a rebuttal. Although from what they had seen of Southport Memorial, neither expected its records to be very illuminating.

The procession straggled down the corridor and came to a halt in the doorway of the office entered by Philip Wittke. They could see two women already in the office. One wore hospital whites, the other black.

The one in white spoke first.

"I'm preparing a list of condolence messages, Dr. Wittke," she said, her eyes flashing a warning.

"Of course, Miss Reese." Wittke nodded his understanding and moved forward. "But, Lucille, should you be out? Miss Reese could have gone to you. You should take better care of yourself."

He looked hesitantly over his shoulder and decided against introducing the widow to the men who had scarified the reputation of her husband.

As for Lucille Martin she paid not the slightest attention to the knot of men hovering on the threshold. Even Philip Wittke's arrival barely seemed to register with her. She had always been a placid woman. Now her grief had transformed that placidity into frozen lethargy. Physically, she had barely changed. Her golden suntan gave her a deceptive, air of well-being. Only blank, unfocused eyes betrayed inner turmoil.

"I have that list ready, Mrs. Martin," Miss Reese said brightly. She offered some typewritten pages, which the widow accepted like a robot.

"And now, Miss Reese, please get us Dr. Martin's records on the Freebody case. Then we won't bother Mrs. Martin any more."

"Yes, Dr. Wittke." Miss Reese moved swiftly to a filing cabinet. She realized that Wittke wanted to remove his visitors before Lucille Martin recognized the name of Pemberton Freebody.

But Lucille Martin was miles away, waiting for the interruption to end. Torpidly she scanned the list in her hand.

"You can take care of these, can't you, Miss Reese? It's only . . . oh, look at this hypocrisy!"

Something had caught her attention. Suddenly she awoke from her torpor.

"How could they? Where is it?" She began to riffle through the pile of condolence cards. Then she seized one and tore it, halving and rehalving it viciously. "That's what Dr. Harley Bauer can do with his condolences! And that scheming little wife of his! They think I don't know what they did to poor Wen!"

Alarmed, Wittke strode to her side and grasped her hands. "Now, my dear, you mustn't let these things upset you. You've overtaxed yourself, coming out. You must sit down and get control of yourself."

Drawing her to a chair, he saw the pulled-out drawers of the big desk and tried using them to distract her. "And you've been looking for something in Wendell's desk. You only had to ask me. I'll gladly do anything I can."

As quickly as it had flared, the widow's brief spurt of emotion faded. Her shoulders shuddered briefly, and she drew a hand down her cheek.

"I don't think there's anything you can do. It's very strange," she said almost absently, "but Wen hasn't left much money. Next to nothing."

Wittke started back and let her hands fall.

"Money?" he repeated stupidly.

Behind him, John Thatcher's ears pricked up.

The widow's dreamy indifference persisted.

"Yes. At first I thought maybe he hadn't been doing as well as he told me. Wen did so like to boast to me. But then I realized I was trying to avoid the truth. And that never helps, does it?"

With a harassed glance over his shoulder, Wittke patted her arm soothingly.

"We can discuss this some other time, Lucille."

She almost succeeded in smiling at him.

"Poor Philip! How embarrassed you must be. But, putting it off won't make it any easier for me. I have to face it. And I thought I understood Wen. That's what hurts so. It's incredible. That Wen could behave like that and, even more, that I didn't realize it."

Wittke's tone was perfect. In John Thatcher's opinion, however, his wording could scarcely have been less fortunate.

"You must try to understand. Wendell was devoted to you, Lucille. But there are some burdens a man wants to spare his wife."

She was incredulous. "Spare me?"

"Lucille!"

It was a peremptory cry. From behind the visitors, Dr. Neverson pushed his way to front and center. He had decided, Thatcher saw, to end this grotesque encounter. Brutally, if necessary.

"Lucille," Neverson said emphatically, "there wasn't any other woman in Wendell's life!"

Sleepily she turned to him. "Oh, Roy, you don't have to lie to me. I know that the wife is always the last to know."

There was slyness in her voice as she went on:

"Was it that way with Julie too, Roy?"

Neverson took a step forward. But Dr. Philip Wittke, engulfed by Victorian shock, erupted:

"Lucille, you mustn't say things like that. Or even, my dear, think things like that!"

Lucille Martin stared at him. "What else is there for me to think?" she asked. "Wen's money is gone! It must have been a woman! It's not easy for me . . . to realize I've been a failure. . . ."

Thatcher, obstructed by Paul Jackson and Dexter Loomis, followed this scene with fascinated horror. Neverson, he could see, was also shaken.

But Neverson rallied. He turned away from the widow with eloquent distaste. Then, seeing the faces in the doorway, he turned to the nurse.

"Get those records!"

Miss Reese scurried to obey.

This was enough to remind Dr. Wittke of his bigger responsibilities. He thrust the folder upon Edmund Knox, who stood nearest him.

"I doubt if we can be of more assistance to you. I hope you'll leave those with my secretary. . . ."

The scene had generated its own paralysis, however. Dr. Wittke's guests remained immobilized for a moment. That moment was enough.

"I must know one thing," Lucille Martin said with terrible finality. "Who was she, Phil? Roy, you've got to tell me. . . ."

After this, as John Thatcher would have been the first to admit, neither Jackson & Jackson nor the Sloan Guaranty Trust stood on ceremony.

They fled.

Atlantic Mutual was scarcely a step behind them.

"All in all, it was quite a day," Thatcher said some hours later, as he took a drink from the barman while they waited to file into the banquet room. In the offing was a speech on credit guarantees for export shipments. But at least he was safely back on Manhattan.

Tom Robichaux disapproved. "You should leave your troubles in the office, John."

"I'm not sure these *are* troubles, Tom. In fact it's almost too good to be true. The people in Southport are practically promising to go on the stand and say their surgeon killed our client, simply to get a speedy decision. I find that very odd, considering their united front a short week ago."

"Well, he's not their surgeon any more."

"No, but they should be thinking of the hospital's reputation. It's all very fishy."

"Covering up something?" Robichaux ruminated silently for a moment. "Kickbacks? But, hell, they all do that. Why make such a fuss?"

Thatcher looked up, surprised. Knowledgeability outside the office was not Tom's strong point. Unless Kickbacks, Inc. was being sold on the Big Board, Robichaux should have been lost by now. Of course there was one other way he picked up information. Thatcher narrowed his eyes as he tried to recall.

"Veronica," said Robichaux helpfully. "You remember Veronica."

No, Thatcher said truthfully, he didn't remember any Veronica.

"Hell, I'm not surprised. I was married to her for two and a half years, and I barely saw her. In and out of hospitals all the time. Sort of a hobby."

There was a respectful silence as old memories stirred into life.

"Wonderful the way that woman could eat, considering she was missing most of her digestive system. And money! Went through it like water!"

Thatcher delicately suggested that expenses in every Robichaux marital ménage ran pretty high.

"That's different. But when you can't tell the drugstore bill from the Tiffany bill," said Robichaux in a burst of nostalgic irritation, "I say that's a hell of a way to take your fun!"

Gravely Thatcher agreed. "One of the other features of this Freebody mess is that today Martin's widow said he's died without leaving any estate. She put on quite a blood-curdling performance. Tom, have you ever heard of a forty-five-year-old surgeon dying poor?"

"Ha!" snorted Veronica's ex-husband. "Don't you believe it! There'll be a safe deposit box, stuffed with cash, somewhere. The tax boys will find it, even if the widow can't."

That, Thatcher had to agree, was possible. But it was one more oddity to be added to Southport's growing pile. However, he reminded himself that this purported to be a social occasion and turned to other questions.

"Whatever happened to Veronica? Do you know?"

"Oh yes, after a couple of tries, she finally settled down with a gynecologist. Been with him a long time now."

"Of course, it's more economical, that way."

"That's not it. Ronnie wasn't a penny pincher." Robichaux protested unnecessarily. Financial prudence had never been the hallmark of a Robichaux rib. "No, this gives them a common interest. Something to talk about, don't you know."

Thatcher found it impossible to contemplate.

8 House Calls

In all honesty Thatcher had, until now, been unable to bring more than a modicum of attention to bear on the entangled affairs of Pemberton Freebody and Southport Memorial. As a man, he had honored the pyrotechnic brilliance used by Paul Jackson to salvage a lost cause. As a banker, he was duly appreciative of the hundred thousand dollars to be netted by this brilliance. The trouble, however, was that John Thatcher did not share the American fascination with doctors and things medical. He appreciated the legal and medical niceties raised by Dr. Wendell Martin's dubious surgery, but he was incapable of following the expert testimony with the genuine relish of Charlie Trinkam. Willpower kept him listening to voices deposing about hemostats and blood transfusions, but it was willpower shaped by his responsibility to the Sloan Guaranty Trust.

Philip Wittke's smooth announcement of his new policy had changed all that. For the first time Thatcher felt a quickening of real interest. The good doctor would have been aghast at this result of his tactics.

Sudden changes of position, particularly following sudden deaths, were, in Thatcher's experience, worth examination. Wendell Martin's death might be simple enough. But the strange reversal at Southport Memorial impressed him as far from simple. Then there was the widow. Her revelations seemed to bear out Tom Robichaux's prediction; there must be a safe deposit box or its equivalent elsewhere.

Safe deposit boxes, not hemostats, were right up John Thatcher's alley.

It was time, he decided virtuously, that the Sloan gave something more than moral support to the efforts of Paul Jackson.

This decision boded ill for his subordinates as Kenneth Nicolls, arriving at the relatively respectable hour of ten minutes after nine, discovered.

"But, Miss Corsa, I've got to finish that pension fund study for Mr. Trinkam by noon," he protested to the phone.

"Mr. Thatcher," said Miss Corsa, in effect dismissing pension funds, Mr. Trinkam and the Western world, if need be, "will require you for the rest of the day."

This announcement, final and adequate for Miss Corsa and possibly Thatcher, left Ken to beard Charlie Trinkam in his den. Charlie was rarely at his best in the morning, and today proved no exception to the rule.

"Oh, great!" he said as Nicolls reported the summons to higher duty and deposited bulky documents concerning the Kosher Butchers' Pension Fund on Trinkham's desk. "Just great! I'll have Phil Cook do what he can, but Gabler has him busy with another cost breakdown on the Pennsy-Central merger. God knows how many Ev wants! Besides, what does John need you for, anyway?"

Ken replied to this unflattering question by admitting that he had no idea.

"I could call and say I need you," Charlie thought aloud. This was an idle threat and they both knew it. Members of the staff did not call John Putnam Thatcher with such comments. Exasperatedly, Charlie returned to his desktop. "Kosher butchers! Still, now that Southport is folding, I suppose I should be grateful for comic relief. . . ."

Ken paused on his way to the door. "You think the *Freebody v. Atlantic Mutual* case is over, Charlie?"

Charlie was already making rapid marginal notes. "Sure. All fine! The hospital is rating. Even Atlantic Mutual can see when it's being double-crossed. The fun's over. We've got to get back to work . . . kosher butchers!"

As he strode down the corridor to Thatcher's corner suite, Ken reflected that Charlie Trinkam, a determined worker despite his airy manner, deserved the recreation proferred by *Freebody v. Atlantic Mutual*. For his sake, it was a shame that the show was closing.

Five minutes later, Thatcher had once again startled Ken into commencing, if not completing, a protest; the show, it appeared, was not over.

"As I see it," Thatcher announced, "there are two lines of approach. One is through those two patients Jackson's men have unearthed. The other is an inquiry into Wendell Martin's financial affairs."

Kenneth Nicolls permitted his eyebrows to ask the question for him. Reports of the Southport conference had stressed only Wittke's betrayal of Atlantic Mutual.

"Ah, you haven't heard? Martin's widow was making

strange statements. Strangest of all, she says her husband left virtually no capital. And he had been a successful doctor for over twenty years."

In many ways Kenneth was still young and innocent. He was not, however, that innocent.

"She's got it wrong," he said with certainty. "Probably there's a portfolio at the broker's or something."

Thatcher nodded. "If so, I think I can undertake to find it. But it will be interesting if there is no such simple explanation. Very interesting."

"Well, yes," admitted Kenneth, "but I don't see what good it would do us."

"You never can tell," said Thatcher enigmatically. "In any event, I want you to tackle the patients. See if they picked up anything at all about the operation on Pemberton Freebody. With luck, you'll find them both out in Southport today. Charlie has the names."

Impetuous questions hovered on Ken Nicolls's lips, only to die unuttered as Thatcher waved dismissal and plunged into some research reports forwarded by Walter Bowman. Not until the door closed did Thatcher permit himself to grin; issuing impossible orders was one solace to the burdens of high office. Then, with a sigh, he paid the price and returned to Bowman's analysis of Major Foods Co., which was planning to expand into a line of polyunsaturated food additives for the weight-conscious canary.

"He wants what?" Charlie Trinkam asked absently, phone at his ear.

"He wants me to start talking to those patients out in Southport," said Ken bitterly.

"Better you than me," commented Charlie, rummaging through his desk for a paper. "Here . . . oh, Ev? Listen, Ev, I want to talk to you about that Pennsy-Central study you've got Phil Cook wasting time on . . . yes, I said wasting time. . . ."

It was after lunch before Kenneth Nicolls drove into what he was already thinking of as Old Southport. He had just treated himself to an elaborate meal on the grounds that he needed it. His morning interview had been frankly terrifying.

There had been no intimation of the horrors in store when he pulled into the driveway before the solid, substantial brick house. Mrs. Furness herself had answered the bell, a trim white-haired lady in sharkskin slacks. Kenneth had taken the trouble to work out a rather elaborate opening, designed to conceal the bare-faced impertinence of his questions. He needn't have bothered.

Mrs. Furness, charmed by his interest, had immediately taken him into her confidence. There had been no question of illness. Far from it. The lady had had an expensive job of face-lifting as preparation for what she intended to be a rambunctious widowhood.

"Edgar died a year ago," she explained. "When I was able to think at all, I looked around at other widows of my age."

She had not liked what she saw. They had all arranged things so that their lives were even drearier than before widowhood. Some of them had gone so far as to marry again—men who were fifteen years older than the husbands they had already lost. This was not what Mrs. Furness had in mind. Edgar had been staunchly conservative. Like a good wife, she too had extolled the virtues of Home, God and Country. She did not rate this experiment a success.

"I gave it thirty-five years," she announced judiciously. "And that is long enough. Now, I please myself."

She was preparing to remove to an artistic enclave in Colorado. She confessed she was not the least bit aesthetically inclined, but—here, the merry eyes twinkled shrewdly—she rather thought that a widow with plenty of money, a desire to entertain lavishly and no rooted objection to overpriced works of art would probably fit in beautifully.

"Because," she concluded forthrightly, "I am interested in men younger than Edgar, not older. Lots of them! And I prefer them as unconservative as possible."

Naturally Kenneth did not inquire into the specifics of her interest. Nor did he understand why he became so alarmed at this point. In any event, it was not a reaction he cared to probe. He did blame himself, however, for allowing his alarm to show.

Suddenly both the twinkle and the shrewdness intensified.

"But, my dear boy," Mrs. Furness laughed, "I can see that you are a very respectable young man, and I am sure you have a very nice wife and children."

Kenneth had withdrawn shortly thereafter, half relieved and half offended at this kindly dismissal. He had a dismal suspicion that he had been classified as a young Edgar. However, no matter what else he had to reproach himself for, he had covered his business. It was abundantly apparent that Mrs. Furness, during her stay at Southport, had been too preoccupied planning her future to have an interest in anything else. And unless Wendell Martin had had unsuspected Bohemian depths, she probably hadn't even noticed her surgeon.

That had been New Southport. He was now entering Old Southport, Kenneth Nicolls realized, not for the first time, that unless a new community is cast up in the wilderness, it never acquires total homogeneity. Where housing developments accrete around an established community, no matter how valuable the land becomes, there is always an old section. The mansions and the estates go, but this remains. It consists of aged ramshackle frame houses whose occupants are mostly old-timers; its storekeepers know all the ins and outs of Main Street business. It wields political power out of all proportion to its population—its residents control the local civil service, win the local elective offices and run the town weekly. This situation persists until a new generation of locals rises to effect a natural redistricting.

The home of Mr. and Mrs. Eugene Perkins was very much Old Southport—sagging porch, weathered siding and all.

"Good God!" Ken's exclamation was involuntary. A venerable gap-toothed picket fence enclosed a small balding lawn and twelve very small children. For a moment Ken fastened on a triviality: why had Southport Memorial put the fecund Mrs. Perkins in the fourth floor Post-Op when sixth floor Obstetrics was all too clearly her spiritual home?

But a second glance dissipated Ken's mental fog; the youngsters, digging holes, playing in the sandbox, swinging in an old tire roped to a malnourished elm, banging on drums and pails, were all of them between three and six years old. It was technically impossible that they should all be young Perkinses.

They were not. A sober fourteen-year-old, rounding the corner with a weeping little boy tucked under her arm, directed him up the walk to the living room and Mrs. Eugene Perkins.

"Oh, call me Nancy," she said exhaustedly, admitting him after he yodeled through the defective screen door. "No, only three of them are mine. But I'm taking care of the others—you see, I simply can't get out to work, not with the children and everything. . . ."

Sinking onto a sofa, she smiled and waved Ken to the overstuffed chair. Ken did see. Nancy Perkins was so thin she seemed transparent; blue lines of fatigue circled her eyes. Only a wiry disheveled mop of curls and the smile showed vitality.

". . . and since the operation I've been so tired! But I'm getting better every day—Freddy! Put that down!"

This last was to an infant who had crawled into view from the adjoining dining room and was purposefully imperiling the end table.

Slowly Ken began to extract facts. They were simple enough. Nancy Perkins had been doomed to die. Dr. Wendell Martin had performed an extremely delicate heart operation. Now, Nancy Perkins was not going to die. She told Ken frankly that she wouldn't be willing to talk with him if Wendell Martin were still alive.

"I wouldn't lie to you," she said steadily. "I just wouldn't let you in. We owe too much to Dr. Martin. But now I'd be willing to help you if I could. What was the date of the operation on Mr. Freebody?"

Kenneth told her.

"Oh, no!" she ejaculated instantly. "I couldn't possibly help. You don't understand. That was the day I was operated on, too. For the next week I didn't really notice anything. I was under sedation most of the time, anyway."

"Then I'm sorry to have bothered you—"

But Nancy Perkins waved him back into his chair. She was frowning and thoughtfully rubbing a snub nose.

"You know, Gene is the person you should talk to, my husband. He practically lived at the hospital all that week. At first, of course, he was terribly worried, but later on, when we knew it was going to be all right, he made friends with everyone. Whenever I was asleep he'd be wandering around, talking to somebody. He might be able to help you."

It sounded very unlikely to Ken Nicolls. A distraught husband, his wife barely snatched from the jaws of death, was not going to be interested in other people's problems. But if Mr. Perkins could be worked in this afternoon, Kenneth was willing.

"When do you expect him home? At five?" He glanced at the battered mantel clock. It was already three.

"Oh, I'm afraid not. He's got the chance to put in some

overtime. And, of course, he's glad to get it. We have so many bills to pay off. And, even then he may not come back from Houlihan's."

"Houlihan's?"

"That's where Gene works. They do bookkeeping for small businesses. That's why it's hard to reach him during the day. He goes from place to place."

Kenneth nodded comprehension, but at the same time declined offers to set up a meeting with Gene in the evening.

"No, I have to get back to the city. Then I'll check with the office and see what they say. If I wanted to reach your husband by phone during the day, could you locate him for me?"

Nancy grinned. "With a little time I could." The grin faded into a more thoughtful expression. "Yes, you talk with your office. But the more I think about it, the more I realize that, if there was any talk, Gene might have heard it. Why, he might even have picked up something at the garage."

"The garage?"

"Yes. That's Gene's *Sunday* job. He's awfully good with cars. I know he always does the tune-ups on Dr. Neverson's sports cars. And I'm almost sure that Dr. Bullivant takes her car there, too."

Kenneth began to wonder about the size of those bills. Here was Nancy taking care of children when she obviously ought to be resting. And the way she said Sunday left Ken in no doubt as to how Gene spent his Saturdays. He looked at the woman on the sofa with sympathy, before he realized the emotion was misplaced. Nancy Perkins had been handed back her life on a platter, and she was still starry-eyed with wonder. Three small children, she had said, Kenneth thought of his own wife and child. No, Nancy Perkins didn't have a single complaint against her world.

But she was quite level-headed enough to understand the positions in *Freebody v. Atlantic Mutual.* As she was seeing Ken off the porch, she had a final word.

"I suppose you don't want me to ask Marie about this?"

"Marie?"

"Marie Gentilhomme. The nurse in the Freebody operation. We got to know her while I was in the hospital, and she's a friend of ours now. She comes over sometimes on her day off." Nancy suddenly smiled with a hint of mischief. "If you'd come yesterday, you would have run into her."

As Ken drove back to the parkway, he realized that his earlier observations had been fully justified. Old Southport was right in the middle of things.

If Kenneth Nicolls had taken the trouble to scan the in-bound traffic as he returned to New York, he might very well have spotted the figures of John Thatcher and Charlie Trinkam. They, too, had unexpectedly spent the afternoon in Suffolk County.

The phone call from Paul Jackson had come in the morning, only ten minutes after Ken Nicolls had stalked off in the general direction of Montauk Point.

"Sure . . . no bother, Paul," said Charlie genially and un-truthfully. "Anything new? . . . What! . . . No! Not on your life!"

He continued in this vein for some minutes, but Paul Jackson was widely known as one of the most persuasive advocates in Manhattan with good reason. After an hour of tremendous productivity that reduced his secretary and one statistician to tears, Trinkam presented himself in Thatcher's office with suspiciously brushed hair and a somewhat shamefaced statement of intent.

Thatcher listened calmly. "By all means go, Charlie. If you enjoy funerals, I'm sure you'll enjoy this one. Mind you, I don't see what you'll get out of Wendell Martin's last rites—but there's no accounting for tastes."

Charlie grinned at him. "Now, John. Paul seems to feel that it's the right thing to do. Ed Knox will be there—and Dexter Loomis, too. I might be able to get a little business in."

Thatcher did not bother to project skepticism. Instead, recalling some of the exchanges between these various par-ties and the late Dr. Martin, he said: "Am I to take it that this turnout is designed to show that, notwithstanding our bitter business and legal contests, we all have a high regard for Wendell Martin? Or had, rather?"

Everett Gabler, whose conference with Thatcher on the Pennsy-Central merger Trinkam had interrupted, snorted impatiently. The staidest and most proper of the trust of-ficers, he was chronically suspicious of Charlie Trinkam's motives, and currently inflamed by a difference of profes-sional opinion. Since he could scarcely interpret a funeral as one of the extravagant extracurricular ventures so characteristic of Trinkam, he fell back on a second line of attack.

"From what I gather, Martin was no loss to anybody! He was knife-happy!"

Gabler was a firm advocate of Nature's healing power (with proper diet and exercise), so his views on eminent surgeons carried little weight.

"Well, I'm meeting Paul at noon," said Charlie. "Sure you don't want to come, John? Paul is touting this as a golden opportunity to see the entire Southport staff, let alone the mystifying widow. Sure you want to miss it?"

When it was put that way, John Thatcher didn't want to miss it. Moreover, in the hour at his disposal before Everett Gabler beat down the door of his office, he had managed to call an impressive array of financial correspondents in Suffolk County. Several of them might well be present at the funeral. It was this second thought that made him speak as he did.

"All right. But tell Jackson to meet us here. If we're going to do this, we might as well do it right. Miss Corsa can get a limousine for us!"

Shortly thereafter Thatcher realized that he had pleased Miss Corsa. This rare feat was always accompanied by surprise, but this time he should have anticipated it. Miss Corsa had a high regard for dignity and ritual. On both counts a funeral could scarcely fail to please. As for the limousine, she was constantly trying to intrude it into Thatcher's life. She deplored his habit of hopping onto the IRT. The fact that the IRT was more efficient in Manhattan cut no ice with Miss Corsa. She had long since realized that after a certain level, efficiency was no longer quite as useful as it might once have been. But there was always mileage in dignity.

There was also a good deal of mileage on the parkway. The drive was enlivened by Jackson's description of the state of affairs at Atlantic Mutual.

"Chisolm and Loomis both know they have to settle this. But they're stalling, and you know why? Loomis is looking for some medical testimony to square himself with his company."

"You're joking," Charlie accused. "Why doesn't he just file some of the headlines that Martin was getting? He was their star witness."

"It's a big claim," Thatcher reminded him, "and a big settlement."

"That's it. Loomis figures he can't be too careful. He wants a watertight file. I hear he's talked to DeLuca, asked him if he'd do a report once the settlement's gone through.

"He can have *all* our experts, once he's paid up," Charlie offered generously. "If the settlement's big enough, even Ed Knox would probably do a report for him. He can't ask for anything better than a Nobel prize winner."

On this happy note, the limousine came to a smooth halt.

"I'm afraid you'll have to get out here, sir," said the chauffeur, as he stopped several car lengths from the church steps.

Southport, the medical community of Southport Memorial Hospital (as well as St. Anne's and Southport Community), the county medical association, patients, friends, relatives were doing Dr. Wendell Martin proud. The steps before the entrance were already crowded, and as Thatcher, Jackson and Trinkam approached, their car was directed by a uniformed policeman to the end of a long cortege of gleaming black enamel. There, representatives of August Pfost ("Serving Southport for Fifty Years With Reverence and Understanding") were hustling up and down appending tasteful insignia to fenders.

As Paul Jackson and Charlie amused themselves detailing to Dr. Knox their plans for his future employment, Thatcher drew slightly aside.

He was particularly interested in the changes in mourning costume during his lifetime. It was especially noticeable in the women. But on this warm July day, some of the men were hatless. Thatcher could remember that when he had been a very young man, fresh to Wall Street, a senior had stressed the advisability of having a hat at a funeral. It didn't make any difference whether you wore it. That way, old Deming had said, whenever you are in any doubt about what to do at a funeral, you can always lay your hat respectfully across your breast. Thatcher had followed Deming's advice through the years and found it sterling.

"They tell me you're John Thatcher," a voice said in his ear.

He turned to discover a spry, elderly man examining him with interest. He acknowledged his identity.

"Benjamin Edes, Southport National Bank," said the other, extending a hand. "We were on the phone with each other this morning."

Thatcher was delighted at the encounter and again thanked Edes for his promise of assistance.

"Haven't done anything yet," Edes said gruffly. "But

I've put some people onto it. Wouldn't be surprised if we had something for you."

"I'd be very interested in that,"

The elderly man chuckled.

"Bet you would! Well, can't talk here. Not that I mind a good funeral." He raised a valedictory hand and melted back into the crowd.

Thatcher then found himself being herded into a knot with Paul Jackson, Trinkam and Dr. Knox.

"Yes, it is quite a turnout," said a mellifluous voice. It was not Dr. Wittke but a younger, slighter edition. "Shall we be getting inside?"

The little group obediently began to move toward the church; Dr. James Wittke bestowed a bloodless smile on them and oozed his way to other mourners.

As they entered the First Presbyterian Church, powerful organ throbs drowned Paul Jackson's strictures on this evidence of over-organization. To the mighty strains of "Nearer My God to Thee," the mourners filed in, introducing an antiphon of coughing and shuffling.

By the end of the anthem, the church was filled. Ushers slipped over to close the great doors and cut off the sunlight streaming into the nave. With the sudden dimming of light, the organist began a discreet musical doodling along Bachian lines. There was a collective hush of awareness, like that which greets the bride, then four men, bending slightly to indicate solicitude, escorted a black-draped figure up a side aisle. Behind them was a small, embarrassed band: a middle-aged man, a troubled-looking matron keeping an eye on two teen-agers. Bringing up the rear, a youthful couple, the woman visibly pregnant.

Barely moving his lips, Paul Jackson swayed toward Charlie: "Three to one we get the 'In the midst of life' dodge."

Thatcher was too preoccupied to hear Trinkam's reply; he had caught sight of Mrs. Doyle, watching the widow's progress. Her expression was unfathomable.

Wendell Martin's assorted nearest and dearest finally were ensconced in the front pew. The organist, unseen but watchful, stepped up the tempo. Dr. Rudolph Simpson, Bible in hand, mounted the lectern, looked down sorrowfully at the flower-bedecked, closed casket, raised his eyes and stared pugnaciously at the waiting congregation.

A muted flourish from the organ, and there was silence. Dr. Simpson continued his measured appraisal. Charlie

Trinkam shifted slightly, but Paul Jackson watched the minister with professional interest.

Dr. Simpson bowed his head briefly, opened his Bible and fell into silent communion.

From the front pew, there came an ominous echoing moan.

Without undue haste, Dr. Simpson finished reading.

"My friends," he began in a reedy tenor.

A strangled wail, followed by controlled activity in the front pew. To a man, the congregation averted its eyes from the assembled Martins and stared at Dr. Simpson. Dr. Simpson compressed his lips, presumably in a moment of silent prayer, then began again:

"My friends . . ."

"Wendell!" The voice was harsh and rasping. "Oh, dear Lord! They've taken Wendell away from me! And nobody will do anything! Al, make them do something! Don't let them get away with it. . . ."

A positive frenzy seized possession of the front pew; fascinated, Charlie watched one of the men rise and bend over the black-draped figure. At the aisle, an usher hovered. There was a murmur that reached to five pews back.

"Lucille, my dear . . ."

"Do you have a handkerchief, Madge?"

"Please relax . . ."

Cutting through this an octave higher, Lucille Martin's voice rose in lament.

"My God! Wen is dead! Doesn't anybody understand! They're going to let him get away with murder! Why doesn't somebody do something . . ."

Dr. Simpson looked upward, away from the drama roiling at his feet. The rest of the church simply gawked at the front pew.

With unconscious theatrical timing, Lucille Martin shook off restraint and comfort and struggled to her feet. Turning her back on Dr. Simpson, she staggered forward to clutch at the casket, then turned a taut, skeletal face toward the congregation.

"He's dead! Do you understand me? He's dead! Why are you sitting there? Why don't you find the man who killed him! Just because he's a doctor . . ."

These words broke the spell gripping those present. There was an almost palpable shrinking among the mourners, a frisson of horror. It was, Thatcher realized, trying vainly to locate familiar faces, professional outrage. Or perhaps it was individual apprehension. Whatever its nature, it produced a belated stir of activity. Dr. Simpson waggled his skimpy eyebrows at adjutants who came hurrying up the aisle. From a pew not far behind the Martins, a portly figure rose and began to edge toward the aisle. Philip Wittke, to do him credit, was hurrying to offer his services—which was more than the other doctors present could rouse themselves to do, as Charlie pointed out some hours later to Thatcher. Her family were plucking nervously at Lucille Martin's draperies.

With anguished vigor, Mrs. Martin straightened.

"They know he killed him! They're going to protect him because he's a doctor! But I won't let him get away with it! Harley Bauer always hated Wendell—Wendell told me! He was jealous and he killed him! And you'll let him go! Why doesn't somebody do something? Oh my God, Wendell, Wendell . . . !"

Her voice had risen to an intolerable pitch. With sudden release, she buried her face in her hands and broke into unnatural, inhuman gasping.

Was there a tremor of response at Harley Bauer's name? John Thatcher—and Paul Jackson later confirmed this—was listening but could hear nothing other than involuntary response to Lucille Martin's hysteria. Throughout the church, women wept openly. Many more clutched their escorts with terrified rigidity.

The removal party, led by Philip Wittke, finally converged on Lucille Martin. Under Wittke's whispered directions, two ushers and her brother-in-law firmly but gently eased Mrs. Martin away from the casket. Half carrying, half leading, they bore her to a side door.

The organist alertly plunged into Handel's "Largo."

A rustle of commiseration and surmise was quickly silenced by Dr. Simpson. As soon as the oak door closed behind the weeping Mrs. Martin, he signaled the organist for silence and, this time accusingly, continued Wendell Martin's last rites.

"My friends. . ."

10 Irregularity

The rest of the funeral was inevitably anticlimax. In whispers, the New York City group agreed that the defensiveness of Southport Memorial against intrusive strangers must have been increased ten-fold by Lucille Martin's outburst. There would be no information forthcoming now. Better to slip away quietly after the burial. Veteran funeral-goers to a man, they took up strategic positions and occupied one of the first cars to pull away from the cemetery.

In spite of this achievement, they had not been half as foresighted as some other interests.

Hasty consultation at graveside among the powers of Southport Memorial had resulted in a division of labor. Philip Wittke was needed to speed to the side of the widow, preferably with a good strong tranquilizer. Supported by his wife—a motherly woman already murmuring "poor dear"—he dutifully prepared to undertake this task. More immediately important, however, was the necessity to soothe Harley Bauer.

Roy Neverson was ready to try, but he wanted assistance. Dr. Wittke was a firm believer in the enormous reserves of tact bestowed at birth on every woman (in spite of the evidence of his daughters-in-law, famed throughout Southport for their ability to put a heavy foot in the middle of whatever was going on). He suggested Dr. Edith Bullivant as an appropriate second.

Neverson stared.

"Have you gone mad, Phil? With what Harley knows about Edith?"

"I forgot." Wittke recollected the status of Dr. Bullivant with a start. Tactful she undoubtedly could be. Unfortunately, she would also be a red flag to Bauer.

In the end it was Dr. Kroner who converged on Harley's left flank as Neverson approached from the right.

Harley stood rigid, looking unlike himself. Doggedly he had remained throughout the funeral and accompanied the casket to the cemetery. But he was paying for this endurance. With the shiny, uncreased skin of youthful corpulence, his face was normally a ruddy mask of good nature. Under emotional or physical exertion, it turned bright red.

86

Roy Neverson knew he was in for trouble at his first look. Harley was dead white; the flesh on his face might have been marble.

"Now, take it easy, Harley," said Neverson, cautiously touching the younger man's elbow. "I know how you feel."

"Do you?" Harley demanded flatly. "And how many times has that bitch accused *you* of murder before the entire county medical association?"

"I know, I know." Neverson almost stuttered in his anxiety. "It was terrible. But, Harley, don't blame us! I'm your friend."

"You're everybody's friend. My friend, and Martin's friend and Wittke's friend. Being your friend doesn't seem to prevent people from getting socked in the stomach."

Neverson bit down hard on a retort. He had spent the better part of a week last winter trying to persuade this pigheaded zealot that only grief would come of tangling with Wendell Martin.

"I'm anything you want, Harley," he said evenly, "But don't go away like this. It's got to be thrashed out. This is an hysterical woman trying to wreck your life."

Neverson's words were making no impression at all. Harley had immured himself in a soundproof cell. But suddenly Dr. Kroner spoke and, in spite of his imperfect English, he spoke with earnest authority.

"I will not permit that you leave alone. You are a boy, and it is your whole life at stake. What you say about the medical association is true. They have all heard, and now they are watching. If you do not wish to speak to us, then it shall be as you say. But you must be seen to leave with doctors from Southport Memorial."

Roy Neverson had chosen his second well. The little European did not pause for argument. He started to turn toward the gate and made of himself a pivot around which the two others could swing. Dr. Bauer marched out of the cemetery between Dr. Neverson and Dr. Kroner.

They walked in silence until they reached the cars. Then Neverson said:

"I thought the three of us could go up to my place for a drink."

Bauer stiffened for a moment, then suddenly he relaxed. Perhaps it was because he had sensed the genuine concern in Dr. Kroner's voice, the concern of an adult holding himself responsible for a young person. For Harley Bauer did feel like a child whose balloon had burst. The funeral was to have given him an opportunity for a few discreet words with old friends at Southport, friends who knew the inside story. Instead he had been singled out from hundreds of mourners and accused of murder. Harley Bauer was almost incoherent with shock.

When they were seated in Neverson's apartment, he exploded immediately.

"The only thing I could think of was 'Thank God, Joan isn't here!' It was the only thing that made me able to go through with it. And she almost came!"

Neverson's bright eyes darkened with sympathy. "My God, that would have been terrible!"

Harley did not doubt his sincerity. Ever since his own wife had divorced him, Roy Neverson had been solicitous about everyone else's marriage. Now that he could give his wife and children nothing but money, he showed more consideration for the sensitivity of others than he had ever shown to anyone, including his wife, during marriage.

Harley thawed further. "I don't know what that woman wants!" he said in a voice more like his own. "They got me thrown out of the hospital, isn't that enough? After all, I'm not the one who's done anything!"

Nothing but fight city hall, thought Neverson silently. He left the vocal response to Dr. Kroner.

"She is upset now, of course. That we understand. But still it is odd." Dr. Kroner struggled for expression. "I think maybe she tries to reject his death. It is easier for her to think of a continuation of his quarrel with you, Harley."

In the doubting silence that greeted this pronouncement, Neverson busied himself making drinks. They were an odd trio sitting there in the luxury apartment surrounded by rosewood bars and stereo tape recorders. Roy Neverson lived next to the boatyard and pursued a sailing, skiing, sports car version of the bachelor life. At first this had jolted colleagues used to associating him with the large split-level house in Green Acres, two small children and a washing machine whirring in the background. Many of their wives still did not like it. But he looked the part with his bronzed countenance and lithe movements.

Little Dr. Kroner, by the simple expedient of wearing a dark armband to a colleague's funeral, had managed to place himself not only a continent away, but a generation as well. And as for tubby Harley Bauer—in spite of his youth, Mrs. Furness would have instantly diagnosed his oddity against this background. He was hopelessly domestic.

Dissimilar they might be; they were joined by a common problem. Each man wanted to erase Lucille Martin's accusation from the tablet of history. Dr. Kroner remained realistic:

"There is only one thing that can be done. Everyone sees that she is not responsible for what she is saying, scarcely knows what she is saying. It must be made clear that Southport Memorial knows this is nonsense."

"One other thing," Neverson added grimly. "Phil Wittke can damn well make sure she doesn't get another chance to sound off. He's got to keep her shut up."

Harley Bauer laid down his glass and prepared to leave. He spoke slowly and carefully:

"He'd better, Roy. I just don't know how much more of this I can take."

Kenneth Nicolls heard the grisly details upon his return to the Sloan.

"Good lord!" said Ken, belatedly aware that his lot, Nancy Perkins and Mrs. Furness notwithstanding, had been free of naked human passion.

John Thatcher, who shared Ken's instinctive recoil at the thought of female hysterics, was prepared to utilize any information they conveyed.

"Mrs. Martin had mentioned Bauer before, as a matter of fact. When we were at the hospital. At that time, she seemed to have a grudge against both the man and his wife."

"Do you think there's anything in what she says?" Kenneth asked.

"I doubt it. There hasn't been any suggestion that Martin's death was more than an ordinary mugging, and the widow was slashing out at Bauer in any way she could." Thatcher shook his head in dissatisfaction. "It isn't our business, after all. We're interested in the financial situation, and, apart from her wild attacks on Dr. Bauer, this Martin woman didn't really say anything. Nothing about missing money, for example."

Charlie replied by pointing out that Lucille Martin had been hustled away before she could really get warmed up. Then, since he was the kind of extrovert who hated to dash hopes, he added that he personally had no doubt she could have gone on and on.

Ken found both John Putnam Thatcher and Charlie Trinkam regarding him. With a chill, he realized they were weighing the advantages of dispatching him into the orbit of a widow who had just burned her husband. Before he could protest, Thatcher shook his head.

"No, I don't suppose that we can get any more information from Mrs. Martin at the moment. Then, too," he broke off and swiveled his chair around to gaze out his window, "there seems to be a crowd of people determined to shut her up whenever she does start talking. I wonder . . ."

The wave of relief crashing over Ken Nicolls made his ears buzz momentarily. When he had recovered, he found Thatcher looking at him with something like sympathy.

"I don't suppose your day has produced anything as colorful as Mrs. Martin," he said. "Did those patients have anything of interest to say?"

"Well . . ." Ken answered the question with a brief description of his encounters with Mrs. Furness and Nancy Perkins. Thatcher listened, he noticed uneasily, with great attention.

Charlie Trinkam, on the other hand, rose. "Sounds like a washout to me. Unless the Perkins husband's got something. But I'll put my money on the widow. There's something funny going on, and they won't be able to keep her shut up long."

On this cheery note he departed to resume hostilities with Everett Gabler.

Thatcher roused himself from his abstraction. "And I," he said severely, "will put my money on the missing wealth of Wendell Martin. But that may just be the congenital bias of a banker."

Ken had had an unrewarding day, and this emboldened him beyond his wont.

"I thought Mrs. Martin decided the money had gone on another woman."

"A little calculation as to how much money was involved will disabuse you of that suspicion, Nicolls," Thatcher said crisply. "The fact may not have been brought to your attention, but suburban American men do not keep mistresses on the scale of the Shah of Iran."

Kenneth struggled with a sense of resentment. First Mrs. Furness and now John Thatcher! Any minute now, there would be a reference to his nice little wife and child.

But Thatcher had kindly changed the topic. Why, he wondered, was young Nicolls blushing like a sunset?

"I think Charlie was right when he said this Perkins might have some information. The man seems virtually inaccessible during the day. If you have an evening free this week, see if you can catch up with him. I'd keep it as informal as possible, if I were you . . . what? Oh, yes, Miss Corsa, I'm ready to dictate."

Ken marched off, wondering if the life he was leading was too restrictive.

Miss Corsa, dictation pad at the ready, settled herself. Thatcher did not give his preliminary cough.

"Tell me, Miss Corsa," he asked, "what do you and your family do about medical care?"

Miss Corsa rarely indulged Mr. Thatcher, but, given a decently limited question of fact, she was prepared to try to cooperate. Despite this, Thatcher had drawn a blank: Miss Corsa, her father and those of her brothers old enough to work, had a wild array of complex, health insurance schemes paid for by the large institutions employing them. Moreover, one Dr. Mario Sodaro was a close family friend, his mother, like Miss Corsa's, having hailed from Termini in the province of Naples. All of this was preparation and no more—despite a diet of saturated fats and carbohydrates, despite girths (excepting Miss Corsa) to turn cardiologists pale, the Corsas were a remarkably healthy and long-lived breed.

"Disappointing," said Thatcher.

Her instincts toward helpfulness prompted Miss Corsa to search her family's medical history.

"My grandfather has high blood pressure," she proferred doubtfully.

"And how old is your grandfather?"

"Ninety-seven," said Miss Corsa. "Dr. Sodaro gives him some medicine, but he always forgets to take it. It's nothing serious."

"I see," said Thatcher.

Regretfully he dismissed the Corsas as a source of information about the peculiarities of modern medicine and turned his attention to the New York real estate entrepreneur whose dubious investment plans were his immediate concern: "Dear Frisch, I have asked our accountants . . ."

11 Deficiency

Nothing in this world is really certain, doctors and lawyers are in the habit of saying. John Thatcher often suspected this was a rationale for the disproportionately high input of wasted energy and fruitless discussion that characterized both professions.

Still, he had to admit *Freebody v. Atlantic Mutual*, the death of Dr. Wendell Martin and now Southport Memorial's grand right-and-left might justify unusual activity. Whether it did or not, the offices of Jackson & Jackson, like the law department of Atlantic Mutual, hummed. Proposal met counterproposal, references to settlements in Kansas were capped by recondite cases from the Hawaiian Islands. Thatcher, at the Sloan, and Dexter Loomis, at Atlantic Mutual, both grew accustomed if not reconciled to calls bristling with *unpredictable interventions, contributory causes and standings to bring suit.*

The medical pot was boiling, too. Up at Hanover, Dr. Edmund Knox and staff, including two young Englishmen boning up on U.S. medicine before ultimate return to the British Isles (or so they claimed), pored over alumni lists to locate allies and drafted complex suggestions for the disposition of one hundred thousand dollars. At the medical grass roots, Dr. Philip Wittke let lesser fry remove tonsils, deliver twins and test overweight executives. He reserved himself for policy-making, namely, holding conferences and keeping a weather eye on Lucille Martin.

Even the police, so Paul Jackson privately assured a surprised John Thatcher, were still asking questions about Wendell Martin's murder.

It was all tiring to contemplate, Thatcher reflected. Yet, on his rarefied level, he too was active, although convinced he was the only one in the whole lot not simply thrashing around.

Of course, when Thatcher decided to look into the financial background of Southport's personnel, he was in a strong position to do so. Over the years, the Sloan Guaranty Trust, with its customary foresight, had dispensed favors to many financial institutions scattered throughout the greater New York area. Possibly more important from the viewpoint of banks in Suffolk County, the Sloan remained a source of future assistance. Since there can never be too

92

many sheet anchors to windward in the money market, Thatcher's inquiries received prompt attention in many quarters and, more to the point, a frank response. Without exception, his contacts promised to call a few friends and check around. With discretion, of course.

As a result, many a luncheon conversation in Islip, in Babylon, in Huntington, was gently steered into channels centering around the names Martin, Wittke, Neverson, Bullivant. Indeed one conversation—on the outskirts of Southhampton—was pushed in that direction by three lunchers simultaneously.

With this kind of wholesale cooperation, Thatcher confidently anticipated information. It came, however, in rather unexpected form.

"Benjamin Edes," his phone identified itself. "Southport National Bank. We met yesterday at the funeral, you recall,"

"Yes indeed, Mr. Edes. It's good of you to call. . . ."

Thatcher was interrupted by cackling.

"Never hurts to cooperate with the Sloan," the phone told him candidly. "I understand you're still in the market for that information. Think I've got something for you if you'd care to join me for lunch. . . ."

Thatcher would. Two hours later, he stood in the foyer of the Southport Yacht Club which, Mr. Edes had assured him snappily, served pretty poor food but still the best available in Southport. It was a deliberately ramshackle structure some three miles from Southport Center, occupying a spread of scrub beach. Neither the parking lot to the west, nor the horrors uncovered by low tide to the east, improved its overall appearance. Within, the Southport Yacht Club compromised between the nautical (buoys and nets draped against dark wood walls, windows giving onto the bay) and the suburban (a mature houri hostessing, a well-stocked bar opening off the dining room). In the evening, and possibly over weekends, the Southport Yacht Club might well shelter tanned and happy sailors in sneakers from Abercrombie's; on working days its prime function was to provide a suitable place where business could be talked. The large dining room was exclusively male save for one female foursome growing hilarious over martinis and plans for a dinner dance.

Edes was the spry, angular septuagenarian who had been so chipper at Wendell Martin's funeral.

"Sorry I couldn't come into town," he said, imperiously

directing the hostess to place them at his usual table in a choice alcove. "Always like to get into the city. They say it's crashing to the ground, what with race riots and rising taxes. But hell, I've been sitting here in Southport for seventy years listening to 'em say it. Every time I go, it's still there. Hear you fellows want to move the Exchange now." Mr. Edes lowered himself into a captain's chair, waved Thatcher to a seat and examined him closely. "You won't like it much up in New Hampshire."

Thatcher, who had left New Hampshire almost fifty years ago, decided that Edes was going to require a firm hand. (He had no intention of disclaiming personal responsibility for the New York Stock Exchange's more venturesome plans for emigration.)

"I'm very glad to have a chance to see more of Southport," he said firmly.

With patent glee, Edes topped him.

"Reason I couldn't get in," he said, studying the hand-written menu, "is that I'm going to attend a meeting of the Board of Trustees of Southport Memorial Hospital. Wife's been on it for dog's years—I told her she ought to rest today. Only reasonable for me to stand in for her, don't you think? . . . Here! You there! We'll order drinks now. Thatcher . . . ?"

Thatcher, no fool, took Benjamin Edes's measure and left the pacesetting to him. He was not disappointed.

Over cocktails, Edes said:

"Normally would have had my girl ring you back. Then, when things started coming in, I decided you and I ought to talk."

"Yes?" Thatcher prompted cautiously.

His host eyed him.

"Don't know whether you were guessing or not, but you're on to something!"

Calmly, Thatcher finished his drink. This was just what he had wanted. Insurance claims could come and go. His sense of smell had told him that there was something bigger in the wind. Here was Benjamin Edes with confirmation.

Edes was high-handedly ordering lobster for both of them. "Only thing they know how to cook," he confided. Then, without changing tone, he returned to business. "Don't know what it is yet, but there's a helluva lot of money missing!"

Thatcher's reaction was disappointment.

"Money missing, eh? That's what Mrs. Martin was saying—in her way. . . ."

"It's not just Martin," Edes told him severely. "The others, too. Wittke and Neverson. And probably others . . ."

Thatcher savored this.

"Now, that is very interesting."

Edes wheezed happily.

"Knew you'd say that. Said it, myself. Let's see, do you know about the quarter of a million?"

Thatcher put down a breadstick. "No," he said invitingly. "Tell me about the quarter of a million."

"There's about a quarter of a million dollars missing from Martin's estate," said Edes. "The tax people were standing by when we opened up his safe deposit boxes. And do you know what they found? Nothing but junk! . . . Here, boy! Get us some more melted butter. . . . Now where was I?"

With considerable amusement Thatcher told him that he had arrived at a safe deposit box full of junk.

"Oh yes. Well, things weren't like that two years ago. About that time, Martin went into cash. Sold out of the market, slapped a mortgage on his house—turned everything he could lay his hands on into ready money."

Benjamin Edes brandished a claw for emphasis. "And there's no record—at all—where that money went! The only thing left is what he's accumulated in the last eighteen months."

Thatcher thought about this for a few moments. Then he fired a test shot. "The widow must have been upset."

"She was!" Edes was in full agreement. "Not, of course, the way she was later at the funeral. Just stood by the safe deposit box in a trance, moaning her husband's name." He shook his head and added, "I have to hand it to those tax people. They didn't turn a hair. Of course, they run into this sort of thing all the time!" Again he peered at Thatcher with a wicked gleam. "And what do you think! She came into the bank first thing this morning—with Al Martin, Wendell's brother. Back to life! Sad of course—but normal, if you know what I mean."

"And what do you think caused that?" asked Thatcher, who was enjoying Edes.

"She knows where the money went, not a doubt about it.

And sure as God made little fishes, Martin's brother told her. He's a stockbroker, you know. Only natural to help his brother out—in money matters."

Thatcher addressed himself to his lobster for a while. "It's natural," he agreed finally. "But that does suggest some sort of family arrangement, doesn't it? Of course, that's just a guess. These doctors seem to follow a policy of studied confusion about money, don't they?"

"Confusion?" Edes asked scornfully. "I'd call it downright stupidity! You should have seen them the day we asked for their social security numbers. That damn fool Wittke made a special trip to inform me that he was not on a salary!"

Thatcher could visualize the scene. "You said that money was missing from other accounts, too?"

Edes nodded vigorously. He was supremely untroubled by this spilling of clients' beans. Perhaps it was his advanced age. More likely, thought Thatcher, it was because of the clients.

"Martin's mortgage reminded me. I recalled some talk, so I checked around. Wittke got a mortgage at the same time. For that matter, so did all the Wittkes. They went to different banks, but the word got around. . . ."

"All the Wittkes?" asked Thatcher, who thought that one was enough.

"He's got two boys," Edes replied. "They're not associated with the hospital. They took over that private clinic Wittke built up. Do very well, let me tell you. No matter what you've got, it's chronic. That means a visit every week. Special medicines you can only buy at their pharmacy. It's a gold mine! Well, all this made me curious. Couldn't approach the Wittke broker myself, you understand. Don't know the man well enough."

Thatcher nodded gravely. "But you know somebody who does."

Edes beamed. "That's it."

Really, it was a shame to think that Benjamin Edes had been wasted in Southport all these years.

"And guess what? The Wittkes sold out of the market about two years ago. The same story. There's nothing in their portfolio except the little they've put in this last year."

Thatcher murmured he felt sure Edes had followed this up by examining Dr. Neverson's finances. Edes had, but confided that he had hit a snag.

"He's an exception to this rush for cash?" asked Thatcher in surprise.

Edes raised a restraining hand. "Maybe yes—then again, maybe no! You see, Neverson and his wife got divorced just about then...."

Thatcher did see. Divorce frequently triggered financial upheavals— with assets scurrying into hiding. Edes's leisurely description of Roy Neverson's recent business transactions confirmed this:

"... didn't mortgage that big house of his, but sold it outright. For that matter, it was already mortgaged up to the hilt. He's the only one who doesn't buy his houses free and clear—course, he's younger, you know. Now he's got a cooperative apartment, so that gives him a tax break...."

After hearing Benjamin Edes out, Thatcher summed up. "We know that Wendell Martin took a quarter of a million dollars and did something mysterious with it—something with no records. We know that at the same time, some other doctors were getting their hands on cash. Of course, they're not dead, so we can't be sure they didn't do something perfectly aboveboard with the money...."

"Hah!"—said Edes, automatically loading a monstrous churchwarden pipe. "It may be aboveboard, but it isn't normal! Not investment in real estate or anything like that! They moved right out of standard banking channels. Otherwise, I'd have heard about it...."

Thatcher believed him and said so. He added that, in all fairness, Roy Neverson had to be exempted for the moment. His financial change of life might be the result of divorce.

A gigantic puff of smoke momentarily obscured his companion. Reappearing, Edes passed judgment on Roy Neverson.

"He's got more brains than the rest of them combined," he said. "I don't think he's pulling any funny business with his divorce settlement. He's still close to his family. Two little girls, you know. They spend the summer with him and his mother. And he pays their school bills—whopping big ones, at that!"

"So you think that his move into cash means that he must be associated with Wittke—all the Wittkes. And Martin, too?"

"I do," said Benjamin Edes decisively. "I can tell you one doctor who isn't, though. That little German. Kroner.

You've met him? He and his wife have an open financial life. Not that there's very much of it," he added. "She's some sort of teacher."

Edes pondered his own words, then, apparently at random, commented that he had not finished his research. Next on the list was Dr. Edith Bullivant. She was, he said, a pretty sharp businesswoman. He would be interested to learn if she was involved in whatever it was. Suddenly serious, he put down the pipe.

"That's what I've been wondering about," he said. "You know, I've been around Southport a long time. Hell, I knew Philip Wittke back in the days when doctors weren't rich. That was before Edith Bullivant married that husband of hers. And Martin was in the bank the day he got out of the service in forty-five and settled down here. And I remember Neverson when he was a resident. . . ."

He looked back at his memories and Thatcher waited.

"You know," Edes said, "I can think of a lot of reasons why Wittke and Neverson might be up to something. But Wen Martin wasn't a gambler! He never took any chances! That means that whatever this is—it's a sure thing!"

"A surer thing than being a doctor!" Thatcher amended. And that, for the moment, was that. Benjamin Edes sincerely advised against any dessert that the Southport Yacht Club could produce. It was over coffee, therefore, that he ducked his head at Thatcher in his first and only conspiratorial gesture.

"Look there," he said. "Martin's brother."

Casually, Thatcher glanced across the room. There, behind the four convivial ladies who had still not progressed beyond martinis, two men were advancing on a table. The short tubby man bore no resemblance to his celebrated brother; the tall dark man with the good looks was familiar.

"Roy Neverson," Edes told him unnecessarily.

He ordered more coffee as autocratically as he had waved it away earlier. "Of course, perhaps they're just friends. Nice chance to get together, after the funeral."

Was Edes being caustic? Thatcher wondered something else.

"I wish I knew," he said aloud, "I wish I knew what they're talking about."

Had he been able to eavesdrop, he would not have been much enlightened.

"I wonder what they're talking about," Al Martin muttered when Neverson, detained by one of the ladies for a moment, finally sat down.

He had sighted Edes and his companion upon entry.

Neverson looked at him quizzically. "Stop worrying, Al! What difference does it make now? You're too wound up! You should get more rest!"

They had to give their orders (no drinks because of Al's ulcer and Neverson's acute understanding of how Southport likes it doctors to behave, no matter how it behaves) before Martin could reply.

"Wound up! You bet your sweet life I am! And you would be, too, if you'd been through what I've been through. . . ,"

Deliberately misunderstanding, Roy looked up from his chowder. "I'm sorry, Al. I keep forgetting that Wen was your brother. . . ."

This insincerity mollified his companion. It also had the less desirable effect of restoring his feeling of intimacy with Neverson.

"You know," he said, "what I keep forgetting? I haven't seen you for . . . God, it must be two years now. I wanted to tell you how sorry we were to hear that you and Julie had split up. . . ."

He blundered on without noticing Neverson's constraint. The Martin brothers, though physically dissimilar, shared certain family characteristics, among them insensitivity. With Wendell, this had been glazed by arrogance. Albert Martin, a much less prickly personality, was just one of those men who are clumsy in personal relationships. He was, however, a competent stockbroker.

Roy Neverson's distaste was not obvious, although anyone from the hospital would have been alerted by his sudden stiffness. A man of many moods, he protected himself from intrusiveness with practiced reserve.

And that, he thought ruefully as Martin rambled on, was one of the costs of divorce—one of many. Divorce was a fissure, flawing the shell that protected vulnerability.

". . . always think of you and Julie and the kids at that beautiful house on the point," Martin was saying. "What a great location, Roy! And the docks . . . !"

"I sold it," said Roy Neverson shortly.

Martin was a fellow boating enthusiast. "You didn't sell that nice little ketch, did you? Remember when we went out . . . ?"

"I traded up. Got a thirty-two footer now."

This, as Roy Neverson had known it would, set Al off on a disquisition on docking charges in Delaware Bay. Interjecting the correct responses left Neverson free to think his own thoughts. These circled and touched down on many subjects these days—he, who had always prided himself on self-discipline. First and always were Julie and the girls. The apartment had every comfort known to man, from maid service to vicuña rugs, but it would never be a home.

Well, maybe Julie was right. He was too self-centered, too calculating to be part of a real home. That was pretty much what Harley Bauer had said, too. Neverson cut into his steak, reviewing the efforts he and Kroner had made to calm young Bauer. That was something else he should check up on . . .

He discovered Al Martin waiting for a comment.

"Why don't you stay over another day, Al?" he said easily. "I could take some time off and we could go out on the boat."

Regretfully, Martin shook his head. "That'd be great, but I've got a seat on the eleven o'clock plane, and I ought to get back. It'll give me time for dinner and another talk with Lucille tonight. . . ."

Neverson was concerned. "You're sure she's all right?"

"She's all right *now*," Martin corrected him. "She's still miserable because Wen is gone"—here he shook his head incredulously—"but I explained things to her. I didn't go into details, you understand. But she didn't want details. As soon as she understood that there was no other woman and that Wen was thinking of her—well, that made the difference. I still don't see why one of you didn't explain things to her before the funeral."

Neverson grimaced. There was no use pointing out that, if anybody had contemplated the unfortunate scene at the church, somebody would have.

"Did she ask many questions?" he wanted to know.

"She didn't ask any," Al was bemused. "Lucille's a funny girl. Really devoted to Wen. I think she'll spend the rest of her life mourning him."

Cleverer men than Al Martin would have found Lucille Martin incomprehensible.

"It wouldn't do any harm if you or Phil ran around to see her once in a while," he began before breaking off suddenly and narrowing his eyes.

Roy Neverson turned.

Benjamin Edes was leading Thatcher out of the dining room. Their path took them near a table where an elegant, white-haired man sat with two younger companions.

"Well, Giles Bullivant!" said Benjamin Edes, all surprised pleasure. "You usually lunch here a little earlier, don't you?"

Confusion on the handsome, if ineffectual, face yielded to recognition.

"Hello there, Edes," he replied in vaguely British accents.

Edes plunged into introductions ". . . and Giles here is Director of Admissions up at our new community college," he told Thatcher. "We'll be having four hundred students this year, won't we?"

"Actually," said Giles Bullivant rather defensively, "four hundred and fifty!"

"You don't say!" Benjamin Edes marveled. "Well, sorry we can't stay. . . ."

As they continued their exit, Thatcher glanced at his host. He was just filled with information.

"Dr. Bullivant's husband?" he inquired.

"What? Oh, yes. Interesting talker. He used to give a lot of time to the club before he got this job. Committees and things like that. He's always been popular. He—and Edith of course—have been members of the club for years. . . . We don't see much of Edith, but Giles is a regular,"

As intended, this gave Thatcher more food for thought.

In the dining room, Giles Bullivant took a quick quaff. And, at the table by the wall, Al Martin munched a full lip.

"I don't like it, Roy! That was Thatcher from the Sloan with that old fool Edes. What did they want with Giles? Hell, do you suppose . . ."

As if he had not heard, Roy Neverson looked across the table and said:

"I'm still sorry you can't stay over for a day or two. And you know, I'm not the only one. Sid Segal dropped in my office today. Told me to tell you he was sorry to miss you after the funeral. You should drop in and talk to him. He's a pretty sensible guy, Al . . ."

These observations did nothing perceptible to allay Al Martin's fears.

12 Retention

There are many rungs on the ladder of banking as in all other careers. While John Putnam Thatcher was lunching with the president of the Southport National Bank, Kenneth Nicolls was arranging to interview Eugene Perkins, bookkeeper, mechanic and cashier.

His arrival in Southport for that meeting after dinner proved that surroundings mirror rank. The Southport Yacht Club, whatever its other deficiencies, had been quiet; Ken Nicolls found himself deafened. Screams, shouts and explosive clatter echoed under the arched low ceiling and smote his ears. More voices were raised, to be crowned by distant explosions.

Dino's Bowladrome was busy. All twenty-four lanes were in full operation; in the banks of seats behind the lanes, many men and women impatiently waited. Threading neatly among them, trimly uniformed waitresses efficiently hurried trays of beer to bowlers and onlookers. In the background, a cash register rang out and a jukebox throbbed tympanically. There were groans of mock sympathy, yelps of pleasure, cries of encouragement rising from every lane, together with the endless swish of heavy bowling balls cannoning down the alleys to strike pins into brittle disarray.

Ken turned and sought out the cashier's desk, where Eugene Perkins put in three nights a week. When Ken learned this, during his telephonic hunt, he had suggested postponing their meeting until tomorrow night, only to be told that it was easier to talk at Dino's Bowladrome than at Grossman's Meat Packing Company where Perkins worked two nights a week.

In the view of the din prevailing, Ken wondered about Grossman's as he introduced himself to Perkins, a jaunty carrot-topped young man sporting a red open-necked shirt. Perkins finished dealings with four men labeled "Babylon Hammer and Drill," then invited Ken to join him behind the counter. Between a bowling team from the Suffolk Construction Works and four ominous teen-agers, their conversation continued.

First, Perkins put his cards on the table. "Nancy says she told you how we feel about Dr. Martin?" Ken ignored the discomfort his sober gray flannel was

102

causing in this sea of informality and replied that the Sloane's interest had shifted away from Dr. Martin himself, to the rest of the staff at Southport Memorial.

"Stands to reason," said Gene, knitting his brows. "Well, the week that Nancy was operated on, I was there most of the time . . . let's see . . ."

His effort, which cost a tremendous scowl alarming several regular customers, was unproductive. This did not surprise Ken, who had chalked Perkins up as an uncomplicated young man, inclined to think the best of everybody, including the new friends he had made at the hospital when his wife was sick. Nobody who accepted things at face value was going to be able to see behind the kindly mask of hospital staffs, particularly when he wanted to trust their professional optimism.

On the other hand, Ken recalled two comments by Mrs. Perkins. Miss Gentilhomme had become a family friend; and Gene Perkins—who must certainly be one of the most active young men in Southport—worked in a garage where Neverson and Bullivant cars were sometimes serviced. So, Ken squirmed on the stool, and listened to an uncritical assessment of Southport Memorial Hospital. Two years earlier he might have cut Gene Perkins short and escaped; tonight he took a leaf from John Thatcher's book and decided to invest the rest of the evening.

"Not that I know anything about the doctors," Gene Perkins said with untroubled humility. "Gosh, I don't think we actually spoke to Dr. Martin more than twice . . . that's seventeen, Mrs. Ballou. Have a good game!"

Suddenly Perkins snapped his fingers and turned a dismayed face to Ken.

"Hey, I forgot," he said in distress. "I hate to break this up, but I've got to take off early."

Perkins was not going straight home. He was detouring to Southport center, to pick up prescriptions at Segal's Drugstore. Already on his feet, he was explaining that, since his car had broken down that morning, he had to hurry to catch the last bus.

Ken seized his opportunity and offered a lift.

"Gee, that'll be a big help!" said Perkins with enough warmth to make Ken feel faintly remorseful. "I've got to change first . . ."

Thankfully escaping from the tumult, Ken went outdoors to wait. In the warm summer night with its dark star-spangled sky, the world seemed older and homelier, he reflected, firmly ignoring the solid blaze of headlights on the highway and Dino's multicolored neon sign. Within minutes, Gene joined him, now in a sweat shirt since, he explained, they were saving on shirts.

"This really makes a difference," he said, setting in Ken's station wagon. "I won't have time to fix that fuel pump until the weekend."

On the trip to the business district of Southport, Ken learned that Gene Perkins was not only a repairer of his own car, but a baker of his own bread. Under the best of circumstances, the Perkins budget had been stretched thin. Nancy Perkins's operation, together with hospital checkups and special medicines, had blasted the Perkinses deep into debt.

"So, whenever I can," Perkins said cheerfully, "I use elbow grease, instead of dollars!"

His world too had been handed back on a silver platter.

Segal's was fully lit, but far removed from its daytime bustle. A solitary man in Bermuda shorts stood leafing through *Playboy*; at the back door a leisurely janitor was already wielding a long-handled broom. Otherwise, no one was in sight. Perkins threaded his way to the prescription counter without hesitation. Ken, following, looked around with the vague interest of the non-shopper, a tourist in a new country. Segal's was an orderly jumble of clocks, cosmetics, stationery, thermometers, hard candies, deodorants. Everywhere signs featured young women transformed by hair spray into goddesses.

This array of consumer goods triggered the usual husbandly response. Ken decided to buy something for Jane. He moved past candy and mothballs, mouthwash and hair curlers, combs and suppositories, to the glass case filled with perfumes and colognes that stood near the prescription counter where Sid Segal had materialized. Three small boxes stood between him and Perkins.

"I've got two new ones," said Perkins, digging two squares of paper out of a pocket. "Dr. Wittle says that she should take them for a couple of weeks."

Segal clucked. "Still," he said, "she's getting better—that's what counts." Affixing his glasses higher on his nose, he peered through them and mumbled something as he studied the prescription. Just then, he caught sight of Ken. "I'll be with you in a minute, sir . . ."

Gene Perkins's introduction drew Ken into their exchange. Segal disappeared from view with Perkins's prescriptions, but he continued speech.

"Why am I working tonight? I'm working tonight because I've got nowhere else to go. My wife's in Florida. Somebody talked her into trying the west coast and she says she's dying from boredom. But my God, what expensive boredom!"

"But, Sid," said Gene, winking at Nicolls, "why isn't Harry here? Or Art? I thought they usually took over nights."

Sid reemerged with two more small packets.

"Art and Harry? You mean my sons? My sons and their wives have more important things to do. They are spending tonight at the Community Theater! To see a play about a man who sits in a trash barrel! Culture! This is more important than working, Dr. Wittke, he's filling in at the clinic tonight, too. His sons and their wives—they too have to go see this play about garbage! And not just see. They're sponsoring it! Wonderful!"

During this monologue, he was totting figures on a brown paper bag.

"I said to Dr. Wittke today, when we were young, we didn't have bicycles. But our sons—they have to have Rolls Royces! Sponsoring plays! Gene, it's forty-three dollars. Make it forty...."

He sighed fatalistically.

Perkins counted out bills. "Don't worry, Sid. Your friend Dr. Neverson is paying tonight."

This comment succeeded in puzzling Segal. Perkins explained:

"He had a split carburetor on that Jaguar of his," he said. "And boy, do those foreign cars cost a mint! I had to spend four hours on the darn thing...."

With a shrug that dismissed anyone foolish enough to waste money on exotic sports cars, Segal turned to his other customer and the question of perfume.

"Who knows what women will like?" he asked rhetorically. "Here, take this. It's the most expensive so it must be good...."

As Ken was fishing out a twenty, a small fold of white caught his attention.

"Say, I've got a prescription too!"

"It couldn't happen in a better place," Segal assured him. He reached out and again studied.

"No," he sadly decided after consulting a leather-bound volume, "I don't have it. I can order it for you."

Ken thanked him and replied that he would pick it up on Wall Street the following day. He caught up with Perkins, who was waiting at the door.

Segal watched them leave with his usual air of melancholy. Then, pursing his lips, he turned away. "Eddie," he called out. Then, "Switch off the window lights. I don't want any more customers."

Segal's was darkening by the time Gene and Ken pulled away.

Ken had not been in a small town on a summer night for a long time.

"Want to stop off for a beer?" he suggested.

Gene Perkins brightened with innocent pleasure, then rejected temptation. "I'd better get on home. Want to be sure that Nancy isn't overtired. . . ."

"Well then," said Ken.

So, armed with twelve cans of beer they invaded Nancy Perkins's kitchen ten minutes later. Mrs. Perkins, sitting at the table, was glad to see them. Since Ken was able to say, with truth, that she was looking much better, this brought a wide grin to Gene's face. It was good spirits on all fronts—save one.

Marie Gentilhomme, who sat across from Nancy, looked very nervous.

"Let's all go into the living room," Nancy suggested.

"Hey, Ken's not company!" her husband reproved her.

"Hi, Marie! You want a beer, too?"

Predictably, Marie shook her head, although she managed a shy smile of greeting. Ken, who drew up a chair and accepted the can that Perkins proferred, knew better than to throw her into total confusion by a direct remark. He simply nodded acknowledgment of introductions and remained silent.

The kitchen, scuffed linoleum, chipped enamel, wheezing refrigerator and all, was gay with yellow paint and bright red and white gingham curtains. Ken could guess who had done the painting.

"No, we don't want glasses," Gene told Nancy. "So what's new, Marie?"

Release came to poor Miss Gentilhomme in the form of a distant honking.

"That must be Uncle Dominic!" she exclaimed, jumping to her feet. "Night, Gene! Mr. Nicolls . . ."

By the time that Nancy Perkins returned from escorting her to the front door, Gene and Ken had passed onto their second beer. She was half resigned, half angry.

"Uncle Dominic," she explained when Gene demanded enlightenment, "He saw Ken's car, and he wants to know who was here . . . you know. I feel so sorry for Marie! They're so old-fashioned."

Gene began to laugh.

"What?" his wife asked suspiciously.

"Uncle Dominic and Alice Doyle!" he chortled.

Ken looked on politely while the Perkinses shared a family joke until Nancy Perkins remembered her manners.

"It isn't really funny," she said, giggling a little, "but do you know Mrs. Doyle? Alice works with Marie, or she did until they transferred Marie. Well, somehow or other Uncle Dominic found out that Alice was getting a divorce. . . ."

"Now, Nancy, if you're going to tell it, tell it right," her husband insisted. "A big fight, you know, and the husband got custody of the two kids. . . ."

The look in Mrs. Perkins's eyes told Ken that she would have a few words for Gene after company was gone. "Well anyway," she said, "Uncle Dominic actually went up to the hospital and insisted that it wasn't right to put a young girl next to someone like that! Marie nearly died!"

Gene Perkins listened while his wife described Marie's difficulties at home, meanwhile placing the little packets from Segal's Drugstore in a line.

"Say, drink up. . . ."

By their fourth beers, Ken and Gene were moving to the point that requires wifely indulgence.

"Sure, I grant you medicine's too expensive," said Perkins with tremendous emphasis. "We know that better than most people, don't we, Nancy? But hell, it's not money thrown away! Not like spending two-fifty for a ten-buck item just because your car's a Jag . . ."

"That's the point I'm making," Ken said. "Here you are, working your head off for these bills. And what are doctors doing . . ."

"Have another," Gene interrupted. "Now, Ken, doctors deserve to make money. I don't grudge a doctor his Jaguar even when he doesn't know one end from the other, even when he parks it in an alley full of broken bottles. Look, they saved Nancy's life, didn't they? That's worth money. . . . Look, do you have kids?"

Ken refreshed himself and prepared to clinch the argument. "Sure, I've got a baby, but that just proves my point. I know life is important—but it's no excuse for price-gouging. Just for the sake of the argument, tell me how much Dr. Bullivant charged for delivering you—"

"What?"

It was an involuntary protest from Nancy. She and Gene Perkins exchanged looks that startled Ken.

"Dr. Bullivant didn't deliver my babies," Nancy Perkins said firmly, lowering the temperature by the chill in her voice.

Although he did not understand why, Ken found himself muttering apologies. Nancy Perkins took pity on him.

"Yes, yes, she is very . . . popular here in Southport. A lot of people swear by her. As a matter of fact, Dr. Bullivant is the only thing I do remember about the night when that Dr. Martin was killed. She was up in the ward just when I was going back to my room. She said I looked well enough to be up in Obstetrics."

Gene Perkins was opening another beer can with concentration. This time the words that would bring a wife's censure were not uttered.

"No, Dr. Wittke delivered my babies. Young Dr. Wittke," Nancy continued. "I used to go to Dr. Philip, but he's too busy . . ."

"Yes," said Ken, who had lost the thread of his argument if he had ever had one. "Well, I only wanted to point out that bringing life into the world is as important as saving life, and it doesn't seem to cost as much . . ."

"But it can cost more in other places," Gene Perkins picked up the ball. Only the other day, he reported, a drug salesman had been complaining that in Southport he sold far too little. "He said that all the doctors here want to do is cut, cut, cut!"

"Gene!" his wife reproved him.

But the discussion ended indecisively, and shortly afterward the evening did also. Ken parted from the Perkinses amidst warm and sincere invitations to return, to bring his wife. Yet, as he headed home, he was wondering exactly what there was about Dr. Edith Bullivant that proved too much for the Perkins's quite remarkable benevolence.

13 Digits

When Kenneth Nicolls left the Sloan and prepared for the long haul out to Dino's Bowladrome, he was convinced that he had been singled out for one of life's more bizarre tasks. Unknown to him, that conviction was shortly to be shared by John Putnam Thatcher.

With the approach of six o'clock, Miss Corsa finished the last of her letters, closed her typewriter and checked her superior's calendar for the following day. She picked up the letters and crossed to the inner office, smiling.

When the signing ceremony was completed, she spoke:

"Mr. Thatcher, I've left the morning open until eleven tomorrow. So that you can pick out a puzzle for Geoffrey."

Momentarily baffled, Thatcher abandoned the Pennsy-Central report and stared.

"Your grandson," Miss Corsa explained kindly. "It's his birthday next week."

Thatcher opened his mouth to protest. He had been cherishing that free morning in the hope that it would dispose of Gabler's *bête noire* once and for all. Miss Corsa's next words silenced him.

"I've spoken with Mr. Durrant and he's saving several models for you. He has one in particular he wants to show you."

Leaving a cloud of indulgence in her wake, Miss Corsa withdrew.

Accordingly, the next morning found Thatcher emerging from his hotel and deviating from his regular course. Instead of plunging into the subway, he walked briskly toward the large toy shop on Fifth Avenue that enjoyed his patronage. And that patronage was by no means negligible now that his role as grandfather was extending so dramatically. (His sons, both late starters, were nosing out their sister in the fertility stakes.)

The day was perfect, not too cool, not too warm, with enough breeze to sweep away the smog and give the illusion of fresh air. Nevertheless, Thatcher felt resentful. He was caught in one of those social traps from which there is no escape.

Two and a half years ago, in preparation for a Christmas holiday to be spent with his son and daughter-in-law, he had been buying some last minute toys. With every name on his list crossed off, he had happened upon a pile of small, complex Japanese wood puzzles, the kind in which all the pieces interlock in an asymmetric fashion defying reconstruction. He had not seen one for over twenty years. Promptly he cut short his shopping and retired to enjoy an evening devoted to mastering the refinements of the post-war models of oriental cunning. Christmas afternoon had been spent relaying this virtuosity to a fascinated grandson.

The spectacle of a gray-haired man and a very small boy absorbed in the same pastime is irresistible to the intervening generation, which suddenly sees itself as the transmitter of a powerful genetic force. Before the holidays were out, family folklore had firmly established John Putnam Thatcher and Geoffrey Kincaid Thatcher as sharers of a common passion for wood puzzles. All very seemly, very proper.

Five months later a letter from his daughter-in-law reminded Thatcher that Geoffrey would be expecting for his birthday "one of those puzzles you and he adore." The letter was opened by Miss Corsa. Thatcher dutifully plodded over to Fifth Avenue, where he was served by the same young man, a Mr. Durrant. The next Christmas, no letter was necessary. Miss Corsa had become self-starting. She called Mr. Durrant, who arranged to hold back three or four specimens for Thatcher family use.

The speed with which a legend can become deeply entrenched is too often underestimated. Within eighteen months, son, daughter-in-law, Miss Corsa and Mr. Durrant were all convinced that they were doing Thatcher a kindness by providing this outlet for an insatiable avocation. On his last visit to the West Coast he realized the lengths to which this process had gone when he found himself being introduced as, "My father-in-law, whose hobby is wood puzzles." He was naturally hardened to that shock of non-recognition experienced by everyone upon being introduced with an erroneous synopsis of salient characteristics. But this seemed excessive. The experience had one salutary result. The next time a lady was presented to Thatcher as mad about pottery, he reserved judgment. She had probably once filled an awkward conversational pause with an innocent query about some vase, thus dooming herself to be publicly branded a ceramics enthusiast from that day forward.

The disheartening truth was that, after unraveling the second puzzle, Thatcher would have been perfectly content to allow another twenty years to roll by before his next bout. He had a shrewd suspicion that this attitude was shared by young Jeff. (Alas, no parent is interested in carrying the genetic seed for a mild and easily satisfied interest. Only a burning passion is worthy of the conduit.) But Thatcher had reconciled himself to the situation. He was, he admitted, not man enough to face his daughter-in-law and say: "Now listen, Susan, I'm fed up with all this wooden puzzle nonsense."

No, the only salvation lay in Jeff's inevitable transformation from small, polite boy, considerate of others, to boorish, self-centered adolescent. Then he would say it for Thatcher. Unfortunately, Jeff showed no signs of being an early-flowering hood. He was still wearing ties and shaking hands.

It was all very discouraging.

Pushing through the revolving doors of the store, Thatcher checked briefly before an enormous stuffed lion with an engaging expression. It was chastely labeled with a price tag for one hundred and fifty dollars. Well, that was one thing to be said in favor of puzzles. At least they were cheap.

Mr. Durrant spied his approach and waved a cheerful welcome. He produced four puzzles, each a marvel of intricacy. Mendaciously, Thatcher discerned a peculiar excellence in the second, thereby sparing himself exposure to the others. Then he selected the present proper—a miniature but powerful set of bagpipes which should settle Susan's hash—to which the puzzle would serve as garnish. Mr. Durrant undertook the mailing of the parcel, and Thatcher was a free man once again.

More than free, almost light-headed. It was like leaving the dentist with no further appointment for six months. (Little did Thatcher know that his expert insights and exacting standards had been a mistake. Dr. Durrant could be a self-starter, too. With his customer's interest now more than confirmed, the young man decided that henceforth he would call Miss Corsa whenever a particularly desirable specimen arrived from the mysterious East.)

Full of virtue at having discharged the requirement of the Protestant ethic, Thatcher contemplated killing the rest of the morning. If nothing had come up at the Sloan, he might be able to find a game of squash at the club. He strode toward the nearest phone booth. Thus do events make the man. Five minutes ago Miss Corsa had been a goad of conscience. Now she was merely a source of information.

"Oh, Mr. Thatcher. I'm glad you called. Mr. Edes has been trying to get you. That's Benjamin Edes of the Southport National Bank."

"Yes, I know. Did he say what it was?"

"No, he was just anxious that you call him back as soon as possible."

"All right. Do you have his number?"

Miss Corsa relayed the endless string of numbers required for direct dialing, repeating them twice. She was always unnerved at the thought of Mr. Thatcher making his own calls. When she dialed a number, she not only got the number, but the party was available. If Thatcher tried to call an insurance company in Hartford, he was infallibly connected to a bar and grill in St. Louis. It was surprising how long conversation could be sustained before the error became apparent.

But this time he was in luck. The reward of virtue, no doubt. Mr. Edes was not only in, he was champing at the bit.

"Thatcher?" he demanded. "I've got something for you." Thatcher was genuinely startled. He had already had such a lucky strike with Edes that it did not seem reasonable to expect another lode.

"You haven't found out where that money is?" he demanded incredulously. Visions of co-opting Edes for the Sloan's Board of Directors danced in his head.

The old man chuckled with satisfaction.

"No, I haven't found out where it is, but I've got some news about what it's doing."

Thatcher arranged himself comfortably in the booth, propping one shoulder against the wall, with coins at the ready for a prolonged conversation. Not for the world would he have deprived either Edes or himself of the pleasures of a leisurely examination into these latest developments.

"Don't tell me that after taking the trouble to go into cash, Martin let something flow back into his account?" he asked.

"That's it!" said Edes triumphantly.

"How in the world did you spot it?"

"Well now, that account's been getting a lot of attention. The tax people have been examining every transaction." There was a long pause. "Naturally I thought it my duty to assist them."

"Naturally."

The phone cackled in high glee.

"As you can imagine, Martin's account was pretty active. Hundreds of entries every month. There was a deposit for six thousand eight hundred last December. It was a check on his brother's brokerage outfit, down in Delaware. There was another one in March, Nobody paid much attention to them on the first go-round. They were sort of buried in the mess. But I remembered them when I saw the mail this morning. Guess what? Another check for sixty-eight hundred."

Hastily Thatcher recalled the day's date.

"What did you say those dates were again?"

"December 5, March 5 and then June 5."

Edes paused for effect.

"Quarterly dividends," Thatcher murmured unconsciously.

"Sure. And he does his normal investing with a broker here in Southport. If he'd just changed brokers, he would have had the portfolio transferred."

Meanwhile Thatcher's mind had been pursuing a well-oiled banker's track. Absently he obeyed the operator's demand for small change.

"But that," he said in outrage, "is over ten percent!"

"Damn close to eleven percent," Benjamin Edes replied cosily.

There was a moment's silent appreciation.

"We agreed they must be on to something good," Thatcher reminded him.

"It's so good, it's the next thing to counterfeiting."

"My God," continued Thatcher, still digesting Edes's information, "if this is being run like a normal business, they're not distributing anything near their total profits. They'll have all sorts of reserves as well."

"Not to mention expanding the business. And who wouldn't expand this kind of business?"

"I'm not surprised the widow became suddenly carefree after talking to her brother-in-law," Thatcher observed tartly.

"Not exactly carefree. She's just stopped worrying about

money and is concentrating on murder, instead." Edes paused discreetly. "You remember the funeral? And what she was claiming about Harley Bauer?"

"I do," said Thatcher. "Tell me, is she still calling him a murderer?"

"She sure is!" said the Southport banker comfortably. "The hospital people keep trying to shut her up, but it's causing a lot of talk out here."

Thatcher was always inclined to clear up finances first; that emotions could be dealt with later. He knew perfectly well that this elderly Sherlock had not completed his disclosures.

"I suppose you've checked to see if the others are getting the same kind of income from Delaware?"

"Wondered when you'd get to that. They're all getting checks from the same place on the same date. But not for the same amounts. All of them except Edith Bullivant, as far as I can see, Philip Wittke is getting the same as Martin got—sixty-eight hundred. The Wittke boys are each getting thirty-four hundred. Neverson is getting forty-seven sixty. Got a pencil?"

But Thatcher was already busy casting up sums.

"The way I figure it," the voice rolled on with quiet elation, "if we count Martin and Wittke as having a thousand shares apiece, then Neverson has seven hundred and the boys have five hundred."

"Yes. That's what I come out with. It would be interesting to know how many people in Southport are getting these checks."

"I thought so myself. If you want to hold on, I'll see if anything has come in."

Thatcher braced the receiver and stared bemusedly at his calculations. There was nothing more to be gained from them. He transferred his stare to the glass door of the booth. Over ten percent! By men who were doing far too well in their professions already to take the risk of peddling marijuana on the side. And who wouldn't set up a Delaware corporation to do it, anyway. He shook his head in vexation. There was no point in blind speculation. It was enough at this point to know that Wendell Martin had been mixed up in something very fishy, indeed. And that, as soon as the inexorable spotlight of publicity had been fixed on him, Wendell Martin had very conveniently died.

Thatcher wondered if things were getting out of hand. His modest objective of forcing Atlantic Mutual to cough up one hundred thousand dollars by proving the general culpability of Southport Memorial Hospital and its staff was becoming small potatoes. It was beginning to look as if Southport Memorial was a front for the numbers racket.

Well, closing it down had not been his intention, but, in view of Pemberton Freebody, it did not appear that doing so would constitute a disservice to humanity.

Thatcher's roving gaze at last found something to hold it, Indignantly he noted that someone was actually buying that stuffed lion. Someone in a short skirt and figured stockings who didn't look a day over nineteen. He had assumed the lion was an eye-catcher. In the absence of Christmas he would have regarded it as unsalable. It just showed how old-fashioned he was becoming. He must make an effort to keep abreast of the financial habits of the go-go generation. (Mercifully, duty did not require him to probe other, and less savory, habits.) Not only was the lion being sold, but two men were hoisting a rather mournful elephant into its place. Probably they went through a whole menagerie in the course of a day.

"Thatcher? Still there?"

Thatcher returned to his post.

"There doesn't seem to be anything else. You understand, I can't have the whole place honeycombed. I just had the tellers queried if they remembered anything with reference to doctors' accounts. Just because they don't remember, doesn't mean there isn't something. But we'd have to know where to look." Edes was disappointed.

Thatcher hastened to reassure him. Of course, he wasn't to divert the entire staff into a search. If a specific name came up, Thatcher would alert him. With renewed assurances of friendship and cooperation, they hung up.

All thoughts of squash were now evaporated. Thatcher was beginning to feel on his mettle. Surely, if a little bank in Southport could produce this much information, the Sloan, with its vast resources, was not helpless. He remembered that Ken Nicolls had spent the previous evening on the Great Southport Tangle. It seemed unlikely that he had unearthed anything, but Thatcher intended to hear his report as soon as possible.

"And that's about it, I'm afraid," Ken concluded his summary with a decent show of regret. He could not understand why Thatcher had been so eager to hear the details of his evening expedition.

"It certainly doesn't tell us anything new," Thatcher agreed. He crossed off his name on some routing slips, tossed the attached reading material into the out basket and buzzed for Miss Corsa. Silly to have convinced himself that the boy was going to hand him a solution on a platter. But he had been gripped by one of his powerful, and apparently erroneous, hunches.

Miss Corsa entered, emptied the basket and eyed her employer with disapproval. She was perfectly willing to allow him time off, once every six months, to fulfill family obligations. Playing detective was something else again. Inefficient suicides, inefficient surgeons and inefficient witnesses had no place in Miss Corsa's view of the Sloan. But she was just. She knew this was none of Ken Nicolls's doing and modified her severity in addressing the young man.

"Miss Todd rang through. If you could let her have the tax table back, she'll type up that estimate."

Obediently Nicolls produced an envelope from his wallet pocket and handed it over. Then:

"Oh, just a minute, Miss Corsa. While you're at it, would you give this prescription to Miss Todd and ask her to send out to have it filled?"

Thatcher watched the transaction in some amusement. Did young Nicolls realize that his Miss Todd was beginning to show the powerful organizing potential of a Miss Corsa? She was telling him what to do, and when. She was beginning to edge in on his personal chores. Soon she would be sending him off to buy model boats for his children. Ah well, Nicolls would have to fight that battle himself.

"It's surprising you have any prescriptions left, after an evening in the bosom of a drugstore," he said. Inefficient drugstores apparently could be added to the roster of Southport's shortcomings.

Nicolls confirmed this unfavorable impression.

"I tried to get it filled at Segal's, but they didn't have the right stuff in stock. And just as well, if the prices they were charging Gene Perkins were their usual ones. Did I tell you what he paid for a week's worth of medicine?" Kenneth became heated in recollection. "Why, I figured out that his entire salary from that blowing job must go in—"

"What did you say?" Thatcher suddenly barked. Why had his superior

Nicolls returned stare for stare.

stiffened like a lamp pole? Why was his voice accusing him of every felony in the book?

"I said," he replied very quietly, "that I figured out that Perkins—"

"No, no," Thatcher waved Perkins away. "About your prescription." He was leaning forward, coiled for the spring.

Kenneth, a good deal alarmed, mentally reviewed his earlier comments. They could not possibly have offended anyone, he concluded. His jaw came forward. With careful control, he repeated:

"I tried to fill my prescription in that Southport drugstore. But the druggist told me they didn't stock the necessary . . . the necessary ingredients."

"That's it!" said Thatcher incomprehensibly. "That *has* to be it. You had the answer all along, my boy." Face, as well as voice, was now accusing. Suddenly they softened. Sorrow replaced anger. Not a marked improvement, in the judgment of a bewildered Kenneth Nicolls. "Now I want to get this absolutely clear. Why did you and this man Perkins race over to Southport Center for a drugstore in the first place? Were the others already closed?"

Kenneth resigned himself to never knowing what it was all about.

"No, Gene never mentioned that. He said that he had to go to Segal's to get these prescriptions filled. I supposed his prescriptions called for something not commonly stocked."

"Splendid! And we have already established that you, on the contrary, had to go someplace other than Southport with your prescription. Do you know what it is, by the way?"

Nicolls shook his head.

"No, it's for Jane. But it's nothing out of the way. I've never had any trouble before, and she's been taking it for months."

Thatcher beamed at him.

"Exactly so. And finally, you say Perkins has heard salesmen from the drug houses joking about how little they sell to that drugstore or to the hospital pharmacy?"

Kenneth shifted uneasily.

"Yes, but Gene was a little beered up by then. We were arguing about surgeons versus pill-pushers. I think that was just a trade joke, Mr. Thatcher. That business about the hospital believing in nothing but the knife. You've got to realize that Perkins has been in and out of hospitals and drugstores so much lately he's practically an insider, the way he talks."

"Not an insider, my boy," said Thatcher with gentle satisfaction. "The insiders are making money, not paying it out. And now we have only one more step necessary for confirmation. To think it was only an hour ago that Ben Edes said he couldn't do anything more without a specific name."

When Benjamin Edes returned from lunch there was a neat note placed on his desk. It said:

Mr. Thatcher would like to know if it checks from the same source have been paid into the account of the owner of Segal's Drugstore.

14 Graft

Late that afternoon an excited Benjamin Edes rang through with the information that checks from the brokerage firm of Martin & Bookerman (Wilmington, Delaware) to the tune of six thousand eight hundred dollars had been deposited in the account of Sidney S. Segal (jointly with Rose E. Segal) in December, in March and yesterday afternoon. Moreover, Edes, to whom a wink was as good as a nod any day, had also examined another account. Deposits from the same source had been made by one Ronald Lawson.

"But he only seems to be in for three hundred shares." Edes was contemptuous. He had no time for small fry. "I think you can guess who he is."

Thatcher thought so, too.

"You did say that Wittke's sons ran a big private clinic, complete with pharmacy," he mused. "Lawson wouldn't by any chance be their druggist, would he?"

"Exactly!" said Benjamin Edes. "Pretty smart work, your tumbling to all this. It's beginning to take shape, isn't it?"

Thatcher agreed that it was and rang off, after making an appointment to confer with Edes tomorrow about further developments. He was amused to find himself full of factional pride; the honor of the Sloan Guaranty Trust had been maintained. It was doing its bit to unveil the dubious financial machinations taking place at Southport Memorial Hospital.

With Segal implicated, things were indeed shaping up, as the redoubtable Edes had said. But the information-gathering stage was over. The time had come to approach one of the many interested parties. If tomorrow were really to bring further developments. Thatcher was weighing the alternatives when he was interrupted by a second phone call; this time from Tom Robichaux.

"You won't forget about this shindig tonight, will you, John?" he inquired mournfully.

"I will if I'm given half a chance," said Thatcher frankly.

"That's what I thought. Wouldn't mind giving it a miss myself."

"Then why are you reminding us both about it? It

119

would have been so easy to let this dinner slip quietly out of our lives," Thatcher said with the brutal frankness of an old friend.

"You don't think I wanted to call you?" Robichaux's voice darkened at this final injustice. "I'm doing it because Cousin Bella made me promise to. Said if I didn't, she would! You're not going to tell me you'd prefer that, are you?"

There was no hesitation in Thatcher's resounding negative. He remembered Robichaux's Cousin Bella (Mrs. Arabella Robichaux Hollingsworth) vividly from past encounters. She was a woman who had been born to be a suffragette. Modern movements proving inadequate, the bulk of her energy was discharged on quailing relatives and associates. It was the kind of situation that made Thatcher believe in professional training for young women. A worthwhile career—say, as an organizer for the Longshoremen's Union—would have gone a long way toward providing Cousin Bella with an outlet for those talents now dissipated on Banning the Bomb and Saving the Old Met.

"She's not going to be there, is she?" he asked, mentally considering the advantages of a fleeting attack by some obscure virus.

"My God, no! It's stag. If you ask me, that's what's got her worked up. She says Amory will make a fool of himself."

Thatcher reviewed the recent activities of Cousin Bella's only son.

"He already has," he pointed out.

"Now look, John," Robichaux rumbled peevishly. "Don't make things even more difficult. We all have relatives! I'll meet you at the bar."

He forestalled further debate by hanging up with a decision far removed from his customary dithering farewells. No doubt it was the suffragette influence at work. Thatcher grimaced and abandoned thoughts of further attention to the Sloan. Instead he cleared his desk and set off uptown for the club providing a private suite for the meeting.

The fine assortment of faces which greeted him as he paused to check his hat was a tribute to Cousin Bella's gadfly potential. Her son, Amory Robichaux Hollingsworth, after an undistinguished career drifting along the eastern seaboard from the offices of one family enterprise to another, had decided to place his talents at the disposal of the constituents in his ostensible congressional district.

Happily, his forty-two years of life had been so politically inert that he had a rather unusual freedom in determining the party of his choice—as well as the state.

An expensive poll, with stratified subsamples, in a Manhattan district composed almost exclusively of registered Democrats, had brought him to the acute conclusion that it would be folly to sally forth under the banner of Republicanism. He had therefore styled himself a N.w Democrat. His candidacy had thus far been entirely uncontaminated by association with any organized political group, whether regular or reform.

"Evening, Thatcher," said a voice at his elbow.

He turned to find Dexter Loomis at his side.

"Hello, Loomis. What are you doing here?"

He was reminded of the Hollingsworth interest in insurance.

"Perhaps I phrased that unfortunately," he said as they strolled toward the bar. "I meant what is our presence supposed to accomplish? Do we do anything other than eat our dinner and listen to Amory tell us his plans?"

"God knows! They're calling it a kickoff dinner." Morosely Loomis inspected the martini handed to him. "I was just talking with Carruthers—the downtown lawyer, you know. He says there's not a soul here who has anything to do with politics or who lives in Amory's district."

"A new approach," Thatcher observed blandly.

Dexter Loomis became suddenly combative.

"I can tell you one thing. Amory isn't getting a check out of me. I don't mind being held up for a contribution when the guy is making some kind of an effort, but I'm not subsidizing hobbies!" He looked at Thatcher fiercely, following an unhappy train of thought. "We've got enough money going down the drain these days."

"I assume that means you're settling the Freebody case with us."

"We don't have any choice. But I—"

They were interrupted by the arrival of Tom Robichaux with the guest of honor.

"You know John Thatcher and Dexter Loomis."

"Hello, Amory," Thatcher began.

"Call me Rob!" the candidate trumpeted with a glazed smile.

Remorselessly the amenities proceeded. Dexter Loomis was so hypnotized by the atmosphere that he was soon assuring Hollingsworth that they were all looking forward to his victory over the machine, and ultimately carried him off to meet someone with the makings of a New Democrat.

"Thought Loomis had more sense," was Robichaux's only comment.

Thatcher was more charitable. "He was just carried away for the moment. But I wish you could have waited another five minutes. Loomis was about to say something. There's no justice."

"Oh, things balance out," Robichaux was cheering up now that his responsibilities were over. "What do you think of Amory's Man of the People stunt?"

"Is that why we're supposed to call him Rob?"

"It's all part of the big picture. He's going to put on a sports shirt and tour his district in a station wagon with the wife and children."

It was not an attractive vision, but Thatcher tried to be fair-minded.

"Quite a lot of unlikely people are doing that nowadays. And getting away with it."

"Not with Amory's wife, they're not!"

"Oh." The vision of an all-American family receded. "Difficult, is she?"

Articulate analysis was not Robichaux's strong point. He fumbled for a shortcut.

"She's the sort of woman who keeps reminding herself that she's got to be very, very kind."

"You can say that again!" echoed a newcomer.

Startled, Thatcher turned . . . to find that life's compensations, as predicted by Robichaux, were duly taking place. Before him stood Curtis Hammerton.

And Curtis Hammerton was a vice-president of Japhet Rose, Incorporated, fourth-largest pharmaceutical firm in the United States.

"Just the man I want!"

Quickly Hammerton replied that he made his political contributions to the Republican Party of Connecticut.

"No, no. This is business."

The announcement did not bring the same satisfaction to his companions as to himself.

Robichaux, fortifying himself with another bourbon, said sadly:

"It's creeping up on you, John. Getting so that you can't ever forget business. You want to roll with the punches."

Hammerton's wariness did not diminish. If anything, it increased. Which was not surprising. Hammerton was

Japhet Rose's outside man, its announcer of new wonder drugs, its maker of policy statements.

And, of course, in recent years, its testifier before congressional hearings about drug prices, practices and profits.

Poor Hammerton, a man made to exude confident good feeling, had lost weight over those recent years; he was probably braced to discover that the Sloan Guaranty Trust was about to embark upon its own version of the Kefauver investigation.

Thatcher set his mind at ease. With a smile he watched Curtis Hammerton brighten upon realizing that, for a change, he was being asked to consider the malefactions of others.

Briefly Thatcher outlined the financial discoveries of the Southport National Bank, concealing only one fact—the amount of the sums involved. Then he touched lightly on the peculiar difficulties encountered in filling the Perkins and Nicolls prescriptions.

"Of course," he said in innocent conclusion, "it's not very difficult to guess what they're up to. But I'm at a loss as to how to proceed. These people have gone to considerable lengths to conceal their activities, which suggests that they may be unethical—"

"Unethical!" Hammerton broke in jovially. "In New York State, let me tell you, it's illegal enough to get you sent up the river. That is, if what you are talking about is what I am thinking of. And, given these damned money-grubbing doctors, the odds are ten to one that it is!"

Thatcher's eyebrows rose. Only strong emotion could have made a vice-president of Japhet Rose, Inc., "The Doctor's Partner in Medical Progress," resort to language like this.

Thatcher lowered his voice.

"Tell me," he said.

"The latest dodge for doctors who can't keep themselves happy until they've squeezed every dollar out of the patient," Hammerton began, "is to set up their own private drug companies. These companies range from perfectly reputable, if small, laboratories—sometimes with a chemist or even a pharmacist—more often with one or two semi-trained people. These operations may be quite all right in their way—that is, careful, clean and so on. They are not, you understand, capable of research . . ."

"Yes, yes," said Thatcher to no avail.

"These bucket shops," said Hammerton, his assumption

of impartiality crumbling, "are really in business to exploit the discoveries made by the millions upon millions of dollars that firms like Japhet Rose spend in research. Why, our six hundred trained researchers . . ."

All information-gathering exacts a toll. Thatcher listened to a vivid description of Japhet Rose's magnificent laboratories, its unending battle to conquer disease, its exacting standards. Hammerton spoke with a fluency normally lacking in his discourse.

After five minutes, Thatcher cut in.

"About these small private drug houses?" he suggested tactfully.

"What? Oh, sorry," said Hammerton. "I make that speech so often that it just slips out. Well, as I say these parasites are respectable from one point of view. They produce, brand and market the commoner drugs under perfectly satisfactory conditions. From a health standpoint, that is. The gimmick is usually that the doctor writes a prescription calling for a drug produced by the company that he owns—and there goes the price! Usually two or three times what we would charge . . ."

He paused to refuel and continued, "Then some doctors set up private drug outfits that are nothing more than an office and a business address. What they do is import drugs cheaply, usually from Mexico or Italy. They then relabel them—and sell them at a damned good price by specifying them on all their prescriptions. The pharmacist, you know, cannot substitute a different brand. And, I need not remind you, drugs produced in Mexico or Italy are not subject to the searching standards of the U.S. Pharmacopeia. . . ."

"You need not," said Thatcher astringently. One lecture was enough. "Just go on. I'm interested in this price hike. I don't wish to offend you, Hammerton, but my general impression was that prices . . ."

Again tact prompted him to keep the sentence unfinished, and Hammerton emerged from his glass to give him a man-to-man look. "I know what you're thinking! You're thinking that our prices are too high already! Well, let me tell you, the price of a new drug may be high, but think of the research—oh, all right John. But the fact remains that within a few years, competition brings it down! Look at the antibiotics! Look at penicillin! But when a doctor sets up a firm, he keeps the price up—steadily! He specifies his own firm's drug—no other! So there is no competition—and he can charge what he wants! And these firms do! I'd say that on the whole they are thirty percent more expensive than the open market! And that's not the worst of it—although five dollars for a dozen aspirin is bad enough! But some of these so-called drug firms are a real disgrace! No tests, no safeguards, not even simple cleanliness!"

Curtis Hammerton, carried away by his own emotion, had raised his voice. The mere fact that he was talking about doctors was sufficient to attract the attention of a bystander.

"What's this about doctors?" demanded Dexter Loomis with grim joviality.

Curtis Hammerton turned to the insurance executive in surprise. It took him a moment to recover his non-platform manner.

"Thatcher, here, has come up with something interesting. Another little swindle by these doctors,"

He began to explain. As he did so, Dexter Loomis's grimness became intensified and the joviality disappeared entirely.

"In Suffolk County, I suppose," he said when Hammerton concluded.

Both men turned expectantly to Thatcher, only to find him lost in thought. Dexter Loomis was appalled to discover the makings of another enormous scandal at Southport Memorial Hospital. Such a discovery would serve to discredit the medical staff more, and further weaken Atlantic Mutual's bargaining position. Thatcher had realized this from the start. He was beginning to realize something else as well. . . .

He shook himself free from abstraction.

"Oh, yes," he agreed. "It's our friends, again."

He did not have to amplify. All of "our friends" were part of a system to make more money. The stark simplicity of the system struck him as peculiar to a peculiar profession; only men who were guaranteed incomes roughly ten times the national average could be so uncomplicated in their approach to acquiring wealth.

Loomis was trying to salvage what he could from the latest debacle.

"So, they've got a little racket going. But what in fact would anyone do about it?" He looked challengingly at Curtis Hammerton.

Tom Robichaux had been a disapproving spectator of

the entire pageant. No one seemed capable of having a simple drink in peace. In many ways it was as bad as if they spent the time having a serious discussion of Amory's candidacy. But now, he thought he saw a shortcut.

"Come off it, Curt!" he advised easily. "Let off a little steam if you want. But we all know Japhet Rose makes its money getting along with doctors. You're not going to stir up any stink."

He leaned back, idly twirling his glass as he watched Hammerton and Thatcher.

The representative of Japhet Rose was reminded of his role as public figurehead.

"Naturally, we wouldn't wish to alienate anyone for the sake of . . . the sake of a minor pecadillo," he murmured. "First, we'd call in our own men and get some sort of idea how big the operation was. If it was small potatoes, we'd have a quiet little talk. . . ." He shrugged.

Thatcher inspected the depths of his Scotch. "And if," he suggested calmly, "if it were a million-dollar operation?"

Curtis Hammerton suddenly choked. "Million dollar! We'd raise holy hell! We'd see it didn't spread! We'd . . ."

Under cover of this wave of emotion, Tom Robichaux spoke:

"Nicely done, John," he commented appreciatively.

Within days, John Thatcher learned precisely what Japhet Rose, Inc.—"The Doctor's Partner in Medical Progress"—meant by holy hell. When the Doctor's Partner moved, it moved. Thanks to information swiftly scooped up by an army of drug salesmen and disaffected pharmacists and, just as swiftly, relayed to the district attorney, Thatcher was surveying a rich and satisfying harvest of headlines.

DRUG RING IN SOUTHPORT

FOURTEEN MEDICOS INDICTED

ILLEGAL DRUGS IMPORTED

15 Infected Areas

Among the ten million people who read these headlines, a surprising number were propelled into some form of action. In Washington, the chairman of more than one congressional subcommittee realized that now, if ever, was the time to resume hearings into drug prices. Officials charged with auditing payments by Medicare, Medicaid and every other form of public health assistance instructed subordinates to inspect druggists' bills with special care. Suave lobbyists (representing powerful German chemical interests) spoke persuasively of the salutary effects to be derived from allowing foreign drugs to compete freely in the American market. Several civic-minded groups demanded legislation to regulate the use of trade names in prescriptions.

On a more parochial level, the state police investigating the death of Dr. Wendell Martin also read the headlines with interest. They came to the same interesting conclusion that had caused John Thatcher's sudden abstraction at the kickoff dinner for New York City's New Democrat.

"Makes you think, doesn't it?" ventured Lieutenant Joseph Perenna, drinking cold coffee from a cardboard cup.

His superior agreed stolidly.

"We said that it was too convenient, Wendell Martin getting himself killed just as he was grabbing the headlines. Now we know who it was convenient for. Exactly fourteen people!"

Perenna studied the news story again. After laying bare the bones of the Hyland Drug Company and discussing the role of Albert Martin as its financial front man, the story went on:

. . . also indicated were Drs. Philip Wittke, James Wittke, Theodore Wittke and Roy Neverson. Sidney Segal and Ronald Lawson, both pharmacists in Southport, Long Island, were also cited as being implicated in the illegal operation of the Hyland Drug Company.

It is understood that Dr. Wendell Martin, slain last month in the parking lot of Southport Memorial Hospital, was a substantial shareholder . . .

127

"None of these people are the kind who'd ever expect to see the inside of a jail. And Martin was pushing them down the road damn fast! Before he was through, they would have the tax boys after them. First the Feds, then the state, then the Food and Drug people—and God knows who else! To say nothing of flushing a beautiful little money-maker down the drain!"

Several moments of silence ensued.

"It gives us a motive, all right," the captain concluded at last. "But we still don't have much else. The autopsy didn't give us anything new. One blow, which could mean some thug cracked Martin in an unlucky spot, or else—"

"Or else someone intended to kill Martin and knew how to do it with the least effort!" The lieutenant swiveled to throw his cup into the wastebasket for punctuation.

"And nothing new on the weapon," the other continued imperturbably. "Except that they did manage to pick some rust particles out of the wound. Just a plain metal bar. And you were right about the wallet and the weapon. They were never found."

"Probably at the bottom of the bay by now."

"Oh, I wouldn't be too sure about that. These people haven't had much spare time," he flicked the headline of the newspaper, "and we've had a man down at the boatyard to check. None of the boats have been out."

"So all we've got is a motive," Perenna mused. "And not much chance of getting anything else unless we come out in the open."

The captain came to a decision.

"It's time we did! These people are rattled now, and being asked for alibis isn't going to calm them down. I want to get them off balance and keep them that way. We need to know where these fourteen were when Martin was killed. We need to know how dangerous this insurance thing was for them, how much these people had to lose if Martin went on talking. And while you're at it, find out what else is going on at this hospital. This guy Wendell Martin sounds as if he could have tangled with almost anybody."

The lieutenant was not impressed by the difficulties of penetrating hospital security precautions. He nodded easily and rose.

"I'll get started on it right away," he said crisply.

Philip Wittke did not have to call for an attorney to be present during his police interrogation. His lawyer was already there, trying to explain to the assembled Wittkes that they would require different representation during their forthcoming trial for running an illegal drug company.

"Look, Phil, I'm not a criminal lawyer. You need someone else."

"Well, you do trial work, don't you?" Wittke demanded impatiently. "I know you handle all those car accidents. And I don't intend to have a lawyer whose other clients are in the Mafia!"

"Phil, it's your own interest I'm thinking of. The trial is nothing. They've got all the evidence they need, and it's all documentary. What you need is someone who can do a deal for you with the prosecutor's office."

Wittke stared blankly. Blunt talking had thus far been conspicuously absent in his immediate vicinity. He was still laboring under the delusion that everything would turn out satisfactorily. The jury would realize that he had only been exercising his God-given right to benefit from the American system. It was a moment before he appreciated the full implications of what he had just been told.

"Do you mean to say that *I'm* going to be found guilty?"

The voice started as a roar, but in midstream turned into an uncontrolled squawk of horror.

The lawyer sighed and spread his hands helplessly.

"That's right, Phil."

The younger Wittkes shuffled their feet uncomfortably. The conference had been their idea, designed to bring home the facts of life to Father. But until now, their one contribution had been the heavy announcement that their wives were terribly upset by the whole affair. Significantly they did not ask how Mother felt.

James now began to speak hurriedly.

"In that case, we ought to make the best deal possible." He looked nervously at the lawyer, who nodded encouragingly. "It might even be necessary for us to testify for the prosecution. We have to think about the future."

His father looked at him as if he had never seen him before. Then he suddenly took a deep breath and relaxed.

"You're upset and you've lost your head for a moment," he explained magisterially. "What you're advising is totally inconsonant with our professional dignity. And, if there's one thing I've always maintained, it's that—"

"Dammit, Father! Don't you understand!" the younger man interrupted with a howl of anguish. "I won't be a doctor any more if I'm convicted. It's different for us than it is for you! I'm thirty-eight and Ted is thirty-five. You were going to retire in a year or two. But what about us? We don't have your financial resources."

"Financial resources have nothing to do with it," grated Wittke. "We'll fight this thing tooth and nail!"

"For Chrissake, father—"

It was on this scene of family accord that Lieutenant Joseph Perenna was introduced.

"Just a few questions," he said easily, settling back into a comfort enjoyed by no one else in the room. "I'm lucky to have caught you all together."

"This is completely irregular," the lawyer protested. "The prosecutor must know that I'm not going to allow my clients to answer casual questions. They'll answer questions at their trial!"

The lieutenant's smoothness remained unruffled.

"I think we may have our wires crossed. I'm inquiring into the murder of Dr. Wendell Martin."

"Well, why didn't you say so?" Wittke snarled. "And it's high time the police did something about that!" Some malevolent spirit impelled him to develop this theme. "Apparently you have all the time in the world to probe into pharmaceutical manufacturing and other things no layman could possibly understand! But when criminals attack and murder a prominent surgeon, where are you then? Dr. Martin was a valuable member of the community whose death should be rigorously investigated. It's getting so that a doctor isn't safe on hospital grounds. I don't know how you expect hospitals to be staffed under those circumstances."

Lieutenant Perenna was supremely indifferent to the problems of hospital recruitment. He let the tirade run its course, then said:

"Will you tell me where you were at the time Wendell Martin was murdered, Dr. Wittke?"

The stunned silence that greeted this question was broken by the lawyer.

"You don't have to answer that, Phil," he said hastily.

"Of course, if Dr. Wittke prefers to stand on his rights . . ." the sentence trailed off suggestively.

"I . . ." Wittke took a deep breath. "I don't know how you expect me to remember at this late date."

"It shouldn't be difficult. That was not an ordinary night and, according to our records, you were at the hospital when our squad car answered the call."

"Yes, of course. I was working late at the hospital that evening."

"The call was answered at ten thirty-four. You must have been working very late."

"I frequently work very late. You don't run a hospital on a nine-to-five basis."

"Perhaps you can tell me who you were with?"

But Dr. Wittke could not. He had, he said, been on the move. Earlier in the evening he had spoken with Dr. Neverson and Dr. Bullivant. But at nine-thirty his memory seemed to end. He spoke vaguely of looking into empty offices and walking along vacant corridors. He had been informed of the tragedy over the house phone, after having been paged. It was all very unsatisfactory.

James and Ted were able to report, with manifest relief, that they and their wives had been present at a rehearsal (for patrons only) of the Community Theater in Bayshore. It was, Lieutenant Perenna thought, typical of them.

Exposure of the drug company had caused the Wittkes to take counsel with their lawyer. Roy Neverson was taking counsel with his mother. In many ways her advice was as shrewd and as hardheaded as any that could be offered by a member of the bar.

"How bad is it, Roy?" she asked on arrival, wasting no time on empty sympathy.

"Damn bad. I may go to jail."

"That's going to be hard. On all of us."

Beatrice Neverson knew all about things being hard. She had begun learning when her husband deserted her and their six-year-old son. Within ten years she had become china buyer in the department store where she started as a salesgirl. Now, thirty years later, she had an interest in a specialty shop which spent the summer in Southampton and the winter in Palm Springs.

Her chunky bracelets jangled as she reached for a cigarette.

"What do you want to do about the children? Julie was going to bring them to Southampton at the end of the month."

"That's just it. I don't think they ought to come up. They'll still hear about it, but nobody's going to be very interested in their jailbird father up in Michigan."

Beatrice nodded. "Do you want me to talk to Julie about it?"

It was thanks to Julie's affection and respect for her mother-in-law that Roy Neverson saw as much of his children as he did.

Neverson replied tensely:

"Yes, but there's more to it than just that. I don't see how I can share the house in Southampton with you anymore. Money's going to be damned tight."

"All right, Roy. Let's get it out in the open. What are we going to have to do?"

"That's the trouble. I don't know." There was tortured effort behind the words. "I'm going to lose most of my investment in that drug company, and there's not much left over. If I go to jail, God only knows what happens then. The medical association will throw me out. Hell! I don't know how to do anything else, Bea, I just can't tell what's going to happen."

His voice broke. His mother made no comment on these fears, or on the effort and sacrifice that had been required to send him through medical school. But her jaw tightened as she ground out her cigarette. Beatrice Neverson had never had much sympathy for weakness.

"Then you may as well face it, Roy. First, you're going to have to cut down on your payments to Julie. The sooner that's fixed, the better. There's no point in putting it off." Neverson stared sightlessly out the window. But his voice was as stubborn as hers.

"I don't want to do that until the last minute. You realize what it'll mean? Julie will have to take the girls out of school. Most of the extras will have to go. I'm not going to do that until I have to."

Deliberately she poured cold water.

"They can go to public school. I did. You and Julie both did. It's not a tragedy."

They were still arguing when Lieutenant Perenna appeared. His pointed questions turned Beatrice Neverson rigid, but her son could barely be distracted from his personal anguish.

"Oh my God! So now somebody thinks we murdered Martin! As if we don't have enough to worry about."

"His death was very convenient," said the lieutenant mildly.

"That may be the way it looks to you," groaned Neverson. "From where I sit, it's just another body blow. I suppose it was inevitable, somebody would get that idea. Living or dead, Martin was always trouble. The only thing that would have done any good was infanticide."

"Just tell me where you were at the time of the murder."

"Let me think a minute. Yes, I remember. It was the day after Marie Gentilhomme's brilliant performance in court. I checked out of the hospital about nine o'clock. I came straight home and stayed here the rest of the evening. I didn't find out about the murder until I heard it on the news at breakfast."

"Any confirmation of that?"

"I don't think so. No, wait, I stopped for a bottle at the liquor store on the corner. But they probably won't remember."

"You'd be surprised what people remember sometimes."

Illegal drug companies were not the only headlines Joseph Perenna had seen in connection with Wendell Martin's death. Sooner or later he was bound to arrive at Harley Bauer's house, where the young couple confronted him together.

"These statements by Mrs. Martin are causing a lot of talk. We thought we'd just check into it."

"It's spite, that's what it is," gasped Joan Bauer. "She and I had a fight, if you must know. Right after Harley started at Southport Memorial. She tried to pull the great lady on me. Ever since she's had her knife into us."

"Now, Joan," said Harley uneasily. "The least said about that, the better. Lucille's just upset. Everybody knows Wendell Martin was killed by a mugger."

"Do they?" The lieutenant paused to let it sink in. "Considering all the dark streets in Southport, we think it's funny a mugger should decide to operate in a lighted parking lot with a lot of coming and going. We're ready to look at any theory."

Harley Bauer went white.

"And so," continued the policeman relentlessly, "I'd like to ask where you were at the time of the murder, Dr. Bauer."

"I suppose I may have been at the hospital," Harley said

in a half-suffocated voice. "I went over to Southport that night to pick up some of my things. I got there about eight. It must have been about two hours before I left."

"You talked to people while you were there?"

"Yes. As a matter of fact I talked to Martin himself early in the evening. I saw Neverson and Wittke and Sid Segal, too. Then, later on, after I cleaned out my locker I chatted with Dr. Kroner awhile. He was the last one I talked to."

"And you left before any alarm had been raised?"

"That's right."

"And where had you left your car, Dr. Bauer?"

"In the staff parking lot," said Harley through clenched teeth. "All right, I know what you're thinking. My car must have been close to where the body was found. I was a couple of places over from Alice Doyle's car."

"And you noticed nothing when you left?"

"Not a damned thing!"

Harley leaned back defiantly, daring the lieutenant to make something out of it. But the lieutenant shifted his attack.

"Mrs. Martin claims you hated Wendell Martin. We'd like to know what the trouble between you was,"

Harley began a response which by now had become mechanical. "The disagreement between Dr. Martin and myself was entirely professional. It had nothing to do with his murder, and I see no reason—"

"NO!"

All the protest which Joan Bauer had repressed since Dr. Wendell Martin's funeral exploded in that one syllable. She clutched her husband's arm desperately.

"Don't you see, Harley?" she demanded frantically. "You can't take that attitude about Southport Memorial any more. They stand back and accuse you of murder, and they know they can rely on you to be all ethical."

"Lucille Martin isn't a doctor," her husband objected weakly.

"That's the filthiness of it! They just hide behind her. Do you think they couldn't stop her if they wanted to? Don't you see what they're doing? It's been the same all along at that hospital. They've victimized you from the minute you set foot in there. And they're doing it again. It doesn't matter what they do. They've always got Harley Bauer to take the blame. If you don't tell the lieutenant, I will!"

Perhaps Harley Bauer had learned something from his

wife's outburst. Perhaps it had occurred to him that he, too, had a woman to hide behind. In any event, he made no further protest as Joan turned stormily to Perenna.

"If there was any hating in Southport, it was Wendell Martin who was doing it. Because Harley showed him up! Dr. Martin was supposed to be such a great surgeon."

"And he wasn't?" inquired Perenna.

It did not seem like a dramatic revelation in view of recent courtroom exposures.

"I don't know how good he was technically. But Harley showed that half the time his operations weren't necessary! He was taking out gall bladders simply to make money!"

"Look, Joan," said Harley wearily. "If we're going to have this out, let me tell it." He shrugged helplessly. "Joan's dramatizing, but she's got the basic situation right. Last year, when I went to Southport as staff pathologist, was the first time they had a compulsory tissue review on every operation. I guess they didn't realize what they were letting themselves in for. Before any results came in, the committee adopted the standards of the big teaching hospitals. The standards tell you how many times a surgeon can diagnose an "acute" appendix that turns out to be normal before being called on the carpet by the chief of surgery. Well, my reports showed that Dr. Martin was operating on far too many normal conditions. The trouble of course was that Dr. Martin was chief of surgery. So I was the one who got called on the carpet. He told me in so many words that I'd better change my reports. I refused. Then I got canned. That's the situation in a nutshell."

The lieutenant did not comment immediately. Harley Bauer had described a situation in which feelings could run high on both sides—indeed, he thought, looking at Joan Bauer's flushed face and recalling Lucille Martin's hysterical denunciations, the resentment could extend to both families.

"I suppose this wasn't just a quarrel between the two of you? Dr. Martin had to have support to fire you."

"The Old Guard stood behind him, all right. But they didn't like it much, particularly in view of his other suggestions." Harley was relaxing now that the skeleton was out of the closet. He was more at peace with himself than he had been since the storm broke.

"What were those suggestions?"

"Martin objected to my temerity in disallowing operations by staff members. But he still wanted a check on the outside doctors with hospital privileges. In fact he had the nerve to tell Wittke to cancel some of those privileges on the basis of my findings. Wittke wouldn't go along with that. He had the sense to see he had to be consistent. He took the position that I was a bum pathologist, and Southport wouldn't pay attention to any of my work. But that didn't stop Martin from tearing a strip out of one visiting doctor he didn't like." Harley chuckled in recollection.

"They went at it hammer and tongs."

"And what was the name of that doctor?"

Harley stiffened.

"Oh, now look here, Lieutenant—"

It was a full five minutes before Perenna wrote down a name.

The sign read:

Dr. Edith Bullivant
Obstetrics & Gynecology
2—4 P.M. and by appointment

The house was a handsome Colonial set in carefully landscaped grounds. It was, thought Perenna, a proper setting for the plump, gray-haired doctor.

"Naturally I'll tell you anything I can about Wendell Martin, Lieutenant," she said, handing back the ID card, "but I don't see how I can be of much help."

"We're checking into his relationships this last year. I've been told that you and he had some fairly violent disagreements."

"That's true," Dr. Bullivant agreed calmly. "And it would be true for almost any year during the last twenty. Dr. Martin and I didn't get along."

"I wasn't thinking of your personal relationship. We've been told that this was a professional disagreement."

"It comes down to the same thing. I don't know how much you've heard about Wendell Martin, but you probably know he liked to throw his weight around. He was chief of surgery. Insofar as I am responsible to anyone, it's to the chief of obstetrics. I told him I wasn't in his jurisdiction, and he didn't like it." The lady paused to smile affably. "But he can't have been very surprised. He's been told the same thing by most of the obstetricians on the South Shore."

"I understand he objected to some of the D&C's you performed. That could mean trouble."

"I'm not in any trouble, Lieutenant," she said good-naturedly. "And I won't be, until the objections start coming from the chief of obstetrics. Dr. Martin was no doubt a highly competent surgeon. He was neither qualified nor competent in obstetrics. I am."

She sounded very sure of herself. But then, if Harley Bauer's story was correct, objections from Wendell Martin would have been taken with a grain of salt by the hospital's inner circle. Particularly if he had a long history of poaching on other people's territory.

"I'm glad to get this cleared up. There's just one more item. For the record, we're checking on the location of everybody at the time of Dr. Martin's murder. Can you tell me where you were that evening?"

"Certainly. I was in the delivery room until nine-thirty. The mother was a diabetic, and it was not an easy delivery. I came straight home after cleaning up. I was with my husband the rest of the evening."

Dr. Bullivant's calm remained unshaken during this recital. Lieutenant Perenna duly noted that she was the only witness to display no reaction to his critical question. But that could simply be strength of character. He had a fairly good idea that Edith Bullivant's reactions were under strong control at all times.

Before leaving, Lieutenant Perenna had a chance to meet Giles Bullivant, who unhesitatingly corroborated his wife's story—which was not surprising. The state police now knew what all of Southport had always known. Giles Bullivant led a carefree, elegant life, which was largely supported by Edith Bullivant's efforts. He had more than one reason to desire her continued success and popularity.

Guided by some unconscious obedience to the medical hierarchic structure, Perenna had deferred Sid Segal until last. In many ways, the interview rounded off the day nicely.

"Sure, I know where I was. I was over at the hospital talking to Phil Wittke. I can't have been gone from him more than five minutes or so when they started paging him over the intercom. I found out the next day they were calling him to tell him about the murder."

"That isn't the way Dr. Wittke tells it. In fact, he didn't

mention you at all in accounting for his evening. How do you explain that?"

Segal closed his eyes briefly, in acknowledgment of the world's stupidity.

"Oh, I can explain it all right," he said wearily. "And if you've met Phil Wittke, you'll understand. What we were doing is having a nice, long talk about how something had to be done to shut Martin up before he got the rest of us thrown in jail!"

Expressionlessly, Perenna took notes.

"That's very interesting. And whose idea was it that Martin had to be shut up?"

"Oh, I admit it, I was the one doing the pushing." Segal lifted his shoulders. "Wittke agreed it would be nice if Martin shut up. But he was willing to wait; he said there was nothing for us to do. I wanted to get rough with Martin—explain exactly what dangers he was running."

"You mean you just wanted him to talk to Martin? That doesn't seem very rough."

Segal looked at him from the end of a great weariness.

"You ever had anything to do with doctors, Lieutenant?"

Perenna admitted that this was his first experience.

"Well, you don't say to Wittke that Martin is so stupid you have to explain to him as if he were five years old. Wittke had been passing Martin off as some kind of genius for so long that he believed it himself. And Wittke had kidded himself this drug business wasn't really illegal. Irregular was his favorite word. He likes to wrap things up. I don't mind it myself, but I like to remember what's under the wrapping. The result of all this was that Martin was being allowed to barrel down the roller coaster without anybody telling him the tracks ended at the bottom. Neverson had already had a go at Martin. I was trying to spike Wittke into the same thing."

"But why should Wittke object? His interests were the same as yours, weren't they?"

"Sure they were. I knew it, Roy Neverson knew it, Ron Lawson knew it. But Wittke . . . well, according to him, he didn't see we were all sitting on a barrel of TNT."

Perenna leaped on the reservation.

"What do you mean—'according to him?'" he demanded.

"Wittke's not as simple as he looks. He's no five-year-old. Not by a long shot!" Segal said with calm certainty.

"And sometimes Dr. Wittke doesn't publicly admit what Phil Wittke knows damned well. But, take it from me, precious little gets by him."

"None of this explains why Wittke doesn't admit to being with you on the evening of the murder."

"Wittke is still fighting the drug charge. The less he admits to being with me, the better he likes it. I don't know why I knocked myself out trying to make him see sense. I've got a lot less to lose than the rest of them. I'm not a doctor, my boys are clean, and I'm a rich man."

Well-regulated disbelief appeared on Perenna's face.

"So you're not trying to fight the drug charge?"

"Not enough to take the rap for someone else's murder." Sid Segal spoke with complete finality.

Lieutenant Perenna's instructions had been all-embracing, and he was a conscientious officer. His earlier interviews had been a necessary part of police routine. But fundamental to the life of Dr. Wendell Martin—and probably to his death as well—had been Southport Memorial Hospital. It was here that Martin had exercised dominion; here that the major suspects spent the better part of their time, practicing their professions, waging political war, advancing or retreating in the hierarchy; and it was here that the Hyland Drug Company had its spiritual home, regardless of the fact that its legal domicile was on the seventeenth floor of an office building in Wilmington, Delaware.

Therefore, the lieutenant spent the next day at Southport Memorial, wandering its corridors, asking questions and watching . . . watching . . . watching. By evening he had learned a surprising amount. He knew how the doctors checked in and out, when the shifts changed down in the service and administration blocks, where the orderlies retreated for a quiet, illicit smoke, when the cafeteria was bursting with people grabbing a quick snack and when it was virtually deserted, what arrangements the nurses had made for their creature comforts, when the tide of visitors swelled and ebbed.

Nevertheless, his mission was a failure. Because he knew something else as well. In spite of the fact that people were being born and people were dying all over the hospital, in spite of the ceaseless clacking of the paging system and the deliveries of food, linen and medical supplies, still Southport Memorial—as it had existed last week—was dead.

He was reminded of one of his police courses taken several years ago. The subject had been how to determine death. The lecturer had moved from the absence of cardiac pulsation through a whole series of corroborative methods, ending with the final, daunting statement. *Corruption is an absolute sign of death.*

And corruption was the prevailing smell of Southport Memorial right now. No doubt a new Southport would rise from the ashes, but it would be unrelated to the old. It was only a final galvanic spasm which moved everyone to consult Dr. Wittke and refer to Dr. Neverson. The courtesies were as meaningless as those surrounding a dowager queen immediately after the death of the monarch. The title might remain, the reality was over. The old political structure had been annihilated. A new king would soon be reigning, new courtiers would appear, new loyalties and enmities would be formed.

And everyone knew this. However reticent the medical community may be in its dealings with the outside world, under the best of circumstances it is not above a cozy intramural gossip with familiars. Under the worst—and few doctors reading the headlines occasioned by the death of Pemberton Freebody and the existence of the Hyland Drug Company could conceive of anything more appalling—the tribal grapevine can operate with an efficiency that might be envied by the larger communication utilities. Anybody at Southport Memorial trying to delude himself that he was surrounded by Casabiancas, stoically embracing the burning deck, had only to listen to the hourly bulletins emanating from the administrative suite.

Mrs. Stosser had crowned a lifetime's success in bending to the wind by getting her resignation in first. She had been scheduled to retire in six months. Now, Southport would be without a director of nursing within a matter of days.

Dr. Kroner's colleagues, when they thought about him at all, were wont to pity him his lack of connection with that rich network of professional contacts which is the heritage of the lowliest graduate of an American medical school. Accordingly they were surprised to find the little German second in line. He was relocating, he explained with unnecessary courtesy, because of a sudden desire to specialize in dermatology. Happily, there was an opening in Poughkeepsie.

Scarcely had Karl Kroner cleared the office before the morning mail brought letters from two new residents, expected to arrive shortly for the forthcoming year. They deeply regretted that it would be impossible for them to take up their appointments, but due to personal commitments, unexpected changes, et cetera. An obstetrician, second only to Edith Bullivant in the number of deliveries for which he accounted, found it expedient to book his patients into another hospital for the time being. Not so polite as Dr. Kroner, he explained bluntly that he was getting out fast before any of the mud stuck to him.

Southport Memorial had never figured largely in the hopes of young interns planning the next step in their careers. Now it ceased to figure in anything but their nightmares.

Marooned on its island, the remaining staff was necessarily prey to a sense of abandonment. Lieutenant Joseph Perenna's presence had the effect of joining to that unwelcome emotion a sense of bewilderment amidst shifting standards.

"But, Alice," protested Marie Gentilhomme, "I don't see what you're so worried about."

"Look, kid," Mrs. Doyle replied, "I've just seen fifteen years' work washed away. And there's no time to gripe about it. I'm too busy wondering whether there's anything that can be done about the next fifteen."

"Well, how can all this affect you? You've just been doing your job."

Alice Doyle produced a travesty of a smile.

"Yeah," she said bitterly. "I've done a good job, too. And do you think I'm going to get anything for it—anything but a boot in the rear? Hell, no! Like everyone else around here, my name's going to be dirt. I'm beginning to think we'd be better off opening up to the police."

"Why, of course," Marie's color rose at her temerity in giving the older woman advice. "If you can tell them anything, you ought to."

There was a pause.

"Well, you know I'm right, don't you?" she insisted.

"Actually, kid," Alice Doyle said at last, "it's you that's got something to tell them."

Nor was Lieutenant Perenna's visit to the Sloan Guaranty Trust the next morning any more helpful. He ended by imparting more information than he received. But at least this interview left its participants in a cheerful frame of mind.

"Now that the police are finally digging, they're bringing up mud by the bucketful, aren't they?" announced Charlie Trinkam. He slung a leg over the arm of his chair as an indication that he was not following the policeman from the room.

The other men in the room had also settled down. The state police had wanted to know about the insurance claim, and they had received the united cooperation of Trinkam, Nicolls, Thatcher and Dr. Edmund Knox. Paul Jackson's professional scruples had debarred him from attending the conference, but he had been on the phone to Thatcher as frequently as Benjamin Edes, both men gathering information in the wake of the police investigation almost as quickly as it developed.

Absently, Thatcher pushed the cigarette box toward Dr. Knox.

"The implications were certainly very nasty," he agreed.

"I'm not sure that I understood all the involvements."

"Well, the main thing seems to be the drug conspiracy," Kenneth Nicolls ventured. "That's what would have come to light if Wendell Martin had kept on grabbing the headlines."

"And they were all in it, up to their necks," said Trinkam, who had been following the newspaper coverage avidly. "The whole Wittke Clinic, for instance."

Thatcher shook his head.

"That's not what I mean. That, if I may say so, is the business end of it. I was referring to the medical end—Martin's disagreements with Dr. Bauer and Dr. Bullivant. I find it difficult to estimate how important they were."

Everybody looked at Dr. Knox. The specialist shook his head angrily.

"Medical end!" he growled. "There wouldn't have been any disagreements if these people had been practicing medicine! Every single time, the trouble started because someone was trying to make more money out of something."

This conclusion came as no surprise to three bankers. But they all recognized that Edmund Knox was overcome by chagrin at the activities of his co-professionals. Secrecy was no longer possible. All the activities of Southport Memorial were now doomed to exposure under the pitiless glare of a murder investigation. But the doctor from Hanover had to find his own way to make palatable a discussion of the foibles of the Southport clique.

Trinkam eased into the subject.

"The fight with Bauer is easy enough to understand. The boy was producing evidence that Wendell Martin was operating in a number of cases where no surgery was necessary. I suppose if he'd been allowed to go on producing that evidence, sooner or later the rest of the staff would have found out."

"It's more complicated than that," Edmund Knox glared at Charlie Trinkam as if he were the embodiment of the collective delinquencies of the AMA. "There can never have been any question of 'finding out.' Some of the staff knew all along. You've forgotten they established a Tissue Review Committee."

"I'm afraid I don't see how that comes into it," Thatcher said patiently.

"Bauer's findings didn't go directly to Martin. They went to the committee. Of course, any surgeon is going to be wrong in his diagnosis every now and then. That's why you have standards. And it's only when a surgeon transgresses those standards that the committee reports him to the chief of surgery."

Kenneth Nicolls unwisely belabored the obvious.

"But that means the entire committee at Southport knew about Dr. Martin."

Dr. Knox was now glaring at all of them.

"Yes," he admitted. "That is why Martin was so furious. If the reports had gone straight to him, it wouldn't have involved his reputation with anyone except Bauer. This way, every man on the inside surgical staff would know about it. If they hadn't had the facts, Martin could have explained away rumors of a disagreement with Bauer. He could always say he was having a run of bad luck."

"But with the facts, the hospital would have to do something about it, sooner or later?" Ken persisted.

"They should have done something about it right at the start. How they could hope to have any kind of Tissue Review Committee that would tolerate that sort of thing, I fail to understand!" Knox's heavy eyebrows drew together in massive censure.

"They do seem to have achieved some sort of toleration as soon as they got rid of Bauer," Thatcher pointed out.

A groan was his only answer. Dr. Edmund Knox's life had been spent in the great research hospitals of the big city. His first intimate view of a small suburban hospital was proving a real eye-opener.

"I suppose I shouldn't be so surprised," he confessed. "The last study on the subject revealed an astonishing number of simple operations that were being performed although totally unnecessary."

"What operations are they?" asked Trinkam.

"Appendix, gall bladder and hysterectomy are the common ones."

"I'll remember that," said Trinkam darkly. "Anybody who wants to take a knife to my appendix or gall bladder is going to have a fight on his hands."

"I had my appendix out three years ago," Nicolls contributed gloomily. "I hate to think it was just to satisfy the surgeon."

Knox came to the defense of his profession.

"Quite a few of these operations are necessary," He searched for something else to say but apparently was unsuccessful.

"Well, then, the Bauer-Martin tangle is at least comprehensible. But what about Dr. Bullivant? Jackson was almost chortling with glee when he told me about it." Thatcher wondered if he should admit that he didn't have the faintest idea what a D&C was. He decided to offer bait. "Something about her D&C's. No tissue for the pathologist, or something."

"Ah!" Dr. Knox expelled his breath softly. "That could be grave, very grave."

Trinkam had no inhibitions about launching into a full-scale gynecological discussion. "What's so grave about it? I thought it was the same racket. Just make-work."

"By no means," said Dr. Knox sternly. "It sounds very much as if you're talking about D&C's after alleged miscarriages."

"So?"

"Criminal abortions," said the specialist shortly.

Charlie Trinkam whistled.

"They don't miss a trick out in Southport, do they?" he inquired genially.

"Obviously not." Thatcher sought to depress Trinkam's exuberance, which was having an unfortunate effect on Dr. Knox. "But the important thing is that it could mean a speedy end to Dr. Bullivant's practice."

"Not quite that. It's a long way from a fuss in the hospital to a question of criminal prosecution."

"In Southport," said Trinkam irrepressibly, "the distance seems endless."

Dr. Knox threw up his hands. He had abandoned his halfhearted attempts to find excuses for Southport.

Thatcher groped for a conclusion. "It really depends on the kind of man Martin was, doesn't it? I gather it would be extremely unethical for a doctor at Southport to report Dr. Bullivant to the authorities. But what about ending her privileges at the hospital? Would that be a blow?"

"A devastating blow. An obstetrician, after all, needs a hospital more than most. But I scarcely see how Martin was in a position to exercise any influence in the matter, considering his own history with the pathologist's reports."

"He seems to have had enough influence to fire the pathologist. I wonder just how safe Dr. Bullivant felt, with Martin on the warpath."

They all considered that. Then Kenneth Nicolls raised another point.

"If Dr. Martin was really interested in the pathologist's reports, he might have been threatening other doctors as well. I think the only reason we know about Dr. Bullivant is because she and Martin went in for a big public fight. You can't tell how many of these scenes were taking place on the quiet."

"Bauer would know," Thatcher pointed out.

"But, Mr. Thatcher, Bauer isn't doing much talking."

"The time has come," said Edmund Knox decisively, "for someone to explain to Dr. Bauer that the interests of the medical profession require a thorough investigation of the situation at Southport. The young man seems to have behaved very properly until now—and under singular provocation. I have every sympathy with the principle of professional discretion. Where irregularities can be rectified without recourse to publicity, it is much more satisfactory to avoid washing dirty linen in public. But the main thing is that they be rectified. And when a hospital has already bemired itself in so much notoriety, no responsible objections can be raised to stringent inquiries and complete disclosure. Dr. Bauer will understand this when I explain it to him—particularly now that he is assured of professional support."

Dr. Knox spoke quietly, without any of the belligerence of restiveness that had accompanied his earlier explanations. For all that, it was as if trumpets had sounded the call to charge.

Dr. Knox's blood was up. He had coolly resolved to declare war on Southport Memorial, and he had an imposing array of forces to throw into battle. The light of the crusader was beaming from his eye as he left them on this martial note. His destination, he said, was the American College of Surgeons. Both Thatcher and Trinkam were reasonably confident that mighty winds were going to whirl through various medical societies, that veterans would be summoned to the theater of conflict, that the New Guard of Southport was going to be charged with an awesome cleansing assignment.

"And has it occurred to you," Thatcher mused as he tilted his chair back contemplatively and studied the ceiling, "that may be just what Wendell Martin's murder was designed to prevent?"

Charlie lit a cigarette and prepared to cast off the conversational restraints which he had inflicted on himself (although Edmund Knox would have found it hard to believe) during the good doctor's presence.

"If that was the reason," he offered, "it wasn't a howling success!"

Ken Nicolls's serious-mindedness was too inherent to be influenced by the mere comings and goings of medical luminaries.

"I don't see how you can tell what the motive was," he objected. "There seem to be so many swindles going on at that hospital—dummy operations, abortions, money floating around, an illegal drug company. Once you know what these people are capable of, you can imagine almost anything going on out there. They might even be running an adoption racket!"

This new game appealed to Trinkam.

"Think of the opportunities in the drug company alone! They were letting Martin's brother handle the financial end by himself. He could easily have been taking a cut off the top of the pile that nobody knew about. Then, suppose brother Wendell catches him with his hand in the till?"

"And remember all the cash transactions that have been going on? There could easily be a blackmailer at work in the middle of them."

The more serious Ken became, the more playful was Charlie Trinkam.

"Now that I don't know about," he said easily. "In Southport, if you step out of line, they seem to crack your skull in. That's not the kind of atmosphere in which blackmailers flourish."

Thatcher thought it time to end his subordinates' flights of fancy.

"I think we can take it for granted that Southport could be the home of almost any malfeasance. On the other hand, we have to ignore the ones we don't know about, as a matter of expediency. I don't think that's a serious oversight, because anything that hasn't been dredged to the surface by the publicity of the last week was buried deep enough to be safe from exposure, regardless of Wendell Martin's antics."

"It's not as if that leaves us with any shortage," Charlie encouraged Ken. "We've got the drug business, first of all. Now that was really endangered. Paul Jackson says the tax people were readying an attack on Martin. Once they started to dig into his income, they would have gotten to Hyland Drug in about three days."

Thatcher brought his gaze down from the ceiling.

"And what would that have meant?"

"Plenty! This Martin was a real fruitcake. The others have been declaring their income from the drug company. But not Martin! He was never satisfied. And the tax boys wouldn't have gone easy on him. It wouldn't have been a simple case of paying up what was owing."

"But the Internal Revenue makes compromises like that all the time," said Ken, mindful of several clients of the Sloan Trust Department.

"Sure they do. But not when it's somebody like Martin. After the Pemberton Freebody business, he would have been in about the same position as Al Capone on a tax rap. The tabloids would have been howling for his blood. The medical societies wouldn't have gone to bat for him. For once, public feeling would have been on the side of the Internal Revenue."

Thoughtfully, Thatcher nodded.

"They didn't expect you to come along, John," Trinkam grinned. "They could figure the drug company was safe, once Martin was dead. In any event, he doesn't sound like the kind who'd cooperate about being a scapegoat. He probably would have done his damndest to paint the others as black as possible. He'd have claimed he was an innocent victim who was tempted by the rest. It's a cinch he didn't have the brains to think up that racket himself."

"I'm sure that's correct as far as it goes. But in one sense, the conspirators would have been better off if exposure had occurred that way. They would have been able to use Wendell Martin as a scapegoat. The others might have gotten off with a suspended sentence."

Thatcher's agreement was now more wholehearted. "That's true. And jail or not, they would have lost their investment. Quite a remarkable number of people will commit murder for a quarter of a million dollars."

Kenneth Nicolls emerged from some private world of his own and shook his head in dissatisfaction. But on such delicate ground, he chose his words with care.

"Even so, we know that there's one woman at that

hospital who wouldn't stop at anything. And there is no doubt that Dr. Bullivant would have gone to jail if Dr. Martin had pressed charges against her. I'm surprised the police bother to look any further."

"I don't see what evidence you have that the others have an earlier sticking point," Thatcher observed. "They were running a criminal system to extort money from the sick. At least Dr. Bullivant delivered at a price that her patients understood. And delivered a service they presumably wanted."

Not for one moment was Kenneth going to admit that, because Edith Bullivant was a motherly looking woman, he was even more revolted to learn that she was coldhearted and venal.

"It is a matter of denying life," he temporized.

John Thatcher had a very fair notion of what was troubling his subordinate and, out of kindness, did not ask him to define an unnecessary hysterectomy. Instead he said:

"Dr. Bullivant's real protection would seem to be in that final phrase of yours—*'if Dr. Martin pressed charges.'* Ed Knox was sure that most doctors wouldn't. As a matter of professional ethics."

Charlie pounced.

"If anything is clear in this whole mess, it's that Wendell Martin wasn't 'most doctors.' As for medical ethics, look at the way he treated this Dr. Bauer. If Bauer's story is true."

"You doubt it?" Thatcher raised his eyebrows. "They can check with the entire Tissue Review Committee, you know."

"Oh, I'm sure the facts about the pathology reports are true. But the way he tells it, he should have been breathing fire and revenge, and Martin should have forgotten the whole thing. After all, it was a victory for Martin and an infuriating injustice for Bauer—as well as a damned good motive for murder, incidentally. But what actually happened? Martin was the one left breathing fire—he must have been, the way that wife of his is carrying on. She seems to have gotten the impression that Bauer was persecuting her husband!"

"You've already given one answer to that, Charlie," said Ken, abandoning his broodings on Dr. Bullivant's iniquities. "Wendell Martin wasn't normal. Any blow to his esteem and he went berserk. Remember what he was like on the witness stand?"

Thatcher intervened smoothly. "There is another answer. That the widow concocted the accusation out of whole cloth—in order to distract attention from herself. In a way, everyone else's motive was negative—to prevent a possible threat. But after all, she alone had a positive motive and a very substantial one at that—over a quarter of a million dollars. Or the police really wouldn't be looking any further."

"You hit it right on the nail!" Charlie Trinkam laughed outright. "That's the first thing the police thought of. Paul says they were almost disappointed when they found out she was playing in a duplicate bridge tournament at the exact moment her husband was killed."

"Do they have the time down that closely?"

"Oh, yes. Not that they need it in the case of the widow. She was still at the tournament when they went to tell her about the murder. They checked back later to make sure she hadn't slipped out during the evening, but she faded as a suspect right from the start. It would have taken her almost an hour to make the round trip."

Thatcher was almost disappointed himself. It would have been a tidy, straightforward solution. And Lucille Martin had not struck him as an adoring wife, although he was the first to admit he had seen her under trying circumstances.

"It's a different kettle of fish for the people at the hospital," Charlie was continuing. "They just needed five minutes to slip out to the parking lot. And none of their stories are really supported. The ones who say they'd already left may not have left; the ones who really did leave may have come back; and the ones seen on the fourth floor at ten o'clock could always have ducked downstairs."

"The murder was at ten then?"

"They place it at ten-fifteen, give or take ten minutes. The reason they can be so precise is that they got there so soon after the killing. The call came through at ten thirty-four, and the police doctor was there by ten forty-five. On that basis, the Gentilhomme girl found the body at about ten-thirty. She must have practically tripped over the murderer."

"The Gentilhomme girl?" Thatcher sat up in sudden interest.

"Sure. The one that Paul Jackson turned inside out. You remember."

"Yes, but I had forgotten she was the one who discovered the body." Thatcher drummed his fingers idly for a moment. "When you pause to think, she has always been a central figure, hasn't she? She was the one who exposed Martin on the stand. And she was on the scene of the crime within minutes of its commission."

"And," Charlie picked up the tale neatly, "she had a fight with Martin that same day. He was threatening to have her blacklisted. The director of nursing out there is finally coming through with a lot of scuttlebutt, now that she's got nothing to lose."

Thatcher was not concerned with the director of nursing's instinct for self-preservation.

"You know," he reflected, "I feel we have neglected Marie Gentilhomme."

The measured silence was broken from an unexpected quarter.

"That's what I thought," said Kenneth Nicolls, "when I met her in Southport."

The two men stared at him. "You do manage to get around, Ken," said Trinkam in congratulation.

Kenneth, on the brink of a hot denial, suddenly remembered Mrs. Furness and desisted.

Thatcher fanned the air with an irritated hand. "Never mind that. Where did you meet her, and did you try questioning her at all?"

"I met her at the Perkins house. No, I didn't question her. I don't think I spoke to her at all. She's a very shy girl. I'd have to get to know her first."

For Thatcher, whose expeditions to Southport had been restricted to the Olympian locales of the Forest Glen Cemetery and the Southport Yacht Club, it was a question of Nurse Gentilhomme, a hospital employee who had tried, albeit unsuccessfully, to parry Paul Jackson's questions. To Ken, who had been among the proletariat, she was Marie, a girl refusing a beer in Nancy Perkins's kitchen.

"What I cannot understand," said Thatcher exasperatedly, "is why you didn't tell me about this when you got back."

Kenneth went onto his dignity. "I don't believe that I ever got beyond the prescription counter at Segal's Drugstore," he said, recalling full well how Thatcher had stiffened like a well-trained hunting dog at that stage of his narrative and then begun telephoning Benjamin Edes.

The beginnings of a reluctant smile dawned on Thatcher's face. He was remembering the same thing. Diplomacy was called for.

"Ah, yes. I believe I may have cut you off due to the importance of your earlier activities that evening. Let's hear what else happened."

Ken recognized the olive branch. He was only sorry that he had nothing to offer in exchange.

"I'm afraid that nothing else happened."

"Tell us anyway." Thatcher had no intention of carrying diplomacy too far. These were no doubt the exact terms in which the boy would have assessed his momentous attempt to fill a prescription with Sid Segal.

But at the end of the recital he was forced to agreement. Nothing had happened, nothing except two men drinking beer in a kitchen while a wife took an occasional companionable sip.

"I could probably arrange it so that she'll be there the next time I go out to the Perkins's," Ken offered as solace. "She might be willing to talk to me on this round."

"Are you going out to the Perkins's again?"

"Yes, Jane arranged everything with Nancy."

"Jane?" Thatcher was bewildered. "Your wife?"

If Thatcher was bewildered, Kenneth was guilty. If he had taken that face into the dock, a jury would have been ready to convict him of almost any crime in the book. Shamefaced, he shuffled his feet.

"Oh, well, when I told Jane about the Perkinses, she started to call people in Brooklyn Heights. She ended up with a station wagon load of children's clothes and toys and things like electric mixers. I'll be taking them out some time this week."

Across the room Charlie Trinkam was showing signs of undesirable jocularity.

"Admirable!" said Thatcher bracingly, determined to avoid emotional quagmires. "If the Perkinses have been put through the wringer by Southport Memorial, I can well understand how they would be hard up."

"They have bills up to the ears. On top of the original operation, they have continuing visits to the doctor, and the weekly checkup at the hospital and druggist's bills. You just wouldn't believe it!"

"I can now. Did you say something about weekly checkups at the hospital?"

Ken nodded, happy to display his expertise on the subject of the Perkins family. "Yes, she goes in one evening every week and stays overnight. They do some kind of tests on her first thing in the morning, when she's barely awake."

Thatcher dismissed the medical details. "But what night? Good heavens, she may have been there the evening of Wendell Martin's murder. Didn't you even ask her?"

"At that time," said Ken stiffly, "we were interested in Pemberton Freebody's death. That's what I asked her about."

"More fool you!" Charlie interrupted cheerfully. "Here

you've got a nice, juicy murder and maybe a red-hot witness, and you let yourself be distracted by an insurance claim. What say, John? Shall we shoot him out to Southport again?"

John Thatcher knew what too many newsmagazines, public relations firms and politicians do not: the snowballing of meaningless detail does not, unfortunately, guarantee the production of truth. Nonetheless, he nodded.

Nancy Perkins had moved the ironing board to the kitchen window in order to be able to watch the play yard as she finished up the laundry. She was so accustomed to policing juvenile disorder and so intent on spray-starching the collar of Gene's shirt that it was several moments before she identified the approaching clamor as adult in origin. That was not the lusty, uninhibited howling of a balked four-year-old; that was the convulsive sobbing of a woman.

Then the door flew open, propelled by a hearty shove from Gene Perkins's right arm. His left arm was wrapped protectively around Marie Gentilhomme; she was red-eyed and hunched over, clutching herself desperately.

Nancy stepped forward in alarm.

"What in the world . . . ?"

"Now, Nancy, nothing to worry about," said Gene. "Marie, here, is a little upset."

Nancy, very properly, ignored this fatuous statement. Instead she pulled out a chair and thrust her guest into it.

"Oh, Nancy, I'm so sorry . . . just silliness . . . thank God Gene was there . . . be all right in a minute . . . ,"

Marie hunted wildly for a handkerchief, looked up at the concerned face hovering over her and abandoned efforts at self-control.

"Oh-h-h-h!" she wailed, the four-year-old triumphing over the woman. Then she flung both arms on the table, laid her head on top of them and surrendered herself to an orgy of weeping.

Gene Perkins looked alarmed and tentatively patted a heaving shoulder.

"Just leave her alone, Gene, and let her have a good cry. She'll feel much better when it's all over. I'll put the kettle on so that there'll be tea when she's ready for it." Nancy Perkins suited action to word, then took her place at the

able. "And, now, suppose you tell me what this is all
bout."

"I don't know exactly where to begin." In perplexity
Gene rubbed the heel of his palm over his crew cut hard
nough to raise sparks. "I was at the garage when Dr.
Neverson pulled up——"

"The garage? Today isn't Sunday."

"Oh, didn't I tell you? We've got the car back! Joe
ound a fuel pump for us in a Chevy they were can-
ibalizing."

"Wonderful!"

For a moment the triumph threatened to distract them
oth. Nancy was already planning a massive raid on the
upermarket to bring back gallons and gallons of the milk
he had been hand-carrying. Gene would at last be able to
et to the dump with the pile of trash gradually engulfing
he entire yard. Marie sobbed in unabated rhythm.

"Anyway, Joe was putting it in for me," Gene sternly
eturned to the subject. "And Dr. Neverson drove up to
rop off a flat he had in the trunk. I asked him how the
ag was running since I tuned it up for him. And we were
idding around with each other. You know, he asked me
ow come I had to have a mechanic work on my car, and I
aid this must be the first time he ever changed a flat him-
elf instead of hollering for the boys at the garage and,
onest, Nancy, he seemed perfectly normal to me! I didn't
otice anything wrong with him!"

He raised puzzled eyes to look at his wife.

Nancy nodded soberly. She knew, as Gene did not, that
hey were neither of them very good right now at noticing
nything wrong with people. Since Dr. Wendell Martin's
uccessful surgery, they had both moved in a cloud of
uphoria that they were inclined to extend, without any
asis in fact, to every friend and chance-met acquaintance.
Dr. Roy Neverson could have assumed a ceremonial squat,
randished a large Japanese sword and proceeded through
he preliminary ritual of hari-kari without Gene Perkins
oticing a thing.

Unless, of course, Dr. Neverson had carefully explained
hat he was feeling suicidal. For the first time, it occurred
o Nancy that this might well be the case. The joys of sports
ars and boats must fade pretty rapidly in the shadow of an
pproaching jail sentence.

"What happened?" she asked nervously.

"Well, nothing happened as long as we were alone. Like I said, we were just kidding each other. Then a car pulled in for gas. It was Alice Doyle, and she was giving Marie a lift."

"Yes?"

"Alice says hello and we say hello, and then Dr. Neverson notices Marie. So instead of saying hello, he makes some kind of crack to me about this being the little woman who started the great big war. He doesn't realize I know Marie. And you know—"

Here Gene broke off to look uneasily across the table. Marie was still weeping, though with less violence. Nevertheless he lowered his voice as if ashamed at some suggestion of disloyalty in his words.

"You know, I think everything would have been okay if Marie had kind of sassed him back. But she doesn't say anything. None of us do, and Dr. Neverson opens up again—but he doesn't sound the same at all—and he says, kind of driving her to the wall, is she satisfied with what she's done, running everybody at the hospital, and it's a pretty good act she's got going, pretending to be stupid when really she's spiteful, and he wouldn't be surprised if she wasn't acting for someone."

"Oh, poor Marie! How awful for her!" Nancy said with ready sympathy.

"Wait! That isn't all, not by a long shot! Before I can even budge, Alice Doyle lets loose. I tell you, you never heard anything like that woman. More like a wild animal!"

Nancy sniffed eloquently.

"Now, I know you don't like her, Nancy," Gene began. "I never said that. I don't really know her. What I said was that she's a cheap tramp. But Marie has always said that she's a hard worker and a good nurse."

"This wasn't just being cheap. I never thought I'd hear a doctor talked to that way. Or hear a doctor talk that way. Gene had been genuinely shocked. "Because Dr. Neverson came right back at her. They're neither of them really nice, you know."

Nancy tried to understand him. She looked at Marie's bent head for inspiration.

"Bad language?" she suggested dubiously.

"That isn't what upset Marie. Although there was plenty of gutter talk." Gene shook his head.

He knew that frank speech is not unheard of in Antigonish, Nova Scotia, where Marie Gentilhomme ha passed her formative years. And even though rural collo-quialisms never sound as nasty as the epithets spawned by city streets, that was not what had upset him, as well as Marie. "It was as if they hated each other, it was pure poison. I've never heard a woman sound so venomous. She said what did the mean, was Marie satisfied? Was he satis-fied? Said he'd ruined the careers of people who had to sweat for a small salary. Then she called him a cheap bum who couldn't keep his greedy paws to himself even though he was making a fortune just to loaf around, him and that SOB Wittke."

"Oh, no!" breathed Nancy in horrified fascination.

"I tell you it was a real set-to. He got started on how she'd two-timed her husband so bad she couldn't even get custody of her kids, and then she called his wife a stupid bitch who'd milked him dry and then walked out and——"

"And it was simply awful, Nancy!" Marie Gentilhomme was now upright. With a last watery sniff, she apologized. "I'm sorry for crumpling all over you this way but this, on top of everything else! I don't understand what's happened to people. Nobody used to act this way!"

Nancy immediately embraced her warmly, then rushed to the teakettle. "Don't be embarrassed, Marie. These things happen. Now you tidy up and we'll all have tea."

A household which includes three small children, a host of transient children, a young woman who has passed through a serious illness and a young man rushing back and forth among countless jobs while economizing on shirts is used to the spectacle of people far removed from bandbox perfection—people in undress, as it were. Marie's disheveled hair, tear-streaked face and crumpled dress did her no disservice in the eyes of the Perkinses. And paradoxically, the woebegone smile she gave them as she rose lent her attractiveness she never achieved in the starched order of hospital uniform.

"What did you mean by 'on top of everything else'?" asked Nancy as she distributed cups five minutes later. "You mean that everybody's acting oddly?"

"No. There's that, too. But everbody is acting as if there were something odd about me."

Clearly she craved contradiction. But Nancy could only ask:

"What on earth do you mean?"

"I suppose it's Alice Doyle, mostly. She seems to be hinting all the time that there's something I haven't told the police." She searched for further illustrations. "And Gene heard Dr. Neverson hinting about the trial and saying I was spiteful. Why should I be spiteful? I was happy before the trial! Of course, I was new at the hospital and I hadn't been a nurse very long, so I was nervous a lot. But there was nothing for me to be spiteful about. Now even Mrs. Stosser and the patients don't seem to behave normally to me."

"Part of that's imagination," Nancy said with assurance.

"No, let me finish. What I mean is that when one or two people are acting oddly to you, it's only natural to think other people are too, to see things that aren't there."

"Well, take it from me, one person who's really being strange is Alice Doyle." Gene Perkins's shoulders shuddered in recollection. "Whew! What a woman!"

"I've never seen her the way she was today," Marie confessed. "But that isn't what I meant. After all, she was sticking up for me. It's that terrible hinting I can't stand."

Nancy studied the salt and pepper shakers with great interest. Her eyes did not shift away from them when she spoke.

"I suppose," she said hesitantly, "I suppose you have told the police everything you know about Wendell Martin's murder."

"Nancy!" Marie lowered her cup indignantly. "You were there! What was there to know?"

Both Gene and Nancy were startled by the counterattack.

"Gee, honey, I'd forgotten that. You were there."

"You both were," Marie pressed home her point. "Don't you remember, Gene? You didn't leave until after I'd given Nancy her ten o'clock medication. That was the first time I was on ward duty."

Gene frowned into the past.

"I remember. You'd had some sort of fuss with Martin earlier. You were crying."

"And Nancy cheered me up." Marie smiled tremulously. "Just like today."

"It's all coming back," Gene continued. "You told me you were going to have to wait for your uncle Dominic."

Nancy suddenly moved to a cabinet drawer, from which she drew a pencil and a pad of paper. She tore off the top sheet, which said *two gallons of milk and peanut butter,* and announced:

"It's coming back to me, too. Let's write down every

single thing that we remember. We can help each other. That way we can settle once and for all whether Marie knows anything."

Half an hour later, Nancy Perkins grounded her pencil. She had been writing steadily except for one dash to the back yard and one dash to the teakettle. She had pages of notes, for the most part representing a minute-by-minute account of the activities of a Mrs. Margolis, who had occupied the bed next to hers. But she had something else as well.

It was that which caused her husband to look accusingly across the table. "You know, Marie, you're just not curious enough, that's your trouble."

"But how could I know? And what should I do? I can't go to the police with a little thing like that."

"I don't know, Marie," Gene said doubtfully. "I think maybe you ought to."

"Well, Marie doesn't have to go to the police alone. We can go with—or, wait, I know. We can call Ken Nicolls. He'll know what to do. Maybe he can go instead."

Everyone was only too eager to lay his problem at other feet. They all had a touching confidence that a banker like Ken Nicolls would carry more weight with the police than they. Cutting off further discussion, Nancy moved to the telephone.

A young woman who is raising three children on no money, however nice at heart, must learn to develop determination in asserting her rights. It was as well that Nancy Perkins had been through her basic training. Because institutions like the Sloan Guaranty Trust employ large numbers of people for no other purpose than to suppress such phone calls.

Marie and Gene watched the back yard from the kitchen while Nancy wrestled with the phone in the hall. Every now and then a bulletin for them wafted across the small living room.

"I've got the switchboard. They want to know who I'm calling for."

Sounds of argument.

"I've got a Miss Todd. She wants me to call back later. Ken is in conference."

Sounds of argument.

"I've gotten a Miss Corsa. She's the only sensible one in the lot. She's getting him."

Sounds of conversation.

"I don't understand. Now he's having a conference about *this*."

And finally, loud and clear:

"Oh, Ken, I'm so relieved you're coming. . . . Yes, of course you can bring Mr. Thatcher with you."

At the Sloan they were just as enthusiastic.

"Well, speak of the devil!" said Charlie Trinkam in the tones of simple pleasure with which he was accustomed to receive any goodies life cared to hand him—whether beautiful women, ridiculous prospectuses, outré social events, outlandish lawsuits or simple opportunities to bait Everett Gabler. "What do you think they've got hold of?"

Ken shook his head. "I have no idea. Nancy sounded awfully solemn. But Marie Gentilhomme is with them now. We'd better go out there, right away."

"Take my car," Charlie offered. "It's at the garage."

But Thatcher shook his head. "No. We're going to Brooklyn Heights first."

"Brooklyn Heights?" Was Thatcher inviting himself to dinner, Kenneth wondered. And if so, was it meat loaf night?

Thatcher looked at him reproachfully. "Naturally we are taking that station wagon load with us." His voice became brisker. "I do not know what the Perkinses have for us, but I will offer odds on one thing."

"What's that?" Charlie was always interested when odds were being offered.

"Three to one Nancy Perkins was in the hospital the night that Martin was murdered!"

18 Quarantine

For Dr. Edmund Knox, busy calling Southport to judgment, the exact day on which Nancy Perkins was accustomed to have her weekly checkup was not important. For that matter, neither was the murder of Wendell Martin. Gripped by an almost biblical fervor, Knox could have watched the annihilation of Southport Memorial's entire staff with no reaction other than a few appropriate references to Sodom and Gomorrah. He was not, however, averse to using that murder to further his own ends.

Dr. Knox had reached a decision in Thatcher's office that he was determined to implement with all the vigor of outraged morality. His methods might lack orthodoxy, but they were grounded in hardheaded realism and unyielding tenacity. Accordingly, as soon as he realized—or was brought to realize—that the success of his campaign could serve other interests and hence command other support, he became an enthusiastic adherent of certain plans advanced by John Putnam Thatcher and Lieutenant Joseph Perenna.

They could not have chosen a better ally. Edmund Knox was a man whose life had brought him into contact with large institutions. He knew all about universities, insurance companies, foundations, banks and medical associations—their power, their inertia, their dislike of trouble, their vulnerability to public outcry. He knew it was hard to make them move and, once they were moving, hard to make them stop. Long ago, he had learned to do both. Within a surprisingly short time, he demonstrated his skill. Fulminating his way the length of Manhattan, he prodded, cajoled, goaded, persuaded and bullied a good cross section of these institutions into agreement with his program.

His hand with individuals was just as sure. When his bristling eyebrows and ringing denunciations burst into a freshly outfitted examining room in Garden City, an emotional compound of gratitude, awe and sheer fright effectively reduced Harley Bauer to an extension of Dr. Knox's will. Stammering with excitement the young pathologist promised full cooperation. Even when it developed that this cooperation was expected to range over some rather surprising territory—which no stretch of the imagination could place within Dr. Knox's province —Harley Bauer was not inclined to cavil.

Edmund Knox's public platform was simplicity itself. He was going to lower the boom on Southport Memorial Hospital.

Present at the boom-lowering were representatives of the American College of Surgeons, Atlantic Mutual Insurance, the Sloan Guaranty Trust and various medical societies. Representatives of the New York State Police hovered, unseen, in the wings. Edmund Knox had shed his worldly affiliations for the occasion. If he was representing anything, it was some powerful abstraction—Justice or Nemesis.

It was certainly a more satisfactory role than that being enacted by the bewildered group in the center of the room, eleven local dignitaries who composed the Board of Trustees of Southport Memorial, and into whose collective lap the whole mess had been deposited. Ordinarily they, together with the absent twelfth trustee, worried about the selection of architects for new wings, the ever-present threat of unionization of non-skilled workers, and fund-raising, fund-raising, fund-raising. Service on the Board was a symbol of achievement, a sign of esteem from the burghers of Suffolk County and an acknowledged form of civic participation. It had nothing to do with knowing about hospitals. The doctors ran the hospital and, to do them justice, until now they had shouldered the blame for any failures in its performance.

"So, what does it have to do with us?" one Board member asked querulously.

Dr. Knox was ready with a stern answer.

"You," he said, "have been responsible for persuading the community to ante up some fourteen or fifteen million dollars' worth of plant and equipment. This investment is placed at the disposal of doctors for the practice of their profession, but it remains the property of the community. It is the responsibility of you, the chosen overseers, to ensure that this loan is used for the benefit of the community, rather than the personal enrichment of the doctors. Failure to fulfill that responsibility constitutes a breach of trust on your part which, in its negligence, is almost as reprehensible as these acts of overt venality. Your laxity has permitted theft! Your sloth has invited greed!"

Not surprisingly, the Board member collapsed. Thatcher noted, with alarm, that Edmund Knox's speech was beginning to assume the stately King James cadence of his favorite reading. Before coming out to Long Island, the outsiders had decided among themselves that a touch of

Knox in this mood would help bring the Board to its knees. But Thatcher hoped Knox was not going to discharge the full load of his displeasure on the heads of these poor unfortunates, who had thought it sufficient to gather together the millions and lay them at the feet of Dr. Wittke and company. Happily, it was now only a matter of harsh words. The real grapeshot was being reserved for the truants; there the Board would have its innings. Everyone had agreed that it would be wiser if Knox and the delinquent doctors did not meet while Knox was still being an Old Testament prophet. Thatcher realized he was weakling enough to be grateful that he would not have to enter the staff room at Southport Memorial Hospital on the heels of a man declaiming: *Woe to them that devise iniquity!*

One lone trustee remained mutinous.

"I don't see what you expect us to do."

In more explicit detail than␣␣that was kind, Dr. Knox told him. No one was misguided enough to leave the situation in their hands. They were not expected to do or to decide anything. All necessary action would be undertaken by those untainted with the stigma of irresponsibility. The Board's sole task was to communicate decisions already arrived at. That way, there would be no possibility of error. Failure was unthinkable. The Augean stables were about to be transformed into a model barnyard.

The solitary standout had stamina, if not intelligence.

"And anyway, what do those people have to do with this?" A heated nod toward the corner indicated the assembled financial interests.

"They," explained Dr. Knox, mimicking the gesture savagely, "are capable of ruining Southport Memorial Hospital with accumulated financial liabilities."

A brittle cough from Dexter Loomis resounded.

"If I may?" he said with meticulous courtesy. "Atlantic Mutual finds itself in a position where it cannot continue with a defense against the claim of the Freebody estate. This is entirely due to the fact that the medical staff of this hospital can no longer be viewed as responsible professional witnesses. There is no reason why Atlantic should shoulder the financial burdens created by this situation. Particularly when we don't have to! We are prepared to bring suit against the hospital to recover our losses. Furthermore——"

"No!" quivered one of the trustees. "If you have a malpractice claim, you pursue it against the individual doctor."

"Not," Dr. Knox intoned levelly, "*not* where there has been a concerted policy by the hospital authorities to cover up, condone and permit further professional misconduct. Failing cooperation by the Board, the insurance companies here represented—who include the writers of the hospital's liability insurance—can subpoena Dr. Bauer's records as staff pathologist and bring to light cases of unnecessary surgery as well as actions open to criminal prosecution."

"What's he talking about?" wailed the innocent trustee.

Two of his colleagues, better informed, whispered hasty explanations.

"Oh my God!" It was a cry from the heart. "That's been going on *here*? Why didn't somebody tell me? We've got to make some settlement and destroy those records."

"On the contrary!" thundered Isaiah in a voice of doom. "Those records are a vital part of the compromise which has been agreed upon. They will be made available to an independent review committee. All offenders will have their association with this hospital terminated immediately. Flagrant offenders will be disciplined by the medical association. The same action will be taken with respect to everyone found guilty in connection with the drug conspiracy. New appointments will be made to the staff from outsiders. This decision will be communicated to the present staff. At once!"

"And who's supposed to tell them?"

For the first time, a hint of humor appeared in Dr. Knox.

"Well, that's the function of the Board of Trustees."

The subsequent meeting between the trustees of Southport Memorial Hospital and the medical staff adjourned in an uproar. The trustees were bent on simple escape. The other participants eddied into the corridors, the lounges and the cafeteria. According to temperament, they were prey to despair, bewilderment or cold fury. The news roared through the hospital like a forest fire.

"This is the end," said Roy Neverson flatly. He was looking into a long, bleak future.

"I don't understand," Dr. Philip Wittke repeated for the fifth time. "How can they do this to me?"

Edith Bullivant's plump good nature had congealed. "If I go down," she threatened, "I will take everyone of these goddamned bastards with me."

"This is very interesting, no?" commented Dr. Kroner as

he and a young resident watched the havoc around them. "My wife, she will have much to say when I tell her."

"I've already said I'll do it, Dr. Knox." Harley Bauer was very nervous in the abandoned office. "They should all be down in the cafeteria in another half hour."

This was not the only exchange aimed at the immediate future.

"Marie, you've got to be very careful." Alice Doyle bent the full weight of her personality on the girl. "One false move and everything could be ruined."

Harley Bauer's estimate had been quite accurate. It had taken half an hour for the truth to penetrate. There was no longer any room for maneuver. The support of colleagues, whether obtained by blackmail or friendship, was no longer an impenetrable defense. Little caucuses broke up. Now, at Southport Memorial, it was every man for himself. But still, misery loves company. They started to drift downstairs, one by one, hoping to submerge themselves in common plaint.

Roy Neverson even roused himself to explain to Philip Wittke the full extent of their predicament, taking a twisted satisfaction as he saw a lifetime's complacency crumbling under the first onslaught of despair.

"There's no point in thinking you can wriggle out of it, Phil. They're going to pin us up like a couple of specimen butterflies. It doesn't make any difference how many important friends you had yesterday. You're not going to have them tomorrow."

"But why? Why?" demanded his senior. "Martin was chief of surgery. It's not our fault what he did. We don't know anything about obstetrics. None of that was our fault!"

"They're out to get us, and they're going to. Just like this," Neverson drew a forefinger across his throat with macabre humor. "And to think that it all started with Martin making a fool of himself in court."

"But that had nothing to do with this!"

Neverson was blunt. "You're behind the times, Phil. Nobody's separating things any more. All they see is one big cesspool. They didn't like the way Wendell was so sloppy with old Freebody. They didn't like the way the staff around here was operating. They didn't like what was going on in Obstetrics. No more rope is being given to anybody at Southport. Particularly, anybody at the top.

They figure, this big a cesspool, we should have noticed."

Wittke shook his head with a stubborn, angry movement. Despair was beginning to make way for anger. The emotions of an innocent victim sustained him. After all, he had made a life's work of holding his nose. How could he be expected to notice a cesspool? On oath, he would have no hesitation in saying he never noticed the Hyland Drug Company. He had been content to draw his eleven percent and leave the details to others. He intended to make that very clear at his trial. Now, he was searching for some focus for his anger. He narrowed his eyes as Dr. Edith Bullivant approached their table.

"I hope you're satisfied, Edith," he lashed out suddenly.

"You've managed to ruin a life's work."

"I don't know what you're talking about," said the lady with open contempt. "I doubt if you do."

A red flush mounted Wittke's neck and face. This was not the tone he was used to on the grounds of Southport Memorial. In fact, it had been a long time since he had heard it anywhere.

"You know perfectly well. I should have listened to Wendell and cut you off the day he asked me to."

"Even, now, you don't know where you made your mistakes," she retorted. "You should have listened to Bauer and gotten rid of Martin last winter. Then none of us would be in this mess."

"You've always wanted to get rid of Martin, haven't you, Edith?" asked Neverson quietly. "You knew he wouldn't rest as long as you were running your little racket upstairs."

"if Wendell was really against it, he was the only one," she shot back. "I never noticed that it bothered the rest of you one single bit."

Wittke sucked in his breath sharply. "What do you mean?" he demanded. "If, for one moment, I had thought that Bauer's work had any substance, I would not have tolerated the situation."

Dr. Bullivant laughed unpleasantly. "What you mean is that you didn't dare stir up trouble about Martin's work. Wendell Martin was never in any position to preach morality. And let me remind you, neither are you. At the moment I'm the only one sitting at this table who isn't under a criminal indictment."

"That is entirely different, it's only—"

Their voices had grown louder until they were drawing

attention from other tables. Marie Gentilhomme and Alice Doyle, a bare three feet away, had abandoned any pretense of conversation. But the muted hum from the further reaches of the room had provided some cover. Suddenly there was dead silence in the cafeteria. Philip Wittke abandoned his protest at the door in disbelief. Roy Neverson turned to look over his shoulder at the cause of the sudden silence.

Harley Bauer was framed in the doorway. He stood for a moment, accepting the dislike, surprise, hostility or speculation in all the faces confronting him. Then he walked quietly toward the coffee urn and drew a cup.

Roy Neverson's quiet voice commanded the room.

"Well, our little collaborator has returned to the fold. You sure picked a great way to get back at us, Harley!"

Solid dignity settled over Bauer's short, round figure. Feet firmly planted, he replied as quietly:

"My collaboration consisted of pointing out the file cabinet where I kept my records and handing over the keys. I don't know what choice you think I had, Roy."

"Handing the key over and giving the learned Dr. Knox an earful, I'll bet," Neverson leaned forward to taunt.

Harley carried his cup of coffee over and set it down firmly. "No, Roy. It wasn't Dr. Knox who wanted my records. It was the police."

Dr. Edith Bullivant went white.

"What were you saying about criminal indictments, Edith?" asked Neverson with malicious satisfaction. "It looks as if you'll be joining our happy throng,"

But again Harley intervened.

"I don't think it was that," he said to Dr. Bullivant. "It was the lieutenant who's been asking questions about Wendell Martin's murder. He seemed to think the records would help him with the motive for the murder."

The quality of the silence in the room had changed. Before, it had been a listening silence, curious, intent, but somehow companionable. Now it was the silence of fear, withdrawn and isolated, as each person wrapped his defenses about him and eyed his neighbor speculatively.

Curiously, Edith Bullivant recovered first.

"Motive," she said softly. "Of course, they've already been working on opportunity. They know who was here late that night."

She looked challengingly at Philip Wittke.

"Being here has nothing to do with it," he said instantly.

His words tumbled out, "I was here, myself, but I was with Sid Segal. I was with him until they paged me after finding the body."

He looked around at the circle of aloof, suspicious faces.

"They only have to ask Segal! He'll tell them!"

"You're not very well informed, Philip," said Edith Bullivant coldly. "We all know Sid Segal would say anything to give himself an alibi. But they asked the girl at the desk, too. She said that Segal had been with her for ten minutes when they started paging you. And that Nurse Doyle had stopped to chat also."

Heads swiveled automatically to the nurses' table. The unspoken question hovered in the air.

Alice Doyle spoke hesitantly, choosing her words with care.

"Yes, I was at the desk when they started paging Dr. Wittke. And Sid Segal was there, too. But I don't know how long he'd been there. Probably the girl at the desk doesn't know either. She'd have to guess. Five minutes, ten minutes, how could she tell?"

It was very well done. The statement contradicted no one, made trouble for no one, left everybody an escape hatch. It was the cautious product of Alice Doyle's training.

But Dr. Bullivant had thrown caution to the winds. She was bent on triumph.

"The girl at the desk has to note times constantly. She is very accurate. She was able to tell the police that I left at nine-thirty to the dot."

"I'm sure she was, Doctor," said Alice Doyle diplomatically. She would have been happy to retreat into the anonymous audience.

"But that was before you came back, Doctor," she said with earnest helpfulness. "Before you met me in the fourth floor ward."

"You've got it all wrong," snapped Dr. Bullivant. "As usual. I saw you before I left at nine-thirty."

The statement was made with hypnotic force, the kind of force which was usually very effective with Marie. But Marie Gentilhomme, a frown of concentration wrinkling her brow, kept the limelight on their table. But Marie Gentilhomme, a frown of concentration wrinkling her brow, kept the limelight on their own, was blind to these evidences of coming trouble.

"No," she said shaking her head, "it couldn't have been. I remember very clearly. I'd called Dr. Neverson and I'd already given Mrs. Perkins her medication, so it must have been almost ten-fifteen. That's when Mrs. Perkins is always scheduled for."

The frown cleared as she settled matters to her own satisfaction and looked up, only to meet the blazing fury in Edith Bullivant's face. The twinkling blue eyes had turned into granite chips.

"It's your word against mine!" the doctor spat. "You're covering up something! You weren't with Mrs. Perkins at ten-thirty! And you were right on the spot when it came to finding Wendell Martin's body!"

Marie's face crumpled.

"Oh, no!" she gasped before raising her hands to hide the welling tears.

Philip Wittke viewed the spectacle with distaste. But the opportunity was not lost on him.

"What makes you think your word is going to be so good, Edith?" he asked, sloughing off the professional veneer long since abandoned by everyone else. "Do you think the police aren't going to be very interested to hear that you tried to fake an early departure from the hospital? No one can prove that Segal and I weren't together until a few minutes before the discovery of the body. But you seem to have been floating around with an hour to spare. And don't think they're not going to hear about it! I, for one am through with all attempts to protect you any more. The time has come for things to be cleared up!"

As Dr. Wittke strode masterfully from the cafeteria, he was followed by many eyes.

But one pair of eyes remained fixed on the bent head of Marie Gentilhomme.

19 Antibodies

Nightfall transforms buildings. The towering skyscraper that vibrates to comings and goings from nine to five becomes a cold, silent sentinel; the school that is exuberant with youth is a chill shell, forbidding and forlorn, in the small hours of night.

Even buildings not abandoned by humanity have a special night presence different from their solid daytime substance. Wartime always brings the discovery that, in factories running round the clock, the odd, inexplicable or antic invariably occurs during the third shift, from eleven o'clock to seven in the morning. Psychologists search for evidence that night-shift workers differ from their daytime brothers. They do not understand that buildings by night (like nocturnal animals) absorb some of the icy madness of the moon. Alone, they shudder. Occupied, they infect.

Southport Memorial Hospital was set back in a small park, its outer limits lost in darkness. Forsythia tendrils waved in a soft, insistent breeze, snaking shadows over the walk; in the parking lot, the spotlights trembled slightly as the wind rose.

"Storm coming up," said Gene Perkins, grasping Nancy's arm.

"We need the rain," she replied, comforted by his warmth.

Yet their anxiety communicated more powerfully than words, and instinctively they moved closer together. Gene slipped an arm around his wife's waist. They continued up the walk.

"Just think," said Gene Perkins, "This is the last time, Nancy!"

"It's wonderful," she agreed.

He tightened his grip on her overnight case. They knew they must behave naturally.

It was only eight o'clock; to the west, lingering pink streamers trailed the setting sun. Yet already it was clear that tonight was going to be dark, with an inky clear sky studded by distant stars.

At the hospital, lights were already lit, still registering yellow against the curiously yellowed sky. Although the Perkinses knew that Southport Memorial was almost as busy by night as by day, they felt the chill of desolation.

170

"I'll be here to pick you up tomorrow," said Gene Perkins.

Nancy too had paused, staring ahead with wide eyes. Now she turned to look at her husband.

"But you've got to go to work."

They were under the old-fashioned portico. Gene Perkins spoke more loudly than necessary.

"When my wife comes out of the hospital for the last time, I'm going to be there to meet her!"

"Oh, Gene!"

"Honey!"

She buried her face in his shoulder, then they turned to hurry inside.

Within minutes, Nancy Perkins was in a routine as familiar to her as her own household chores. Yet this familiarity was still miles removed from her home and her life; as always, it was remote and uninviting at first. Only after hours or days in a hospital does its reality obliterate the outside world.

They walked past the waiting room in which only two small lamps glowed inadequately against the darkness. At the reception desk, Nancy was greeted like an old friend.

"You're up in 4C again, Nancy."

Even Dr. Philip Wittke turned aside from his conversation with Sid Segal to smile at her.

"The last time, isn't it, Mrs. Perkins?" he rumbled.

"Yes, yes it is,"

"Splendid," he said before turning back to bend his head toward the little druggist.

Nancy Perkins stood on tiptoe to peck a swift kiss at Gene's chin, then slipped the night case from his hand.

"Good night, dear . . . Oh, I forgot!"

"Forgot what?"

"My teeth things. We were going to stop and pick some up. Well, I'll just have to do without." She smiled ruefully at the receptionist. "You wouldn't think I could still forget things, would you, Grace?"

Gene Perkins was determined that Nancy's discomforts tonight would not include any that he could prevent. Even a little thing like a toothbrush could loom large under some circumstances.

"I'll pick them up for you, honey. But it'll have to wait until I've gone to the laundromat. Will that be too late?"

"No, that's fine. Marie Gentilhomme will come down for them, I know she will."

"Good." Gene turned with his usual friendly grin to the desk. "I'll leave them with you, Grace, right?"

"Sure. You can leave them in the office. Marie won't be able to come down until the ward's settled in."

Gene nodded, squeezed Nancy's elbow and threaded his way to the door. Wittke and Segal were still busy with each other. A white-faced man huddled in a corner looked up incuriously, then back at his shoes. Nancy Perkins shot him a sympathetic look, then glanced at Grace, who shook her head unobtrusively. They were, they both knew, intruding.

By day, this would not be true. By day, the controlled rustle, the muted footfall, the careful voice of nurse, doctor, visitor, even patient, attest to the demands that illness makes upon life, but conversely they are at once encouraging and soothing, a reminder that life itself, like light and sound, is a powerful primal force.

But by night when vitality is lowered, light and sound are the enemy sapping precious strength. So the quiet is made more quiet, and night lowers the lights, creating shadowy hallways outside rooms where pain and anxiety hold sway. And even sleep, the natural refuge, is suspect. In a hospital, sleep too often indicates not strengthening but the end of resistance. The homely, familiar figures performing welcome chores during the day become furtive intruders at night; terrors held at bay emerge to haunt hospital beds. At night, everyone is alone in a hospital, alone and surrounded by enemies curtained from them only by silence and darkness.

The uneasiness brought by night affects the staff as well as the patients. Night is the easier duty for a nurse in the wards; there are no doctors to visit, correct, blame. There are fewer errands to be run and no distracting visitors to disrupt routine. Yet nurses accustomed to day duty do not like night assignments. They rationalize this by explaining that night emergencies are more demanding, that responsibility is heavier. But they too feel what the patients feel; night is a foretaste of death.

On four, Marie Gentilhomme was sitting at the desk facing the long corridor, bent over some reports, the paper rustling under her fingers as she wrote.

She rose as Nancy Perkins emerged from the elevator and approached.

"Hello, Nancy. This is the last time."

Nancy greeted her. "No," she said when Marie moved to help her with her overnight case. "I know my way."

"Fine," said Marie. "Now, don't stay up too late. Just half an hour . . ."

She was referring to the muted sounds of activity at the far end of the corridor, the patients' lounge. This was a tattered porch-like room filled with wicker furniture, piles of torn copies of *Life* and ashtrays. It was shabby and depressing, yet on the floor it was important. Patients well enough to walk were allowed to visit the patients' lounge to vary the tedium of their days: nurses, doctors, visitors were forbidden. Here, in a strange array of wraps and peignoirs, women with hair carelessly held back by ribbons, with faces naked and plucked without cosmetics, created something fleetingly like the cheerful intimacy of a girls' school. Their talk, inevitably, was of illness, of operations, of doctors, of nurses. Yet there was a certain camaraderie built up by being part of a group, a reminder of what it is to be a human being, not a case. People came and people went, in the patients' lounge, but there was always an authority who knew the ins and outs and advised others; there was always a shy and frightened little mouse; there was always an enigma—a woman who was neither married nor the mother of three children. Despite slow, pain-wracked gaits, hands pressed to sides, eyes bright with fear, the patients' lounge was a haven.

But not tonight. When Nancy Perkins changed into her night attire, put her case in the small closet and slipped down the hall, she found several acquaintances and a newcomer. The newcomer, a brittle, middle-aged woman scheduled for an operation day after tomorrow, was nervous to the point of hysteria and trying desperately to hide it. The other women, who would have been happy to offer unlimited sympathy, could not cope with edgy gaiety. And it was no surprise therefore, that within fifteen minutes, people began drifting to their own beds.

By a quarter to nine, Marie Gentilhomme, looking in to urge her charges to retire, found the patients' lounge deserted. The heaping ashtrays, the neglected pots of ivy, the scattered magazines were no concern of hers—a scrubwoman would make a pass at them early in the morning. Nevertheless, before switching off the light, she walked in, piled the magazines into a semblance of order, plumped a sagging pillow and assembled the ashtrays. Wrinkling her nose slightly at the acrid tobacco aroma that soaked the room, she turned off the light, walked back to her desk, checking right and left as she passed. Most night lamps were already out.

The ward was settling down. Outside, the summer night was just setting and in roadside steakhouses, young couples were finishing their drinks and getting ready to order. But here, in the inner time of the hospital, dinner was long past—served and cleared by four-thirty. Tomorrow would begin by three-thirty in the morning.

Nurse Gentilhomme was at her desk when somebody stopped beside her.

Startled, she looked up. "Oh, it's you!"

"Did I frighten you?"

The voice was hard.

"N-no. But I didn't hear you."

Alice Doyle stood just outside the circlet of light, but the reflection from papers on the desk etched bleak shadows along the bony ridges of her cheeks and forehead, undoing the soft camouflage of cosmetics. It was a harsh and strong death's head beneath yellow hair that looked down on Marie.

"You won't forget what I told you?"

She spoke in her normal hospital voice, low, non-carrying, yet not a whisper.

Marie Gentilhomme reached nervously for the glass of water kept on her desk. After sipping thirstily, she said, "No, Alice, I won't."

With a long last look, Alice Doyle moved away. A moment later, the brief click, then the pneumatic whisper told Marie that she had taken the elevator.

Or had she?

Thirstily, Marie finished the water, then looked over her shoulder. The elevator ranks were around the corner. For all she knew, Alice could be standing in the far corner, waiting. Determinedly, Marie rose and went to refill the water carafe. The thought showed how nervous she was. The next thing you knew, she reflected, letting the water in the small sink in the ladies' room run, she would be getting strange feelings that she was not alone.

Which, in a hospital, was well-nigh madness. Here, within sound of her voice were thirty patients. On the other floors, even on this floor, nurses were on errands, an occasional doctor was still checking a patient. Down in Emergency, there might be a great crowd of people.

Through the silence, there were gentle stirrings—and elevators moved, people climbed the stairs beyond the fire door, doors opened and shut.

At nine-thirty, elevator doors again whispered. Marie looked up.

She had been wrong in thinking that Alice Doyle had not left the floor. Because here she was, coming from upstairs, deep in conversation—with Dr. Roy Neverson. Exactly as if that scene at the garage had never taken place, exactly as if they were doctor and nurse, conferring about a patient. What could draw them together after that shattering explosion of hatred? Inwardly Marie marveled at the brazenness of it. In spite of herself she strained to overhear their words. That would never do, she told herself severely. She had other things to think about. The empty water glass came into her hand automatically. Irritatedly, she slapped it down on the desk.

There was a thread of tension running through the ward tonight, and there was no denying it. Uneasy tremors disturbed the calm of darkness. Of course, the patients were not comfortable. It was the hysterical woman who had done that, She was one of Dr. Bullivant's patients.

But it was more than patients. Southport Memorial Hospital itself was wounded. And the wound throbbed.

"Marie?"

It was Nancy Perkins standing by her desk. She too had noticed the unlikely camaraderie between Nurse Doyle and Dr. Neverson, but she did not comment.

"I'm sorry. I forgot to tell you. Gene is leaving some things in the office for me. Could I get them?"

She had not mastered the hospital tone of voice. First whispering, then speaking so loudly it seemed that her words, echoing down the hallway, must waken the sleeping.

"Oh, no, Nancy. I couldn't let you."

Marie Gentilhomme was affected by Nancy's nervousness. Her own voice was louder than usual.

The wind outside slapped a branch against a loose pane somewhere. Nancy persisted.

"But Gene went specially to get them."

Marie looked up the corridor. "I'll run down as soon as I have a minute. Don't worry."

The wind must have risen. Now the old building was loosing long, low moans. Nancy Perkins's eyes blazed with intensity. But all she said was:

A STITCH IN TIME

"No. No, of course, I won't."

Ten minutes later, Marie stood at the elevator. She had brought Mrs. Ohlmann a carafe of water, calmed Mrs. Palfrey's fears caused by the gurgling of the pipes and checked the patients' lounge for open windows. The ward was peaceful. There was no one about and nothing more to be done. She could slip away.

The murderer, too, had just started downstairs. It had been hard waiting for the time to pass, waiting for the right moment.

But it was hardest of all for Gene Perkins, who had delivered his package and then, under orders, had proceeded to act as he had acted on every other checkup night. But this was not an ordinary night, and every move he made was a violation of his love and loyalty. Reluctantly he walked to his car under the swaying trees, while his lips moved soundlessly over the same words, again and again, as if he were telling his rosary.

"I got her into this. I shouldn't just be driving away like this. What if something happens to her? . . . I got her into this."

But in the midst of his despair he remained obedient and did what he had said he would do. He started to thread his way along the obscure shortcut which would bring him home ten minutes earlier. As if he wanted to be home earlier tonight! Dutifully he pulled his car away from the hospital, drove two blocks along the main street, and then turned right into the alley which would allow him to cut over and miss two red lights.

"I got her into this," he thought desperately and his eyes stared unseeingly at the blank warehouse walls looming overhead, at the solitary parked car. "If anything happens," he concluded, "it will all be my fault."

The elevator responded to Marie's call and now the door opened. For a moment, the bright garish light in the elevator made her blink. She stepped in, punched the ground floor button but, as usual, other commands supervened. The elevator started to rise.

At six, it halted and the doors slid open.

"Dr. Kroner," gasped Marie as the small man joined her.

"Ah, Miss Gentilhomme," he said sadly, stepping beside her in the elevator large enough to accommodate a stretcher. "So I kidnap you, true?"

The doors clanged shut.

"Ach, these elevators! They are all wrong. But they are not the only things wrong here, now, am I right?"

The penetrating look was at variance with the melancholy of his voice. He was asking something. But what?

Marie was incapable of reply. Perhaps Dr. Kroner expected none. He continued his gentle murmuring.

"Something drastic must be done! Like the cancer—the evil must be cut out! Yes, cut out! Or else . . ."

They bumped gently to a halt.

"So, here we are!"

With an unhappy smile, Kroner stepped out on the ground floor and disappeared.

Everybody was behaving strangely, Marie thought, licking suddenly dry lips. Even Dr. Kroner. She liked Dr. Kroner, she reminded herself. *She liked him.*

With a shiver, she marched up to the reception desk, now manned only by the switchboard operator. In the waiting room, she noticed, the white-faced man was slumped in the corner. He seemed to be asleep. But he was no longer alone.

Edith Bullivant stood, as if halted involuntarily by an expectant father demanding something from her. Her head remained reassuringly inclined toward him. But, even though she did not change her attitude by as much as a centimeter, her eyes moved in a slow, horizontal sweep so that for a moment Marie caught the full impact of that flat, hostile stare.

Until the revelations in the cafeteria, Dr. Edith Bullivant had had all the protection of a plausible alibi corroborated by her husband. Marie shuddered and was glad when the doctor shook off a restraining hand and stumped away.

"No, nobody's left anything here," the girl replied to Marie's query.

Marie's nerves were again playing tricks. The switchboard girl was speaking too loudly, too distinctly.

"But say," the girl continued, "that little fellow with the red hair was here about twenty minutes ago, just before Grace left. I think she told him to put it in the office . . ."

Wearily, Marie Gentilhomme turned past the desk to the administrative offices that adjoined. Here were the offices of Dr. Wittke, the dietician and the Board of Trustees. However, in the language of the switchboard, "the office" meant the treasurer's office, the long green room with six wooden desks, endless rows of battered filing cabinets and three calculating machines. Here was where the admission records were maintained. It was the last office in the block.

The murderer was already in that block.

Dr. Witke's office was the first, and light showed through the frosted glass panel. These were hard times for Philip Wittke, and he had been cleaning out his desk today. All the nurses knew that he was staying late tonight. He had explained that he still had "one or two things to take care of."

Marie passed on, turning the corner, into a deserted corridor. Her rubber-soled shoes squeaked slightly on the linoleum floor as she went by two empty, darkened offices, Squeak . . . squeak . . . squeak.

Her rubber-soled shoes, or someone else's? Firmly she thrust back the terror rising to choke her, firmly she refused to vary her slow, steady stride. It would be so easy, by a sudden discontinuity, to test whether other footsteps were synchronizing with her own. Then she came to the treasurer's door. It was closed. Better not to think of that.

She knew what lay behind that door—the three orderly rows of desks, the angled lamps ready to spotlight typewriters and checkwriters. At the far end of the room were two closets, each big enough to conceal the largest of men.

She put her hand on the doorknob, then hesitantly turned her hand slightly. Nothing happened. Her moist hand simply slid around the cold brass. Nerving herself, she clutched tightly and twisted hard, all in one convulsive motion. The door opened swiftly—to disclose an empty room.

The room was not dark, although the overhead light was off. One desk lamp was lit, spotlighting the desk farthest from the door and leaving the rest of the room in shadow. The desk top was clear except for two items. Precisely in the middle of the pool of brilliant illumination lay a green toothbrush in a transparent container and a small tube of toothpaste. Two homey, domestic objects floodlighted as if they were part of a stage set, almost festive in their simple colors. They seemed to beckon to her invitingly.

Temptingly . . . luringly.

Marie hesitated on the threshold for only a moment. Then she forced herself to go forward while the silent, oppressive air around her seemed to shriek at deafening volume: "This is a trap! This is a trap!"

She could feel the blood pounding at her temples. Her

ears were blanked out by an inchoate thundering. She must move now, another minute and she would not be able to. She had almost reached the desk when, behind her, the door clicked shut.

She wheeled about.

He was standing with his back to the door, a dim blurred figure, darker than the surrounding shadow. The outline of his hunched shoulders was feral with menace, the long narrow object trailing from one hand hinted of crushed bone and welling blood.

Terrified, Marie shrank back, gaping at him.

"I don't want to do this," he said in cracked tones that sounded horribly sincere. As if all the insincerities had been burned away by the anticipation of violence. This time he would not have the emotional insulation of a blow delivered in hot blood, out of an unthinking rage. Now he *had* to think it was the only defense left to him, to think quickly enough to remove all danger. There was danger all around him. "You know too much. I have to do it," he concluded in a lost, lonely voice.

The voice was a revelation. "Why he's lonely!" Marie thought wildly. "That's what murder does to you. We're two lonely people trying to destroy each other."

And then he started to advance, his body well under control even if his voice was not, so that he moved with his familiar lithe silence.

Marie gave an inarticulate moan and scurried behind the desk to stand at bay, back to the closets, with no further retreat possible.

He raised his right arm as he came forward, and the light caught the metal as it arced into the range of the lamp. But Marie did not see this. With one last shudder, she pitched forward on her face before he could reach her.

The two closet doors burst open, the rush of trampling feet sounded in the corridor.

As the overhead lights snapped on, Lieutenant Joseph Perenna was the first man to brush by her recumbent form.

"Okay, Doctor! The fun's over!" he said as he wrested the tire iron from Roy Neverson's unresisting hand. "Hey, Sammy!"

The white-faced man from the waiting room entered.

"Him? Well, what do you know? Okay, Joe. Take him away."

Blue-coated figures removed Neverson, now dazed and trembling.

"That leaves this poor kid," said Sammy, indicating Marie Gentilhomme, still unconscious.

Lieutenant Perenna was in good spirits. "What better place for it?" Opening his mouth wide, he loosed a booming, unhospital-like bellow:

"DOCTOR! GET A DOCTOR!"

20 Witch Doctor?

The room rang with the buzz of voices, the clinking of glasses, the flaring of matches. Theoretically, it was the formal reception to commemorate the opening of the Freebody wing of the Institute for Cancer Research. Actually it was Edmund Knox's song of triumph. He had crushed his enemies—and brought home the bacon. In consequence, the proceedings were more exultant than is the custom with institutionally sponsored events.

"Glad to hear the girl's all right," said Benjamin Edes, surveying the room with lively curiosity. "Out of the hospital, isn't she?"

"Oh, yes," Thatcher assured him. "She wasn't really hurt. It was more a matter of accumulated nervous strain, than that rap on the head when she fell. And a week of cosseting from the Perkinses and Alice Doyle has taken care of that."

Edes nodded. By now the characters in the final act of the Southport drama were familiar to him, as they were to every newspaper reader.

"I never have figured out what she was supposed to know, why Neverson thought he had to kill her. Though from what I can see, he must have been damn near crazy by that time."

"An accurate assessment, I would say," Thatcher remembered Joseph Perenna's description of Roy Neverson in jail, resigned, half-stupefied, refusing to see his mother. "He had just learned that Marie Gentilhomme could blast his alibi into smithereens! The scene in the cafeteria sent him into a tailspin. Of course, it upset quite a few people. That's what it was designed to do."

Edes inspected him shrewdly. "Telling me you were surprised it turned out to be Neverson? That you didn't know until the end?"

"Oh no. Neverson was the obvious suspect all along, on the basis of motive. He was, I agree, half-crazy. But to suspect anyone else, you had to postulate a complete lunatic!"

"I suppose you mean that drug company we dug up."

Benjamin Edes' brief career as a detective had gone to his head like May wine. Thatcher had a strong suspicion that the Southport banker now spent his idle moments plowing through his clients' accounts in the hopes of bringing to light further conspiracies that had left their trail, like the slime of an earthworm, across the prim statements of debits and credits. And if that hospital were any reflection of the community, God only knew what he would come up with! He might soon be running an operation second only to J. Edgar Hoover's.

"Naturally I mean the drug company. After all, whatever threat Wendell Martin might have posed for Edith Bullivant and Harley Bauer was not being perceptibly increased by his performance in the Atlantic Mutual trial. If Martin planned to discredit Dr. Bullivant, the only effect of the trial would be to distract him. She might reasonably assume that he would have plenty of other things to occupy his mind. But every additional hour he was on the witness stand made exposure of Hyland Drug more likely. It would be too much of a coincidence to suppose that someone else, for an entirely different reason, stepped in at just that moment to solve the problem for Wittke and Segal and Neverson."

"But that's just it. Narrowing it down to the drug racket didn't narrow it down to Roy Neverson. The whole bunch of them were in it up to their necks." Edes, warming to the story, gestured for another drink with the same lordly assurance he employed in Southport, and got the same deferential service. Whatever else the years had done for him, they had taught him the value of making an impression.

"Certainly, they were all in it. But it's a mistake to think they would have suffered the same losses if they had been exposed. What would have happened to them? The certain loss of their investment, the probable loss of their license to practice, a possible jail sentence."

"For all of them."

"Not necessarily." Thatcher raised a cautionary finger. "But even assuming that to be the case, what did it mean to each man? Sid Segal was in the strongest position. I expect he joined them simply because they threatened him with the loss of a large part of his prescription business if he didn't. And prescriptions play a very big role in the economy of that store. But, quite apart from his investment in the drug company, he's a rich man. He owns that entire block, he has a thriving business which could continue with his sons. His family wouldn't suffer any hardship, and he himself would not be an object of moral revulsion, because he wasn't a doctor. He was only the man who filled the prescriptions the doctors wrote. Except for this last point, much the same can be said for Philip Wittke. He, too, was independently wealthy by now. And while professional censure would be a blow to his ego, he was on the point of retiring anyway. He could always slip away—even after a jail term of six months or a year—and spend his golden years in Arizona as if nothing had happened."

Thatcher belatedly hoped that Edes did not include Arizona in his immediate plans. "In fact, as a general principle, you can say that the older men were not going to be hit very hard, not hard enough to constitute a motive for murder, anyway. It was a very different kettle of fish for the younger men, they were the ones who would suffer. They would lose all their money and their right to practice medicine, with their whole lives still before them. And, bear in mind, these were not ordinary young men. They had all been used to living on incomes which a young man, like Kenneth Nicolls say, would consider fit for a king. You can lose your license to be a real estate agent, or a lawyer, or a pharmacist for that matter, and still have every hope of re-creating the same life in some other occupation. But this is not so with doctors! Roy Neverson, still in his mid-thirties, was making over seventy thousand dollars a year—and without being particularly good at his profession, without being a world authority or even associated with a good hospital. How could he ever duplicate that if he were thrown on the world and told to make his living doing something else?"

"Don't tell me about the young men!" Sounds of displeasure had been emanating from Edes for some time. Now he enlarged on his grievance. "I've heard it all from the Wittke boys. They're selling off their summer place and their boats. Every time they come into the bank, I have to listen to their sob story. Finally told young Jim off! Said he was only getting what he deserved for being mixed up in that swindle. That shut him up." The memory seemed to afford Edes considerable satisfaction. "Hell, why not? He's going to be wanting a loan any day now, and money's tight."

Thatcher was pleased to see that bankers remain bankers under the most outrageous conditions.

"Tight money?" asked an alarmed voice. "My God, what are they up to now?"

Tom Robichaux appeared out of the swirling throng, an unlikely celebrant for the latest attack on cancer. He was reassured on Federal Reserve policy.

"Money's not just tight for doctors in Southport," Edes confirmed with a cackle. "It's non-existent."

"Oh, doctors!" Robichaux waved away the profession and rocked back on his heels to run an expert's eye over the gathering. "Nice little blowout they've got going here. Don't believe I've ever been given decent brandy by a school before."

Somehow Robichaux managed to reduce Hanover University to the level of P.S. 98. But Edes was not prepared to stand on ceremony with him.

"They can afford it," he said dismissively. And, turning back to Thatcher: "So, the Wittke boys were right on the starting line with Neverson."

"Not exactly. They would feel it, I'm sure. But they have something Roy Neverson doesn't have—a rich father. Neverson, on the contrary, was sharing some of his mother's expenses."

Robichaux registered intelligence.

"Neverson? He's your murderer out there. Somehow I expected it to be a surgeon. Nothing they did would surprise me!" He retreated into brooding memories of Veronica.

"That too was a matter of some importance." Thatcher neatly took over the conversation before Tom could carry them all down one of those esoteric, speculative channels in which he specialized. "Because I don't think it's true that all the conspirators would have drawn the same penalties if a prosecution had resulted from Wendell Martin's indiscretions. We were talking about this the other day, and we agreed that a scapegoat would probably have been offered up as sacrificial victim. Naturally, at first sight, it seems that Martin should have been the scapegoat. But Martin undoubtedly would have tried to defend himself. His obvious course would be to claim that he had been led astray by the originator of the scheme. In fact, that he was just a high-spirited boy victimized by a Bad Influence. And, from what Edes here has told me, I don't think there's much doubt that Neverson was the one who masterminded the entire racket."

"None at all!" Edes barked. "He was the only one who had the slightest idea about money. He knew about mortgages and took some interest in the stock market. Hell, the rest of that bunch didn't even understand credit. They took in a lot of cash and put out a lot of cash. Every now and then, they took whatever had accumulated and dumped it with a stock broker. That's about the size of it."

"And the others, bear in mind, were surgeons. Neverson was an internist, what Gene Perkins tells me they call a 'pill-pusher.' He'd be particularly alive to the possibilities of drugs—as well as being the one who was on good terms with Al Martin."

"Put it another way," urged Edes. "He was the only one with the brains to think up that scheme."

"Or possibly with brains enough to comprehend the full menace of Wendell Martin?"

But here Edes jibbed. He shook his head decisively. "No, I wouldn't say that. The one really on the ball was Sid Segal. Still is, as a matter of fact. He's got the druggists association protesting the pressures brought to bear on pharmacists by doctors. I'll bet he comes out of this lily-white. And Phil Wittke isn't stupid, when it comes to protecting his own interests. They both must have known that Martin was a menace. Segal tried to talk to him, and Wittke realized it wouldn't be any use. But that's as far as they were prepared to go. It all comes out of what you were just saying. Neither of them was desperate. And Neverson was!"

Tom Robichaux did not care for these highfalutin emotional flights. It was, in his opinion, a waste of good brandy. He prepared to move on.

"I can see that you're both hipped on this thing. Think I'll find somebody who can chat about something livelier."

It was no accident that his eye rested on an attractive young woman at the bar. She was unaccompanied at the moment. She was also, as Thatcher had been informed by Dr. Edmund Knox, a very promising brain surgeon. Oh well, let Tom make his own discoveries.

"I don't understand what you're doing here anyway," he said to Robichaux.

"Melinda." The gleam in Robichaux's expression was momentarily dimmed. "Seems Hanover has an island somewhere. Melinda's got her eye on it. Well, it keeps her busy."

On this philosophic note, he departed. Things do balance out, as he had once said. Melinda, hot on the trail of her island, would be too preoccupied to notice her husband—also hot on a trail.

"You know, there's another thing you might have considered about Roy Neverson," Edes resumed. "That is, if you'd known him. He really has been a little crazy since his divorce, grimly determined that his wife and children were going to have the best of everything, whether they wanted it or not. He lavished money on them. I think he wanted to prove to himself he was necessary to them, even if his wife did get a divorce. Coming down to a regular job and a regular salary would have been bad enough. Breaking it t... his wife would have have just about killed him."

Thatcher nodded. He was not going to tell the septua genarian he had already figured this out.

"That's interesting. And not so uncommon, where th... husband resists divorce and the wife doesn't remarry."

"Then there's that mother of his," Edes continued hi... character analysis. "She's always been a driver. That's th... real difference between Wittke and Roy. Wittke think... everything is coming to him naturally, and he's no... inclined to make a push. But Neverson knows you have t... go out and take it. When Martin got in his way, his natura... instinct would be to do something about it." He twirled th... Scotch in his glass reflectively. "And he almost got awa... with it. Don't really see how he messed things up."

"I don't know that you can say he messed things up. H... really didn't plan the murder of Wendell Martin. Wha... seems to have happened is that he made one last attempt t... talk sense to Martin on the night of the murder. He wa... forced to the conclusion that Wittke had been right. Talk... ing to Martin wasn't going to do any good. The Freebod... trial was going to go on, with the attention of the entir... country riveted on Southport Memorial. So Neverso... slammed out of the hospital at nine o'clock, exactly as h... later claimed. He stopped for a bottle across the stre... from his apartment house, where his presence was dul... witnessed. There was no premeditation at that point. That'... what he's said to Lieutenant Perenna, and I believe him... Otherwise he would never have been so silly. But by th... time he'd had a few drinks and reviewed his own positio... he'd worked himself into a white-hot fury. If talkin... wouldn't do any good, then it would have to be action."

Thatcher could almost see it. "Scarcely knowing what h... was doing, he went back to the hospital and parked his ca... in an alley. He got out his tire iron and sneaked into th... parking lot to look for Wendell Martin's car. It was en... tirely by chance that the murder took place. The timin... hadn't been planned at all. If Martin had already gon... home, Neverson would probably have drunk himself into... stupor and wakened the next morning, still frightene... about the future but rid of his homicidal rage. In fact... Wendell Martin had worked very late and Neverson ha... been forced to lurk in the lot for a few hours, diving in...

he shrubbery every time someone appeared, he would probably have thought better of the whole thing. But, as luck would have it, the car was there. Martin himself came out in a few minutes."

"You're right about that. Roy Neverson would never have hung around very long. As soon as he started to calm down, he would have been worried at looking foolish if anybody caught him sneaking around."

Thatcher agreed sadly. "He would have been lucky if looking foolish was all that came of his night's work. After he killed Martin, he had sufficient presence of mind to rifle the pockets and try to make it look like a mugging. Then he went home and faced the fact that he was a murderer."

"Admitted, it's not a cleverly planned crime. But it's the kind they always say has the most chance of success. One stiff on a dark night and away you go!" Edes spoke with considerable gusto.

"That's fine as long as a motive isn't apparent. But once the police started concentrating on the drug conspirators, the picture changed. Neverson, of course, simply omitted his return trip to the hospital. His story was that he went home and stayed there."

"What's wrong with that? I'd have said the same thing myself. Nobody saw him, did they?"

"Nobody saw him. But people knew about his activities anyway. He had made the mistake, just before leaving the hospital at nine o'clock, of asking Marie Gentilhomme to call him with the results of a patient's test. It was, he said, very important. So she called him—twice. Once at ten, again at ten-fifteen. There was, of course, no answer. Furthermore, Gene Perkins saw his car. That disaster, Neverson could not have anticipated. Neverson was careful to leave his car in a deserted alley, surrounded by warehouses. But that alley is on Perkins's shortcut home, and Perkins works in the garage that services the car. In fact he services it himself. And it is a noticeable car."

"A big fancy sports car," said Edes disapprovingly.

"Exactly. A Jaguar, I believe. And seen by one of the few men who could identify it without hesitation. Perkins was so impressed he even commented on the doctor's parking in the midst of broken glass."

"You couldn't want anything more damning. One witness busts his alibi, and the other not only places him at the scene of the crime, but in a surreptitious location. No reason in the world for Roy Neverson to park in an alley only two blocks from the hospital."

"Particularly when there was nothing in the alley that he could have possibly been visiting at that time of night Gene Perkins, of course, did not realize the importance o... what he had seen at the time. But he was a man who wa... interested in the death of Wendell Martin, simply becaus... he has very good reason to be grateful to Martin. And h... could therefore identify that night without much difficulty even a good while later. It was not until afterward that hi... suspicions were roused."

"That was when the Perkinses and that girl got ahold o... you, eh?" It had not been an accident that Mrs. Benjami... Edes was absent from the most critical meeting in th... history of the Board of Trustees of Southport Memoria... Hospital. But her husband knew Thatcher's conference i... Old Southport had been the inspiration for that meetin... and all that followed.

"Yes. When Marie and the Perkinses put their head... together, they came up with the phone call and the parke... car. The Perkins remembered something else. Neverso... had dropped off a flat tire at the garage that very day, an... in the course of so doing became involved in a nasty en... counter with Alice Doyle. Naturally everybody's attentio... was riveted by the quarrel. But when that interest faded... Perkins began to consider the tire. Neverson was a ma... who had never done anything himself on his car, ... Perkins's memory. When he had a flat tire, he called th... garage to change it. And rightly so. It was a difficult tire t... change. For an inexperienced man like the doctor, Perkin... estimated that it would take over half an hour—if he wa... lucky. Why then, this sudden change in pattern? Perki... couldn't figure it out, but he was suspicious enough t... then to tell the lieutenant about it. And the lieutenant h... on the answer almost at once."

"The tire iron? Why didn't he get rid of it? It certainl... wasn't still bloody, was it?"

"Neverson was facing up to the problems of living in a... apartment house. He didn't dare put it in the garbage, ... didn't have the time to take his boat out, he had no mea... of disposal. Above all, he didn't want to be seen carrying... in circumstances which would make anybody think. The... he was bothered by the problem of replacement. If he w... missing a tire iron the next time he needed a tire chang... the garage would notice. And he certainly didn't want... go out and buy one. So he came to what was probably sensible conclusion. He decided to leave it in the one place where it would attract no attention. In his car, with the other tools. But almost all the difficulties involved in throwing it away arose when he tried to clean it. He couldn't exactly carry it into the hospital and toss it into a sterilizer. He had to be content with wiping it. Of course, that wasn't sufficient to defeat a chemical analysis. Perenna tells me they are having a field day with it. More important, it might not be enough to escape notice from a mechanic who had used it several times. Neverson was taking no chances. He changed the tire himself."

"All right. Then that brings us to your trap. I don't see how you worked it."

"Properly speaking, I didn't. It was Ed Knox who did. He set up the scene in the cafeteria with young Bauer. It was imperative that Neverson be told about Marie's calls. You understand, he still didn't know about them. When he tried to upbraid her for failing to call him, she didn't try to defend herself. Instead Dr. Kroner stepped in and explained that she had been sent home after finding Martin's body. So Neverson had to be told that Marie Gentilhomme was a danger to him, and under circumstances where everybody else's attention was distracted. Bauer and Marie did a very good job of it."

Edes snorted. "I would have smelled a rat!" he said confidently. "And then you handed him the girl on a plate."

"Naturally." Thatcher was shocked. "You don't think we would invite him to murder her and then leave the time and place to him? Miss Gentilhomme was very carefully guarded until that evening. Then he was given the information that she would be in a lonely, deserted spot at a certain time. I expect he must have been rather impatient by then. They tell me he was trying to get her alone for some time."

"And the Perkinses were in on it?"

"Almost everyone was in on it. The Perkinses, of course. And Alice Doyle was assigned to bring him to the fourth floor where he would overhear Mrs. Perkins asking Marie to go downstairs. That was in case he hadn't picked it up already. They did everything but announce it over the PA system. Even Dr. Kroner was assigned to see that Marie was not in the elevator alone."

"With that much cooperation, it's surprising someone didn't blab."

"People were picked out rather carefully. And being a

murderer is a lonely business. I think Neverson realized that at the end." Thatcher had put this interpretation on Marie Gentilhomme's rather disjointed remarks.

"I'm surprised you let this Alice Doyle in on things. She seems to have been acting up herself."

"That was simply a failure in communication. Mrs. Doyle was present when Roy Neverson complained about Marie's failure to call. After the doctor left, Marie explained her attempts to reach him. At the time it was not very important. Dr. Martin's death was being viewed as a mugging. But Mrs. Doyle did realize the oddity of a doctor demanding to be called with a message about a patient and then disappearing without any word as to his location. When the police made it clear that Martin's death was not a casual mugging, that oddity instantly assumed its true importance in her mind. In fact, the importance was so self-evident she ignored the possibility that it had escaped Marie. That woman is a born politician. She instantly assumed that Neverson had squared himself with Marie."

Edes looked knowing. "Blackmail?"

"Not at all. Give Mrs. Doyle her due. She knows what kind of girl Marie is. She never even considered blackmail. Rather, she thought in terms of some explanation by the doctor and agreement by Marie, out of the goodness of her heart, not to embarrass Neverson. That was why she was so furious when the doctor had the gall, in her eyes, to attack his benefactor at the garage. It was righteous fury, mingled with her own disappointments, that led her to attack Neverson so savagely."

"Disappointments?" Edmund Knox joined them, beaming widely and far removed from the Isaiah of Southport Memorial. "Doesn't Mrs. Doyle like her new job?"

"I didn't know she had one," Thatcher confessed.

"Southport's new director of nursing. There was a little opposition to the appointment, but I soon took care of that."

Thatcher could readily believe it.

"Not exactly in the image of Southport Memorial," Benjamin Edes commented fearlessly. His position was that he could eat Edmund Knox for breakfast.

"The sooner they get rid of their old image, the better," Knox announced genially. "She'll make a first-class director, if you ask me. She knows the job, she's a hard worker, and she's got plenty of backbone. Not likely to take any nonsense from anybody."

It was a quality that appealed to him. Social polish left him indifferent.

"You've been busy," Thatcher remarked. "I hear you offered young Bauer his old job, too."

Knox was virtually running Southport Memorial in addition to his more than adequate regular schedule. He seemed to be thriving on the demands.

"Turned me down flat. He said that he likes general practice now that he's started."

"He'll probably end up being the last GP in the country." Edes was being deliberately provocative.

But Knox was above provocation. He looked around with contentment.

"The medical profession has a good deal to be said for it, in spite of Southport and its little cousins." For a moment he seemed to be readying an attack on the negligence of Southport's trustees. Then he refrained, out of an overriding sense of well-being. "I'm not the only one getting people jobs. You heard about Thatcher's final clause in the Freebody settlement?"

"No," grunted Edes, dissatisfied. "Nobody tells me anything. How did the settlement turn out and who got a job?"

"We got a hundred thousand," said Knox, putting first things first.

"Yes," Thatcher agreed, giving Edes the details he craved. "The settlement was tied in to our little trap. We agreed to drop the double indemnity claim if Loomis would agree to drop his claims against the hospital—provided, of course, that Southport went along with our demands. Loomis was so pleased at finally getting the case off his neck that I was able to talk him into hiring Gene Perkins at a salary that should put a stop to all that moonlighting."

"Nice, very nice. The boy's bank account had even me worried."

"I don't know that I've effected any real improvement in his life. Although he's down to one job, he seems to have some kind of commuting schedule that involves rising at five-thirty."

Knox pointed out the obvious.

"He could move."

Thatcher shook his head. You had to know the Perkinses before you could appreciate their zest for impossible schedules, their talent for overworking themselves, their cheerful concern for the well-being of others. At this very moment, according to Ken Nicolls, Nancy Perkins was scouring the countryside for young men for Marie. She had her eye on a boy just finishing dental school.

"I don't think it's even occurred to them."

"Well, at least, if they stay in Southport, they can continue to protect Marie Gentilhomme. And she seems to need it more than most." Whether this was some obscure comment on Marie's bank account, neither of the two men facing Edes could determine. "Why didn't she tumble to the importance of what she knew earlier?"

"The reason for her obtuseness is very simple," Thatcher reported. "Gene Perkins put his finger on it. She is singularly devoid of curiosity. She never bothered to find out what alibis the doctors were using, even though every orderly was talking about them. She had not the faintest idea that her information was catastrophic, to Edith Bullivant, as well as to Roy Neverson. Not until Nancy Perkins got the whole story out of her."

"Damndest young woman I ever heard of," Edes summarized. "Curiosity is the hallmark of youth."

"Oh, I don't know about that," began Edmund Knox. "One of the troubles we have training researchers——"

He was interrupted ruthlessly.

"Take my grandchildren, for instance." Edes automatically groped in his breast pocket for pictures. "Got seven of them now. But the six-year-old boy is the pick of the lot. Bright as a whippet! Always taking things apart to see what makes them tick. Took my watch apart the other day," he said proudly. "Sometimes he even puts things together again. I tell you it's a real problem keeping him supplied. But you've got to do it. Shame not to encourage that kind of talent. That's the way they develop."

John Putnam Thatcher was visited by a sudden inspiration. He began to speak.

"There's this place on Fifth Avenue . . . very carefully made . . . imported from Japan . . . a challenge to your ingenuity . . ."

He spoke slowly, persuasively, seductively. Ten minutes later, he was saying:

"Mention my name to Mr. Durrant. He'll have just the thing for you!"

The voice was Jacob's voice, but the hands were the hands of Esau.